CAREFUL
WHAT YOU

Wish
FOR

Jackie Calhoun

BELLA
BOOKS
2019

Bella Books, Inc.
P.O. Box 10543
Tallahassee, FL 32302

Printed in the United States of America on acid-free paper.

First Bella Books Edition 2019

Editor: Medora MacDougall
Cover Designer: Judith Fellows

ISBN: 978-1-64247-012-3

Other Bella Books by Jackie Calhoun

Acknowledgment

My first reader and friend, Joan Hendry
My editor, Medora MacDougall
The staff at Bella Books

About the Author

Jackie Calhoun is the author of twenty-seven novels. She lives with her partner in Northeast Wisconsin. Write to her at Jackie@jackiecalhoun.com and/or friend her on Facebook.

Dedication

To Kay Lancaster, who saved me from boredom
To Sandra Schmeck, who makes me laugh
To Diane Mandler, my other half
To Chris Calhoun, my sister and friend
To my daughters, Janet Smith & Jessica Peterson,
who make me proud.

PART I

CHAPTER ONE

1990

Nelson Mandela was free, but she was tied to this woman screaming at her, because of a house, this very house they were in. Chelsea studied the pinched, angry face and thought how ugly rage was. She tamped down a touch of panic as June rattled on about her right to go out with Karen if she wanted to. She and Karen had feelings for each other, June said.

Chelsea had thought Karen was *their* friend, hers and June's. They certainly had spent a lot of time with her. Once when alone together, Karen had intimated regret that she hadn't met Chelsea first and implied they might become more than friends. Though flattered, Chelsea had shaken her head and later told June. Had that been mistake number one or two? How quickly Karen had changed her attraction for Chelsea to June. It was almost laughable.

Chelsea had once been crazy in love with this woman who was yelling at her. Or had it been crazy in lust? When Chelsea knew for sure June was a lesbian, she went about seducing her with relentless determination. She remembered how, after the first thrilling touch, she couldn't get enough—although June was not the best lover, far from it. June had told her she'd had previous lovers, but she apparently hadn't learned how to please. Her lovemaking had no nuance, no imagination. However, her lips were hot, and Chelsea knew how to make her rise to her touch, to pant with excitement, and to come with a cry and shudder.

Although disillusioned, Chelsea was not quite ready to quit. The ache in her chest told her that. She knew it was foolish to attempt to keep someone who didn't want to be kept. Brad hadn't been able to hang on to her. She'd begun to leave him as soon as June had shown an interest in her. By the time Brad had realized what was going on, she'd had one foot out the door—following her desire.

She wondered, as she had many times, how she'd been transported from married woman to lesbian lover. It had surprised her to find out that hearts actually do leap with joy and break into pieces, like the books said. And oh, how they can hurt. She was ashamed that she had done to Brad what was being done to her.

June's face had turned red from shouting. Chelsea emerged from her funk and studied the angry hazel eyes, the cascading dishwater-blond hair, the Slavic cheekbones, and the sturdy yet womanly body. Was she really in love with this person who was cheating on her?

She laughed softly, bitterly.

"You think this is funny?" June snapped.

"Not at all." She stood up, heart thudding heavily, and stretched to shake the hurt away. "I'm going out."

"Where?" June demanded.

"Actually, I don't know, but I won't be gone long," she answered, thinking that it had been nervy to ask. June had lost that right when she took up with Karen. Although she knew she had to get away, she feared even more coming home and finding June and Karen in the house or, worse, in the bed. Maybe that's why June was asking.

She picked up her keys and headed toward the nearest door. *Don't slam it*, she told herself. *Don't let June know how upset you are.*

She paused to check out her appearance in the floor-length mirror by the door. Her short auburn hair was shot through with silver, her blue-gray eyes looked back at her tiredly. She checked out her face, the straight nose and high cheekbones, and wondered why she wasn't cute enough. She'd lost weight since Karen had come on the scene. Skinny wasn't necessarily attractive.

As she closed the door quietly behind her, she thought maybe June would run out and try to stop her. And tell her what? That she didn't want to lose her? Like that was going to happen. Even so, she gave June a few minutes to redeem herself before backing out of the driveway and heading for the bridge. Where would she go? She hadn't made any friends of her own—she had only been here six months. She felt as if she had made a huge error in judgment, one that could not be rectified.

It wasn't too late to go back to Brad, she knew. He hadn't wanted her to leave. It had taken all her resolve to pack and move from the house she and he had called home for over twenty-five years. If she returned, though, she knew she'd never be able to leave again. She winced at the thought of living there, knowing it would be a huge mistake, unfair to Brad and untrue to herself. Now that she knew who she was. What she was.

Her kids were angry. Her sister bemused. Her best friend, Gina, had helped with the move. Chelsea hadn't thought to ask how Gina felt about her leaving. When Gina had asked why she was going, Chelsea had said her girls were grown and she wanted to go home, back where she came from—something Gina already knew.

Thinking about Gina brought a smile. They had spent so much time together over the years—taking care of each other's children, going on trips with or without their kids, sharing hobbies, even painting each others' houses. They were more like sisters than sisters. Gina was better than a best friend. And

Chelsea had lied to her. Yes, she had wanted to go home, she had never wanted to leave in the first place, but she had been unable to tell Gina why she was going back for good. After all these years, how would she explain that if she couldn't have Gina, she would have another woman—especially when she had never admitted to how she felt about Gina.

She had loved Brad, but she had been in love with Gina without ever acknowledging it. Not to herself, not to anyone. It stunned her when she finally "saw the light." Anyway, it would have been impossible even if Gina had felt the same. Their families were tied together. The kids loved their dads, who were good friends. Gina worked with her husband. Although Chelsea hadn't actually worked with Brad, her life was bound with his in so many ways—children, money, and property. She had managed the family finances and balanced the books at Brad's dad's welding company—a job she took when Lizzie, her youngest, went to pre-school and the empty days stretched before her.

She drove to High Cliff State Park and walked to the edge of the cliff that was part of the Niagara Escarpment. A hot, strong wind pushed against her as she looked down at the trees growing out of the limestone wall, resisting the urge to jump. Did anyone else feel this strange impulse? Boats bobbed like toys on the huge lake beyond. Was she beginning again, alone this time? It would be lonely, and she had never been good at making friends—too shy. She was very good at keeping them, though.

Maybe June had been a catalyst, the nudge she'd needed to leave Brad and move back home and live the life she had been meant to live. She had broken free, even though everyone she loved had disapproved. She had tried to convince herself that her behavior would give her children the liberty to ignore convention and find their own ways in the world, that she had actually done them a favor. Of course, they did not see it that way, and despite her protestations, they were sure she'd left their father for another woman—one they disliked. They were right, but even if she was brave enough to tell them the truth, and she wasn't, she was afraid she'd lose them for good.

She'd met June at the family cottage. She had actually saved her life. June had been hit in the head by her own ski after she'd fallen in front of the cottage. While her mother and daughters were eating lunch, Chelsea had gone down to the beach to pick up the book she'd left there and had witnessed the accident. She had jumped into the water and cradled June until the ski boat looped around and returned to the site of the fall.

She had watched them drive away, realizing only then that it was the boat owned by the dykes, or the women who her cousin, the uncle of her girls' second cousins, called the dykes. He would say, "Here come the dykes." And she would ask how he knew that. "Vibes," he'd say and laugh. He was gay. He was also her favorite cousin.

Later that hot day, June had kayaked over to thank her. She had told Chelsea she was visiting friends at a cottage down the lake. Later Chelsea had called one of those friends and asked for June's number. She had called her one evening when Brad was out and they had begun a conversation that had continued to the present.

When Chelsea returned to the home she and June shared during the owners' absence, the house was empty. Not even a note on the fridge to tell her where June had gone. She plopped down on the sofa and stared out the window at the sunny day. Piled on the coffee table with mail on top of it was a package—a manuscript. She leaned forward and opened it. The enclosed letter read—

Dear Chelsea—
This mms is the work of Mimi Kincaid, a new writer we decided to publish if she agreed to one condition. We asked that she change it from first person to third person, so be alert for mistakes. After your read-through, let me know what you think.
Best, JG

Joan Gordon was the person Chelsea dealt with at FemBooks, a lesbian publishing company for whom she'd been working as a manuscript reader for about six months.

She had seen an ad by FemBooks, looking for a reader in *Lambda Literary Magazine*, a periodical June subscribed to. Chelsea thought it was something she could do since she'd majored in English with an emphasis on journalism and communications. She'd also worked on school newspapers and successfully submitted her own short stories to the college magazine, *The Raven*. And she'd won a short story contest in a teen magazine. She was grateful when she was given the chance. Being a reader was not the same as being an editor. As a reader she gave feedback as to the merit and potential of new manuscripts. She did not make corrections or suggest changes, except, in this case, she would be making notes of the I's, we's, our's and the like that should have been changed to he's, she's, they's and their's.

The manuscript was titled *Fire Works*. Chelsea tore open the package, glad to have a distraction, and began to read. The book was aptly named. The protagonist was a thirty-nine-year-old woman, just coming out. The daughter, home from university, was furious with her mother because the woman was splitting with the girl's father. The mother's lame lies only made the nineteen-year-old young woman angrier. The protagonist could have been Chelsea trying to explain her leaving Brad to their daughters, Abby and Lizzie.

She became so engrossed in the book she failed to hear the door open and jumped when June entered the room.

"Have you got another book to work on?" June thought what she did was glamorous.

"A new author," she said.

"Good. I'm going away for the night. I'll be back late tomorrow," June said abruptly and gestured toward the bedroom. "I have to pack a few things."

She knew it was a mistake to ask, but she couldn't help it. "Where are you going?"

"Not your business."

She followed June to the bedroom and leaned against the doorframe, her hands in her pockets. "You asked me where I was going." Her heart had squeezed itself into a painful knot.

June looked at her and sighed. "Look, why don't you go to Dana's? She's been asking about you."

"Why don't we both go to Dana's?" Dana Cooper was June's friend, not hers. She and June taught at the same high school.

"No, I'm serious. Dana wants you to come over. Her girlfriend will be there and a friend of theirs she wanted us to meet. I have to get away."

"From me?" The knot that was her heart tied itself tighter. Breathing hurt.

"Yeah, Chelse, from you."

The intense pain caught her off-guard, although it shouldn't have. She hated herself for being so needy. She turned abruptly but thought to grab the manuscript and her pencil before she fled. She never went anywhere without something to read, because she might end up stuck somewhere with nothing to do. She heard June's voice but not what she said as she went out the door.

Normally, she would ride her bike, but she wasn't sure how far she was going or if she would be coming back before dark so she took the car.

For an hour she drove aimlessly around the neighborhood where she'd grown up, which she remembered as happy times. She couldn't locate the place where they'd first lived when the family moved to the Fox Cities, the one where the mouse jumped out of the toaster one morning. It must have been torn down when that side of town had been spruced up. The triangular lot where she and her sister, Celine, had played softball with neighborhood friends had been turned into a park. Celie now lived in Colorado with her husband and two sons.

Their dad had long been dead, but she still heard echoes of his voice. Her mother's death had been more recent. She was very much alive in Chelsea's mind. In fact, Chelsea often talked to her. A year or two after their mother died, Celie had sent her *Kinflicks* and *Other Women* to read, and Chelsea had admitted her sexuality to herself.

She parked at the boat landing in a small space next to vehicles with empty trailers. A hot breeze washed over her sweaty face. She wondered if she showed up at Dana's what they would have to say to each other. What did they have in common, besides June? She sure didn't want to talk about June. Nor did she want anyone's pity. She was certain June had told Dana about Karen.

She went anyway, because she needed to hear another voice besides the one in her head. She'd only been to Dana's once and June had been driving. After a few wrong turns she found the way to the apartment complex, but once there she realized she didn't know which building Dana was in or the number of her apartment. Sorting back through her jumbled memories, she came up with the right building. Inside the foyer, she studied the names next to the buzzers, found the right one, and pressed the button next it. Dana let her in the building.

As she raised her fist to knock, Dana opened the door and drew her inside. "I'm so glad you're here." She looked into Chelsea's eyes as if searching for something. Dana was tall and commanding, but right then she was also reassuring. "You remember Mickie, right?" Dana asked, pointing to a young woman who looked more like she was thirteen than eighteen. Dana was breaking school rules by dating a student, but who was Chelsea to judge? "And this is our friend, Barb Dunhill." Barb looked to be around Dana's age.

"I do remember Mickie. Hi to you both." She smiled and wiped the sweat off her forehead. "Hot out there."

"Come in and sit." Dana pointed to an empty rocker. "I'll get you something cold."

"Just water, please," she said.

An uncomfortable silence fell, which Dana filled. "Barb teaches music and coaches girls' sports at a high school south of here."

Barb made the muscles in her upper arms bulge and burst into song. "Oh, solo mio, I am so strong. Look at my muscles. They'll take you down…"

Astonished, Chelsea erupted into nervous laughter and couldn't stop. She howled until she nearly wet her pants. "Sorry," she panted. "Where is the john?"

She heard the others laughing when she closed the door and ripped down her shorts. "God, don't do that again without warning," she said when she came out.

Barb picked up a doily from the end table next to her and put it on her head. "I'm doing penance," she said.

They all broke into laughter. Chelsea wondered how she could laugh when a minute ago she had been so sad. "Can you come home with me?" she asked. "I need some humor in my life."

CHAPTER TWO

1968

It had been a bad year so far anyway. She had been in shock when Dr. Martin Luther King, Jr., was assassinated, and she'd cried and cried when Bobby Kennedy was killed. Brad hadn't seemed terribly upset, which made her think he might vote for Richard Nixon. She'd called her mother and they'd commiserated together. On the next Saturday she'd taken the kids to downtown Indianapolis, put them in their buggy and marched with the Women's International League for Peace and Freedom, protesting the Vietnam War.

Chelsea nursed loneliness like a cold sore, touching it with her mind instead of her tongue. She tried to ignore it, but like a cold sore, she couldn't leave it alone. She had married Brad Browning—well, actually, she'd become pregnant first—and moved to Indiana, every turn of the wheel taking her away from the state she loved. She'd thought marriage would be more meaningful. But it hadn't played out that way.

Outside the bay window the grass stretched at least a football field-length to the road. Brad had planted a row of pines to shield the house from public view, but the trees were only a couple of feet tall. He had also placed two ornamental trees near the house, a redbud and a magnolia, and a tulip tree a few feet farther out. It would be years before they offered shade. In the meantime, the small house they lived in with their two little girls baked in the sun, like a pile of stones in a kiln.

"Look, Mama, the grass is running!" Abby exclaimed.

The green blades leaned away from the warm May breeze as if they had somewhere urgent to go. "It does look that way." She smiled at her daughter's imaginative observation and placed a hand on the little girl's ginger-colored hair, still baby soft at the age of four. Abby looked up at her and grinned.

Chelsea sighed deeply. How she wished they lived in town, surrounded by neighbors—not just for her but the kids too. They needed playmates. She'd been here four and a half years and only knew a few people, none well enough to call up and chat.

It was a Saturday. Brad was landscaping and might not be home before dark. Chelsea loved her kids, she did, but she couldn't have an adult conversation with them. Elizabeth's cries penetrated her thoughts, and she walked down the hall to the little bedroom where Lizzie hung on to the rail of her crib with one hand and stretched the other toward her mother. The baby's wails turned to sobs and then hiccups when Chelsea picked her up.

"Shh, Lizzie. You sound like you've been abandoned." She kissed the tears from her baby girl's fat pink cheeks before placing her on the changing table.

"Was I a crybaby, Mama?" Abby asked.

"All babies cry. Otherwise, how would we know something was wrong with them? Want to go swimming?"

She carried Lizzie to the little pool in the backyard. Lizzie wore diapers. Abby stripped down to her underpants. When Chelsea lowered Lizzie into the water, Abby was already splashing.

"Don't get water in Lizzie's eyes, Abby," Chelsea cautioned as she pulled a lawn chair close enough to put her bare feet into the lukewarm pool.

"That looks like fun," someone called.

Chelsea craned her neck in the direction of the voice. A woman stood on the old railroad tracks that were no longer in use. With her were two kids—a girl and a little boy.

"Can we go in the water, Mom?" The boy pulled on his mother's arm, trying to drag her toward the little pool where Chelsea and the girls gawked.

After a few awkward moments, Chelsea found her voice. "Come and join us. It's not much, but it's wet." She felt stupid, thinking how hot it was and here they were sitting outside next to a foot-and-a-half-deep plastic pool with only a twig of a tree to protect them from the blazing sun.

The woman let the boy pull her through the berry bushes and burdock into the yard. The girl followed, holding her arms high against the prickly branches.

"Hi, I'm Gina Lawrence and these are my kids, Suzy and Matt." Gina's warm brown eyes and wide smile broke through Chelsea's natural shyness.

Chelsea stood up. "I'll get another chair. Watch your sister, Abby."

"I'm Abigail and my sister is Elizabeth. I'm four and she's almost one. Do you live on the road over there?" Abby pointed toward the direction from which the kids and their mother had come.

"Yeah. In that white house." The little boy had taken off all but his underpants. "I'm four too."

Abby laughed, a high trilling sound. She jumped up and down in excitement, sloshing water over the sides. "Come in the water, Suzy."

Lizzie, who had been rocking precariously, lost her balance and fell backward.

"Whoa," Gina said, righting the baby, who sputtered and began to cry.

Chelsea set the chair down and picked up her little girl. "You're okay, Lizzie."

Lizzie quit crying and pushed against her mother, her small finger pointing at the pool. Chelsea put her back in the water.

"I'll watch her," Suzy said, shedding her shorts and shirt and sitting down next to the baby.

An hour sped by. Chelsea knew they should go inside. She put more lotion on the kids and added water to the pool. The children's bare skin had turned bright pink. But she and Gina had begun exchanging information about each other. She feared Gina and her kids would leave, and she wouldn't have this chance again. Reluctantly, she suggested the children dry off and play in the house. It was littered with toys and books.

"The sun is so hot," she said, and Lizzie needed a nap. She was falling asleep in the water.

Gina stood up and said it was time to go home anyway.

"No!" Chelsea protested loudly, embarrassing herself. "I'll get some towels. Watch the baby, Abby." And she hurried into the house before anyone could respond.

When she came out, though, Gina's kids were pulling their clothes over wet skin. The little boy was crying. "I don't wanna go home," he howled.

"I wish you wouldn't leave," Chelsea said, feeling defeated. She swept the baby out of the pool, and Lizzie began to wail.

"Why don't you come to our house tomorrow?" Gina asked with that warm smile. "We don't have a pool, but we have a pony."

Abby jumped up and down. "Can I ride the pony?"

"Of course, you can," Gina assured her.

"It's *my* pony, Mom," Suzy said, glaring at her mother.

"I know, sweetie, but you don't mind sharing, do you?"

"You have a pony all your own?" Abby asked with awe. "You're so lucky."

Suzy smiled, her small chest puffing up. "His name is Rodeo Joe, but we just call him Joe."

Matt stopped sobbing and smiled, tears shining on his burned face. "Will you come?" he asked Abby.

"Can we go, Mama?" Abby's crystal-blue eyes squinted at her mother.

"Yes, of course. What time?" she asked Gina, admiring her tan. Her own skin felt crisp and shrunken. She knew it was burned from the sun.

"Any time after nine. We can always put the baby down for a nap."

The next day they woke to rain. The drops weeping down the windows felt as if they came from Chelsea's heart. Abby cried when her mom told her she couldn't ride the pony in the rain. As if in a trance, Chelsea watched the roses in bloom bend their heavy heads under the onslaught. She'd often felt they lived in a place of frightening fecundity. Grasses, plants, bushes, flowers, and weeds grew with alarming speed. In Wisconsin the summers were not so hot and humid.

Brad had left for his regular job at Better Welding, the company his father owned. Brad loved to weld but disliked the paperwork that came with running a business. Chelsea often wondered why he had gone to college. What was the point, except to please his mom? Of course, they would never have met, thus no babies, had they not gone to the same college.

More to the point, she thought, why had she graduated from college only to become a housewife? Because she had lost her first job when she became pregnant. That was when she married Brad. She couldn't even get a credit card in her name. Just as she was beginning to sizzle, the phone rang.

She figured Brad must have forgotten something. But no, it was a woman on the line. "Looks like we got rained out. How about tomorrow?"

"Gina, is it you?"

The woman laughed with gusto. "Yes, it's me. Matt is moping around like he lost his best friend, and Suze is disappointed too. She wanted to play pony trainer."

Chelsea felt her spirits spiraling upward. She laughed, maybe too loud.

Gina said, "Come at nine. We'll have a picnic lunch. If you have time, that is." The last sentence said with a trace of doubt.

"What should I bring? For the picnic, that is." Chelsea knew she sounded eager; she was.

"Nothing. Just yourselves." More laughter. The boy was shouting in the background. "Do you hear Matt? He's all excited."

"I am too," she said and wondered if she should have admitted it.

"Me too. See you in the morning then. It better not rain."

She felt like dancing. "We're going on a picnic tomorrow," she said to Abby, picking Lizzie up from the floor and swinging her around. Only then did she wonder how Gina knew her phone number.

"Are we gonna ride the pony?" Abby asked, standing on her toes. "Was that Gina?"

"Yes. Watch your little sister for a few minutes, Abby. I'm going to make a path to the tracks for tomorrow." She put Lizzie in the playpen. Before she went out the back door, Lizzie was bellowing.

The next day, Chelsea walked through the yard to the old tracks over the narrow path she had made the day before in the rain. She carried Lizzie and a bag with a dozen deviled eggs and peanut butter and jelly sandwiches that she'd cut into fourths, all wrapped separately in cellophane. Abby whined about the berry bushes scratching and grabbing her clothes and the tromped burdock clinging to her, making her itch.

"You like the berries your daddy picks. They come from those scratchy things." Some days she just wanted to say "Shut-up," but the "S" word wasn't allowed. She was more excited than Abby. Nothing could squash her happy mood.

The little white house had dormers. A Rambler station wagon was parked in front of the garage. Chelsea walked up the front steps onto the open porch and rang the doorbell.

Matt flung open the door. "Mom is in the bathroom," he shouted.

"Oh," Chelsea said, startled.

Suzy came up behind her brother. "You're not supposed to tell if anyone is the bathroom,'" she scolded. "Want to come in?"

Chelsea felt they should wait till Gina appeared, but Abby pushed past her mother into the house. Lizzie banged her little legs against her, and Chelsea set her on the floor where she clung to her mother.

"Hey, how are Abby and Lizzie?" Gina knelt on the wood floor and took Lizzie's hands.

Lizzie screwed up her little face, ready to bellow, and then unscrewed it. "Pony," she said, and Chelsea involuntarily clapped her hands. It was the first time Lizzie had said anything besides "Mama and Daddy and Abby."

"I think she should have the first ride, don't you, Chelse?" Gina said, looking up at Chelsea with a wide smile.

Abby began to sniffle.

"Aww, Abby. You'll get to hold the reins. Do you know what reins are?"

"They're how you steer the pony," Matt said proudly.

"I didn't ask you, smarty-pants," his mother said, ruffling his fair hair. Standing up, Gina gave Chelsea a stern look. "What is in the bag? Diapers, right? Not food?" She laughed. "Don't take me seriously. I love it when other people feed me. Don't I, Suze? She's been helping me with the picnic."

Still savoring being called Chelse, she handed the bag to Gina with a shy smile and then realized she'd forgotten diapers. She hit her forehead with the heel of her hand. Lizzie would be drenched by the time they went home.

Gina peeked in the bag. "I love deviled eggs!" she exclaimed. "And look at the little sandwiches. How clever." She met Chelsea's eyes with a teasing grin. "We have diapers. My sister has a little girl about the same age as Lizzie."

The pony was a little devil—Gina's words, said in an aside to Chelsea. When Suzy put on the saddle, the pony cow-kicked at her. Suze punched Rodeo Joe in the gut and he grunted. The kicking started again, though, when Suzy tightened the girth.

"MOM," Suzy complained.

The pony was tied to a post next to a low building. Gina tightened the girth with no problem. "You have to show him who is boss." She unbuckled the halter and let it fall around the pony's neck. Rodeo Joe immediately pulled back, thinking he was free, but the halter was fastened to the post by a lead line. A little tussle ensued as Gina got the pony to open his mouth and slid the bridle up over its ears. "Got you, you little B."

Aghast at the animal's behavior, Chelsea opened her mouth to say her girls weren't ready to ride, but she didn't want to jeopardize this new friendship.

"B means bastard," Matt explained.

Chelsea burst into nervous laughter.

"What's a bastard?" Abby asked.

"A bad pony," Gina said and roared.

Chelsea laughed so hard she squirted in her panties. "Oh," she said and laughed some more.

Suzy rode the pony first. "To show you how," she told Abby. Every few steps ended in a buck. "MOM," Suzy yelled again.

"I'll straighten the S-O-B up," Gina said, picking up a crop that was balanced on a fence post.

"That means son of a bitch," Matt shouted.

Gina gave her son a severe look and walked beside the pony. When the animal lifted his hindquarters, Gina lifted the crop.

The pony's eye rolled back to keep a watch on her.

"I think Lizzie should wait till she's bigger," Chelsea called. "She hasn't learned to walk yet."

"He's kind of feisty today," Gina agreed.

Abby stood with her finger in her mouth, looking terrified. "You go first, Matt," she said.

When Gina looked away, Joe bucked especially hard and Suzy went flying. The girl's high scream stood Chelsea's hair on end. She watched, open-mouthed, as Suzy arced through the air and hit the ground. The pony ran on past, reins trailing on the ground and stirrups flapping against his fat belly.

"I HATE him. I HATE him," Suzy said between sobs.

Gina bent over and felt her daughter's limbs. "You're okay, honey. Let me help you up."

"I don't want him, Mom." Suzy pounded her heels on the ground. She threw a twig at the pony, but it traveled less than a foot.

"We'll send him back," Gina soothed. She met Chelsea's eyes. "The owner knows my husband. I think he was trying to unload Joe on us. Some friend, huh? We are trying him out. Maybe the kids will change their minds about wanting a pony."

Rodeo Joe stood at the far end of the small fenced-in area, eating the grass under the bottom board. Gina lured him to her with a little grain in a bucket. She took his tack off and turned him loose with a hard smack on his rump, while Chelsea and the kids waited outside the gate.

Gina hugged Suzy. "You okay, hon?" Suzy sniffed and nodded. "Want to picnic down by the creek?"

"Yeah," Abby and Matt crowed.

A spot by a bend in the slow-moving water had been mown short. Gina set the food on a small picnic table that was losing its paint and helped Suzy spread a blanket for the kids. She and Chelsea, who was carrying Lizzie, would sit in the lawn chairs. Abby and Matt had run ahead and were wading in the creek.

Chelsea couldn't remember when she'd been so happy. In her life before Brad, she'd always had close friends and neighbors, but until Gina came down the tracks, she hadn't made any real friends here. At least, she hoped Gina would want to be a close friend.

She laughed when she sat down and nearly missed the seat, and Lizzie yelped with fright. Joy coursed through her as she put the baby on the blanket.

"So, did you grow up here?" Chelsea asked, keeping an eye on Lizzie, who was stuffing a deviled egg in her mouth with both hands.

Suzy was handing Lizzie food.

"One piece at a time, Suze. Otherwise, she'll choke," Gina said.

Suzy steadied the bottle when the baby drank. She fed her bits of sandwiches. Arms waving and legs kicking, Lizzie stared at the older girl with adoration. Abby and Matt sat facing each other, steadily shoving food in their mouths and then opening them for the other to view the contents.

"I moved here in time to go to high school. You know Dan, don't you? He and Brad and I graduated together."

Chelsea had just popped an egg in her mouth. She chewed and swallowed. "Not really."

"The four of us will have to do some things together now that you and I know each other." She looked at Abby and Matt and wrinkled her nose. "It's like living with little pigs, isn't it?" She turned those dark shining eyes on Chelsea. "Piglets are smart, but they grow into hogs—still smart but huge."

"Let's hope we get them trained before they do."

It was late in the day when she and the kids returned home. Lizzie slept heavily on her hip, and Abby dragged her feet and whined. She placed Lizzie in her playpen. Abby fell asleep on the living room floor.

Brad had taught Chelsea how to make his favorite foods, like beef with noodles made from scratch, but there wasn't enough time for that. She decided on dried beef gravy and mashed potatoes and frozen lima beans for greens and set to work.

When Brad came in the door, Abby was awake and setting the table.

"How is my big girl?" he asked, swinging her in the air.

She squealed. "I'm helping Mama."

Brad gave her a kiss and set her on her feet. "Good."

He gave Chelsea a kiss next to her lips, and she smiled absently.

Brad was over six feet tall with broad shoulders. He sniffed under his muscled arms. "I should take a shower."

"You better hurry. Dinner is almost ready."

CHAPTER THREE

When they sat down to eat, Abby told her dad about their picnic.

"I went to school with Gina and Dan," he said, smiling at Chelsea.

"Do you know Matt and Suzy and Rodeo Joe too?" Abby asked, her voice rising in surprise.

"I don't know Rodeo Joe," Brad said.

"He's Suzy's pony. He bucked Suzy off and ran away."

Brad raised his fair eyebrows. "For real?" He shot a look at Chelsea.

"It's true, isn't it, Mama? Joe is a bastard," Abby said.

Lizzie covered her face with her bib and laughed. "Bbbb,"she said.

"Bad pony." Chelsea tried not to smile, but she laughed aloud.

"Sounds dangerous to me," Brad remarked, digging into the dried beef gravy and mashed potatoes. "This is so good, hon." He smiled at Chelsea.

He was so easy to please, Chelsea thought. "Why haven't I met Gina and Dan before?" she asked.

"You have. Remember when the Service Club held a dinner for the wives? I introduced you to them."

Chelsea searched her memories for a glimpse of Gina and Dan. She pictured them dancing.

"I'm glad you met Gina. Dan and I have been friends since first grade."

"Aren't you still friends?" Chelsea asked.

"Sure, just not like high school. We'll have to get together with them."

Chelsea wanted to be Gina's best friend.

Lizzie was napping the next day when Chelsea went out front to pull weeds in the rose bed. The roses were peeking in the windows, and the marigolds she had planted as a border had grown into each other. She knelt in the sunlight and jerked at the weeds. They broke off at ground level, but she didn't care. It was a task she abhorred.

Abby, who had been helping, had fallen asleep on the grass in the shade of the house. Her cheeks were pink from the heat and a fly hovered over her face.

Chelsea crawled next to her and waved the fly away. She stretched her legs out and was leaning back on her hands when she saw Gina coming toward her, a finger over her lips signaling silence.

Gina beckoned Chelsea with a hand, and they went around the corner of the house by the garage.

"I can't stay more than a few minutes. Suze is watching Matt. I wanted to make sure you came to the Service Women's meeting tonight. I'll pick you up around six thirty. I thought maybe you didn't know about them. Brad's a member of the men's group."

"I don't know anybody," Chelsea said as an excuse, mesmerized by the intense brown eyes.

"Well, now you know me. Okay? Six thirty?"

"All right." A few minutes ago, boredom had exhausted her.

But now, because of Gina, she felt full of energy, almost buoyant.

She went inside and made beef and noodles. The noodles she hung from the backs of kitchen chairs to dry. It was an unpleasant reminder of how she had scolded Brad's old dog for eating the first noodles she'd ever made. She'd sent him to the basement, his tail between his legs. He'd been hit and killed by a car a few months later. Brad had carried him home in his arms. Shuddering, she pushed the memory away.

When Brad came home from work at six, having stopped to check on his most recent landscaping job, she was dressed to go. Nervous, she ate quickly. There would be little time to clean up and no time to get the girls ready for bed.

"I'll take care of them," Brad said. "We'll have fun, won't we?" he asked the girls.

But when she kissed them all goodbye, Lizzie began to cry and Abby followed Chelsea to the door, talking. Brad put his arms around the baby and then Abby when she burst into tears.

"Don't worry about us," he called after Chelsea.

She ran to Gina's car and climbed in. "I feel as if I escaped," she said, feeling guilty.

"Me too," Gina agreed.

The meeting was held in Carole Jackson's home. Carole was six months pregnant with her first child, Gina told her as they walked toward the front door. When Chelsea looked around the room, she recognized two women. She and Brad had gone to college with them.

"I know those two," she whispered to Gina, but she was in conversation with another woman. She had neglected to tell Chelsea she was president of the Service Women's group.

Chelsea found a free chair and sat down.

The first order was for everyone to introduce herself. The two women from Chelsea's college days, Jeanne Jalinsky and Trish MacComb, had different last names due to marriage. Chelsea was the only new person. Rattled at being asked to stand up, she felt a flush creep over her skin like a hot red blanket.

The second order of business was getting people to work at the car wash with the guys the following weekend. The money was going to the Carmichael family, whose little boy suffered from renal failure. Chelsea couldn't imagine losing Abby or Lizzie.

"Trish and I will babysit for those of you who want to go." Jeanne Jalinsky waved a hand in the air.

"I'll go to the car wash," Chelsea volunteered and was embarrassed because everyone looked as if she'd spoken out of turn.

Gina winked at her. "I'll go with you," she said.

Flustered by the wink, Chelsea looked away. Her heart was pounding.

"I can take the kids to Jeanne's," Gina said on the way home.

"I better go with you. They were both screaming when I left home tonight."

Gina laughed. "Sure. Did you notice how everyone talks about their kids as if they hadn't just been with them? It's nice to know someone who talks about something else."

She had noticed. "I suppose their kids are their lives." She shuddered and then was ashamed.

"Maybe we should hang out together with our kids, so they are not all we have to talk about."

"That would be fun," Chelsea said, hoping Gina meant it.

"The thing is, I have to paint Suzy's bedroom next week and then, of course, Matt wants his bedroom painted too."

"I can take the kids, or I can help you paint."

"Paint with me. We can keep an eye on the kids together."

Jeanne lived in a ranch house surrounded by other ranch houses. The backyard was fenced-in and full of little kids—a few crying, some wandering about, and several on an elaborate swing set.

Abby clung to her mother's leg until Matt grabbed her hand and ran off with her. Suzy sat down in the living room with Lizzie in her lap. Chelsea felt like a bad mother, because she was excited to go somewhere with Gina without the kids. Maybe she was, she thought.

"Why were all those kids there? Their moms aren't going to the car wash, not yet anyway," she asked Gina as they drove away.

"Jeanne and Trish run a daycare center. Sometimes Carole Jackson helps." Carole had been there as had Trish.

The car wash was in a bank parking lot. The guys were washing and drying vehicles. Chelsea and Gina stood on the sidewalk, waving cars in or at least trying to. One of the guys collected the money. Chelsea would rather have been washing cars. Dan and Brad were not there, of course. Dan had to work Saturdays, and Brad had a landscaping job.

At noon, two other women showed up to take Chelsea's and Gina's places and Gina said, "Let's get the kids and go have some fun. How come women always get the crappy jobs? Like we can't wash cars or collect money."

Chelsea agreed. "Isn't that the way it goes," she said, thinking she would go anywhere with Gina. Gina had saved her from boredom.

It was past lunchtime and Lizzie was crying when they walked around Jeanne's house and into the backyard. The little girl brightened for a moment when she saw her mother and then began screaming full force.

Chelsea picked her up and rocked her. "Shush, Lizzie." She turned to Jeanne, who was holding a bottle and looking stressed. "I hope for your sake she hasn't been crying all morning."

Jeanne handed Chelsea the bottle, and she stuck it in Lizzie's mouth even though it was cool. Jeanne must have seen them coming. "Well, she fell asleep for a while."

Gina drove while Chelsea fed Lizzie. "Poor little screamer," she cooed.

They stopped at a White Castle burger joint and fed the other kids and themselves, then traveled on to Eagle Park. The park was huge. Trails traversed the woods and reservoir. They walked down a steep hill to the shore, where the opaque water was filled with twigs and leaves. A branch was sticking up further out. Lizzie had fallen asleep in Chelsea's arms.

"There is a program on birds of prey in the park building at two," Gina said. "Want to go?"

A bald eagle and a golden were caged side-by-side. The golden eagle dwarfed the other. When Chelsea bent over to look at the huge eagle, it snapped at her. "I'd bite someone too if I were in a cage," she said softly.

A man in a park uniform walked up and down the aisles with a kestrel on a glove, holding the jesses between finger and thumb. He introduced himself as Ranger Ken. The bird was as beautiful as it was aloof.

"This male was found injured in the park," the man said and swept his arm toward the cages along the wall. "None of these birds can be turned loose because, for one reason or another, they can't hunt." He talked about the kestrel being the smallest falcon in the country and explained that a falcon was a hawk with long pointed wings. The beautiful little falcon mostly ate insects but sometimes devoured other things like lizards or mice. "It is often called a sparrow hawk because of its small size, and it is one of the few raptors where the male is colored differently from the female." He put it back in its cage, where it briefly flapped its wings.

He then took a barred owl out of its cage. The owl clamped down on the man's glove and swiveled its head around without changing its body position. Laughter erupted. Ranger Ken smiled. "She does that because she can. Owls have excellent hearing. They eat small mammals, like mice and moles or rabbits. Their fearless relative, the great horned owl, is bigger and is often called the denizen of the night or the flying tiger. It will even take on skunks and porcupines. In the birds of prey, the females are larger than the males."

Lastly, he put a peregrine falcon on his glove. "This is the fastest animal alive. She can stoop, which means dive through the air, at 200 miles an hour and kill ducks on the wing." The falcon chattered and tried to peck him. "She is a feisty one," he said as the bird grabbed his thumb with its beak. "We wear gloves not only to protect us from the talons."

The kids were fascinated when the man allowed them to stroke an unbelievably small saw-whet owl. "Can we have one?" Matt asked his mother.

"We probably do in woods," Gina whispered. "You can hear them at night, saying 'too whit,' if you listen."

Chelsea had noticed the three bird feeders in Gina's yard. Chelsea only had one.

It was after four when they got home. Lizzie was crabby, and Chelsea fed her before starting dinner. The worse thing about being in charge of the food was the planning. *What to eat tonight?* she wondered. She got a beef stew going, but it wouldn't be done till after six. Brad never complained, though.

Abby fell asleep in front of the television before they sat down to dinner. She woke up grumpy. When her dad asked her what she did that day, she brightened and told him.

"Sounds like fun," he said. "I thought you were going to the car wash."

"I did. Till noon," Chelsea said.

"Chelse, do you want to go with us to the Humane Society, you and the kids?" Gina called and asked the next day. "We're looking for a pup. Dan doesn't have time to go with us. You could keep me from getting a dog that's cute but doesn't fit our lifestyle."

"What dog fits your lifestyle?" She wanted to laugh but was pretty sure Gina was serious.

"Probably a Lab or a golden retriever. You know? Good with kids. Obedient. Friendly. Won't bite the mailman or yap when somebody comes over."

Chelsea thought that description would fit her family too, but Brad thought they should wait until the girls were older before they got another dog. "Sure," she said, though she had been planning to march again in protest against the Vietnam War with the International League of Women for Peace and Freedom.

She had thought of asking Gina to go with her, but she didn't know anything about Gina's politics. And usually when Gina called and wanted to do something, she canceled everything else. She'd been grocery shopping at night when Brad could babysit, in fact, so that she'd be home during the day in case Gina wanted to do something. It was shameful, she thought, this fixation on her friend.

The barking at the Humane Society was deafening. She carried Lizzie, who covered her ears with her hands. A skinny woman showed them the kennels. She was dressed in faded jeans and a T-shirt with the letters "Adopt Me" under a photo of a sad-looking dog. Elaine was scrawled on her nametag. In the kennel area, the noise increased measurably. Dogs pawed the cage doors, tails wagging, all of them barking.

The kids squatted before a cage of puppies that were falling all over each other, trying to push their little noses between the bars. The pups looked like a mix between German shepherd and something else. They nipped at the kids' fingers.

"Ouch!" Matt yelled. "Mom, why don't we get one of these?"

Gina stood on the cement, apparently deep in thought. She looked at Chelsea. "There is an older Lab down at the end."

"Let's go take a peek at him." Chelsea said to Lizzie, kissing one of the hands covering an ear.

The black dog was lying on a dog bed, its head on its paws. "Come here, big dog," Chelsea coaxed.

Lizzie took one hand away from her ear and reached for the animal. Chelsea set the little girl on her feet and watched with trepidation as Lizzie took a step forward and clutched the bars. Before Chelsea could pull the baby away the dog stretched its neck and licked her little fingers.

Lizzie screamed with laughter. "Nice doggie," she said, putting two words together for the first time.

Chelsea squatted next to her and kissed her pink cheek. "It is a nice dog, but it looks so sad. I wonder what its story is."

Elaine came up behind them. "His owner died and there was no one to take him. Older animals get the shaft. They're housebroke and don't cut their teeth on the furniture, yet nobody wants them."

"Can we take him out of his cage?" Chelsea asked, backing Lizzie up.

"Sure." Elaine opened the cage door and leashed the dog. It followed her into the aisle.

Lizzie lost it. "Nice doggie," she yelled and threw herself at the animal, patting it with both small hands before sitting down abruptly.

The dog wagged its tail and licked her cheek, and Lizzie squealed.

"His name is Brutus, but his owner called him Brute. Talk about misnamed. He's a softy."

"Boot, Boot, Boot," Lizzie yelled. "Want, Mama." Lizzie reached for the dog.

Chelsea took hold of Lizzie's hands and pulled her to her feet. Gina had come over and was watching Lizzie's attempts to touch the animal.

"Looks like Lizzie found you a dog." Gina laughed.

Chelsea signed the papers and put down money for the dog, while Abby looked stunned and Gina's kids cried.

"We'll come back soon," Gina promised her children. "I told Elaine to call us when our puppy comes in."

CHAPTER FOUR

Chelsea couldn't take the dog home until her reference, Gina, was checked out, which seemed foolish since Gina was right there. "I wonder what Brad is going to say," she said, thinking aloud on the way home.

Gina threw her a smile. "He'll be delighted to have such a great dog."

"He wanted to wait till the kids were older and more responsible. I thought you would want the dog." Chelsea hoped she hadn't taken the dog out from under Gina's nose.

"How could I do that to Lizzie?" Gina smiled sweetly. "We'll find a dog, and then you and I can take them for walks."

Chelsea was almost sure Gina would have chosen the black Lab if Lizzie hadn't made such a fuss over him.

Abby and Matt were pretending to be pigs in the backseat. One would snort, the other would answer, and they both would laugh. Suzy told them to shut up. Lizzie was crying in her baby harness.

"What's the matter with Lizzie?" Gina asked over the bedlam.

"She's crying because we left Brutus behind," Suzy shouted.

"Boot, Boot," Lizzie yelled between sobs.

"We'll go get Boot later," Chelsea called loudly, and Brutus became Boot.

When Brad came home, Abby jumped into his arms. "Guess what, Daddy?"

The news was on the TV in the living room and Chelsea was listening with half an ear while putting Lizzie in her highchair in the kitchen, but she heard Abby tell her dad they'd bought a big dog. Apparently, Lizzie heard too.

"Boot, Boot," she yelled, banging a spoon against the tray. "Want Boot."

Chelsea turned to meet Brad's questioning gaze. "She put two words together," he said with a smile.

Chelsea laughed at the absurdity of it all.

Two days later Gina and the kids rode with Chelsea to get Boot—two days of listening to Lizzie's demanding words. "Want Boot. Want Boot."

When Elaine brought the dog out, his tail wagged hesitantly. Chelsea knelt to put on Boot's new collar. "Poor guy," she said. "He must feel like he's deserting his master." How could the dog know his former owner was dead?

She had told the kids to wait in the car, but there they all were standing next to Gina, who was holding Lizzie. Gina lifted her shoulders. "I tried to keep them in the car. It was four against one."

"Doggie, Boot!" the baby exclaimed, squirming to get down.

"She's an armful." Gina laughed as she struggled to hang onto Lizzie.

"You can pat him all you want when we get home, Lizzie," Chelsea said.

Lizzie learned to walk hanging on to Boot's collar. She took naps curled into the dog's belly while Boot sprawled in the sunny living room. Abby was jealous until her mom put her in charge of feeding and watering the dog. Chelsea also handed her older daughter a brush and told her to groom Boot every day. Now when they went over to Gina's, Boot went with them. On the way he picked berries from the bushes and ate them.

"What a wonderful find he is," Gina exclaimed on one of their walks. They were pulling Lizzie in a wagon. Matt and Abby took turns sitting with her. Suzy was at a friend's house.

Every July Chelsea spent a month with the kids at the family lake cottage in Wisconsin. This year she asked her mom if Gina and her two children could come with her. Her mom worked during the week, and with only the children for company, Chelsea got kind of lonely—at least, that's what she told her mom. Her mom never would have said no anyway, although Chelsea had a not-so-sneaking suspicion that her mother would rather just have Chelsea and the girls visit. Brad always promised to come on weekends, but the past two years he had only made the trip one weekend out of the month. He was always too busy.

They drove Chelsea's Ford station wagon. The luggage was packed behind the backseat and around the kids and dog. It had to come out first in order for everyone to get out. Chelsea drove, and Gina kept an eye on the kids. Suzy sat in the window seat in the middle with Lizzie fastened beside her. Abby and Matt were in the back. The dog took turns standing between two of the kids, his front feet perched on the window ledge and his nose out the window—eyes squinting, tongue and ears blowing.

It took over eight hours to get to the lake. The traffic around Gary and Chicago slowed them to a stop at times. Lizzie cried when Boot rode in the back with Abby and Matt, but Suzy complained when his big body got in her face as he leaned over her to reach the window.

"That's what dogs do," Gina said. "Move closer to Lizzie. Let him have the window."

But then Lizzie yelled because she couldn't pat Boot's behind.

"We need a window between us and the kids," Gina said.

They were inching along behind two lanes of vehicles. "I've thought of that," Chelsea said. "I wonder what the hang-up is."

"Probably an accident." Gina glanced behind her. "Hey, don't open the window so wide. Boot might jump out."

It was late afternoon when they drove down the sandy two-lane driveway to the lake cottage. Chelsea stretched, a hand to her back, before helping to unload.

Her mom came outside, a slender woman with graying hair, and Chelsea introduced her to everyone. Abby clung to her grandma, while her grandma kept an eye on Lizzie.

"Take her hand, Abby. We'll show her the lake." Together they walked Lizzie to the top of the hill.

Lizzie pulled free of Abby's grasp and pointed at the lake. "Pool. Swim," she shrieked.

"I forgot she was a screamer," Chelsea's mom said, laughing.

Chelsea had paused to watch. She laughed too. "Shh, Lizzie. You'll scare Grandma."

"No. She won't. Should we go down and see the lake, Lizzie?" Abby was already running down the steps after Matt and Suzy to where the dog was belly deep in the water.

"Stay off the pier, and don't get in the water until Grandma gets there, all of you," Chelsea yelled. "I mean it."

Gina looked amused. "It's like keeping flies off a dead fish."

"Come on, Lizzie," her grandma said. "Let's leave your mom and Gina to it."

"Thanks, Mrs. Saunders," Gina said. "Don't let my kids give you any guff."

"Call me Jen, Gina. I won't let them drown."

Chelsea threw her arms around her mother and Lizzie. "Thanks, Mom. It's so good to see you. How's Dad?"

"He said to say hello. You'll see him on the weekend." Her dad taught shop at the high school and took on painting jobs in the summer. Jen Saunders worked morning kindergarten during the school year. She said she loved the kids, loved having the afternoon free. In the summer she helped out at a nursery school, also half-days. When Chelsea was a kid, her mom taught fifth grade full time.

"Do you think you can stand us for a month?"

"I've stood you for twenty-seven years. A month is nothing. And where but here do I get to see the kids and you for any length of time?" Jen stood about five feet three and weighed no more than one hundred and ten pounds. Her eyes were the same shade of gray-blue as Chelsea's.

"My kids are here too. Sure you can stand them?" Gina's mouth twitched.

"This is the perfect place for children," Jen said and started down the hill with Lizzie struggling to get down. "Just hang on there, baby, we're going down to swim."

Jen left for home around five. She'd brought dinner but hadn't stayed to eat it. When the kids were in bed, Chelsea and Gina played Scrabble on the porch. In the loft Matt and Abby's whispers had faded into sleep. Even Suzy had turned off her light in the other loft. Lizzie had fallen asleep during dinner. The sun had finally set, leaving a dark red streak along the western horizon. A soft southerly breeze drifted through the screens, along with gnats. Chelsea loved hot summer nights, but she didn't know whether Gina felt the same way.

"It will cool off later," Chelsea promised. "Maybe around midnight." They were sleeping in the two beds on the porch with all the windows open. Insects hit the screens like tiny kamikazes, attracted by the overhead light, while cicadas sang in the trees.

"Look," Gina said, pointing at the half moon hanging over the lake. "It is gorgeous here, Chelse. Thanks for inviting us."

"Thanks for coming." She grinned, and Gina laughed. Chelsea thought she'd never been so content.

The first few days she and Gina sat in beach chairs and read while the kids played in the sand and splashed in the water. Suzy made it her job to look after Lizzie, pulling her out of the lake, only to have her crawl into the water once again. Gina paid Suzy a dime every time she ran up the hill to check on Lizzie when she took her afternoon nap.

"Let me," Gina said when Chelsea argued that she should do the paying. "I want to and it's so much easier than arguing with her."

The dog dropped a ball in front of anyone who would throw it. He retrieved it time after time. When everyone was tired of throwing for Boot, he trotted out on the pier and dropped the ball in the water, watched it for a moment and then jumped in after it.

"Look, Mama," Abby said, standing on her knees in the sand. "Boot throws his own ball."

"Good!" Chelsea exclaimed. "I was getting awfully tired of throwing it for him."

"Mom, I want a dog like Boot." Matt too was covered with sand. He and Abby had been burying each other. Suzy turned her nose up at getting "all covered with dirt." She didn't trust Matt to unbury her. Besides, she was always chasing Lizzie.

By the end of the day, either Chelsea or Gina hosed Matt and Abby off before ordering them into the tub. The kids wore T-shirts to keep from getting burned, but the sun got to them anyway. By supper they were all tired and squabbling.

On cloudy days they went for walks. Lizzie rode in the wagon and Abby and Matt took turns riding when they tired. Gina and Chelsea took turns pulling the wagon and leading the dog. Suzy whined and dragged her feet until she got to ride for a spell. She was only seven.

Chelsea's mom brought food on weekends, and they all ate as if they'd been seriously deprived. During the week Chelsea and Gina often fixed fish sticks and hot dogs and peanut butter and jelly sandwiches in place of what Chelsea's mother called real food. The two younger women gave the kids oranges and celery and carrots for fruit and veggies. All except Lizzie, whose food was mashed or cut up in tiny pieces.

The days were long and lazy, almost fooling Chelsea into believing July might never end. She hated the very idea of going home. She even confided that thought to Gina, who smiled wryly.

"I feel the same way. It's like living in a dream world, isn't it?"

The dream world ended when Brad and Dan arrived on the last Friday of the month. A black mood fell over Chelsea. To her the men were intruders. In a fog she missed hearing whole sentences.

"What?" she asked.

Brad was holding Lizzie in one arm and hugging Abby with the other. He smiled at Chelsea. "How about a kiss before Lizzie chokes me to death."

She stood on her toes to give him a kiss on the lips. All the while, she was tuned in to Gina. She and Dan were acting like lovers. Chelsea hated the kissing sounds. She faked a smile and pretended she was glad to see Brad. She hoped she would fool him. Maybe if she tried hard enough, she would convince herself.

She forced a laugh and took Lizzie out of his arms. The baby immediately began to scream. "Be quiet for once," Chelsea hissed, giving Lizzie a tiny squeeze—something she'd never done. Lizzie looked at her mother with wide eyes and her screams turned to hiccups.

Brad lifted Abby onto his shoulders. "How was your month?" Chelsea wasn't sure whether he was questioning her or Abby, but Abby began talking nonstop.

They were standing in two camps, her family and Gina's, when Chelsea's mom and dad drove in. That night dinner was served outside at the picnic table. The kids were still babbling over each other, regurgitating the month at the lake as each remembered it. Chelsea's eyes flew to Gina's when she felt a hand patting her knee. Gina smiled at her, her wineglass in hand.

She lifted the glass in a toast. "Thanks for a wonderful July."

Chelsea's fingers fumbled for her glass and spilled merlot over the plastic tablecloth. Everyone jumped away while she and Gina mopped it up with paper napkins.

"Bad Mama. Bad," Lizzie yelled.

Chelsea forced a laugh. "Sorry."

She and Gina cleaned the next day, while their husbands watched the kids swim. Chelsea's mom and dad had already said their goodbyes. Chelsea had been unusually teary.

"You'll be back again before you know it," her mom had said as Chelsea's hug took her breath away. She patted Chelsea on the back. "And we'll talk every week."

"I know, Mom," Chelsea had replied. But she wouldn't be back with Gina.

They locked up and drove away the next day, the men behind the wheels. Chelsea and Gina had packed enough snacks to keep the kids happy. Lizzie and Abby slept most of the way home. Chelsea stared out the window, occasionally checking to see that Dan and Gina's car was behind them.

"What's wrong, honey?" Brad asked over the sound of the radio.

"Just tired," Chelsea said.

"You'll be back," he said as her mother had.

"I know."

School would start at the end of August, so they wouldn't be coming back to the lake until spring. Abby and Matt would be in kindergarten. Chelsea would have to find something to do to occupy her time. She knew Gina would be helping Dan part-time at the gas station.

When they pulled into the driveway at home, the yard looked alien—grass and flowers gone wild. Brad looked sheepish. "I didn't have much time to mow and take care of things." He was always taking care of other people's property.

"It will give me something to do," Chelsea said, carrying a bag of dirty clothes to the house. She yelled at Abby to keep an eye on the dog, which was exploring the yard, nose buried in the grass.

Even the house smelled different. It had a closed-up musty odor to it. Dust covered everything. She dropped the bag and went back outside to check on Boot, but the girls were with him. When Lizzie had a handful of his scruff, he stood still or matched his steps to hers.

The grass tickled Chelsea's bare legs. She put a leash on the dog and handed it to Abby. "If he gets away, yell." Boot looked at her as if insulted.

After dinner, Brad put an arm around Chelsea. "It's so good to have you home, hon. I missed you."

She looked up at him, reading the sly smile, the lifted brows. They would have sex that night. She smiled and stifled a sigh.

This was their life together, and she liked sex. She had taught him how to please her. But she couldn't say she'd missed him or that she was glad to be home. Home was the cottage or the Fox Cities.

She looked at the kids and dog and back at Brad. She had to do better, try harder. Besides, Gina was here. Everyone needs a good friend. How lucky she was in having her.

She was riding the mower the next morning. Brad was gone to work. The kids were playing with the dog in the yard. It was heavy going, the grass thick and long. She was in low gear, chugging along, when she noticed an older woman leaning over the fence by the driveway. She idled the engine near her.

"Can I help you?" she asked, thinking the woman must need something.

"Thank heaven you noticed me. I need my yard mowed. My mower man up and quit. It's a big yard, but he says it's not big enough to bother with. Maybe your husband would mow it for me till I find someone else?" The woman was tall and thin and capable looking.

If she hadn't looked quite so able, Chelsea might have done it for free. As it was, she felt guilty asking how much the woman, Mrs. Linkwalter, paid to have it done.

"Twenty bucks a time."

"I'll do it. Just tell me where you are," she said impulsively.

The woman lived half a block from their house. "I might have to bring the kids," she said.

When she told Gina, Gina offered to watch the girls if Chelsea gave her the next job that came along.

As she'd promised, Gina soon brought home a four-month-old puppy, which was as black as Boot. As Lizzie grasped Boots' scruff, Abby and Matt rolled on the grass with the puppy, squealing when Bonnie's sharp little teeth nipped them. Boot remained staid and endured Bonnie's endless attacks.

When Bonnie turned six months, Gina and Chelsea walked the two dogs in the fall evenings as leaves curled down and scuffed under their feet while Dan and Brad watched the kids.

In late August Chelsea and Brad had watched the Democratic Convention turn into a brawl between protesters and police and National Guardsmen. Chelsea was afraid it might cost them the election.

Maybe it's time for a change," Brad said.

"Nixon?" she squawked. "You wouldn't vote for him, would you?"

He hesitated. "I don't know, but plenty of other people will."

"You think?" she asked. "It's time to end that damn war."

"It is," he said.

CHAPTER FIVE

1990

On the way home from Dana's she turned on public radio, heard President George Bush's voice, and turned it off. The sky glowed different shades of red, reminding Chelsea of that summer at the lake when she and Gina swam as the sun set. But time never stands still. Each year she and Gina had grown busier, and the kids had made other friends.

By the time she drove over the Racine Street Bridge, the sky had darkened to purplish gray. So what if things hadn't turned out the way she'd wanted them to? She told herself to stop wondering if she'd made a mistake and get on with her life.

Since she was housesitting, she couldn't walk away from the place till the owners returned from Europe the following fall. Nor, for her own sanity, could she put up with June meeting Karen at the house. She'd have to make that very clear.

She parked in the garage, noting the empty space where June's car belonged, grabbed the manuscript, and went inside. At least, she had something to work on. Settled on the couch with the box of pages and her yellow pencil, she began to read.

Darkness slowly closed around the glare of the lamp and still she read. So far, she'd only picked up a few slips into present tense.

When she came out of the spell the story had created, she was hungry. She scrounged for leftovers. There were none. She stood looking out the open window into the backyard as she ate a peanut butter sandwich. The night was warm. She heard voices as people walked past the house, and she moved to one of the front windows.

Was Brad as lonely as she was? Or had he met some woman to take his mind off her? When she'd told Lizzie she was moving back to Wisconsin, she had denied her daughter's accusation that she was June's lover. She was a coward, no doubt there. She walked around the house to relieve the pain nipping at her like a predator. Locking the door behind her she strode into the beautiful night.

As she walked, she thought of her mother, who had been widowed for many years. Did she have to experience loneliness to understand her mother's? And why had she waited for her mom to die before even admitting her own sexual orientation and coming out? Her mother had liked Brad, maybe even loved him as a son-in-law. She would have understood the gay thing, Chelsea was sure, but she wouldn't have been able to condone Chelsea leaving Brad as she had. She would have had to be honest.

She lifted her head to smell the air. The cicadas were buzzing in the trees, keen to reproduce before they died. As a kid, she had loved summer nights at the lake—the smells, the sounds— even as she'd hung out the window trying to breathe on the way to the hospital for a shot of adrenaline. On the way home, her heart beating crazily, her eyes hollowed and dark from lack of sleep, she'd watch the mist rising from the fields.

Her entire body had yearned to be like that of every other kid. She'd known when an asthma attack was coming on and even so had denied that knowledge till she was struggling for air. Her mom had spent nights in her bed, telling her stories, while she sat up and wheezed and her sister slept obliviously in the other twin bed.

During the day she'd thrown up everything she ate and dreamed of downing cold glasses of milk. Had it been the meds that had nauseated her? Had it been her father's cigarette smoking that had given her asthma, although asthma had run in the family? She'd been so sure she couldn't grow up and live without her mother.

So why, when she turned thirteen, had she morphed from being a nice kid into being a horrid teenager? Stealing her dad's cigarettes, acting as if her parents and sister had been the enemy, skipping school whenever she'd been allowed to drive the car, and sneaking into eighteen-year-old bars at the age of sixteen. It was like she'd been hell-bent on self-destruction after she'd fought so hard to stay alive during her early years. It made no sense.

Asthma had been the reason she quit smoking, though. When she began to wheeze every time she lit a cigarette, it was easy to give up cigarettes. She'd been about twenty-one at the time.

In bed that night she tried her best not to think about June and Karen and what they might be doing. Instead, she relived every unkind thing she'd ever done and said to anyone or anything. She deserved to be abandoned, she thought, before falling into an exhausted sleep.

She woke up to birdsong as the sky began to lighten and lay quietly sorting out the sounds of robins from those of cardinals. Doves cooed from under the eaves. At six she rolled out of bed, dressed, and ate a piece of toast before getting her bike out of the garage. When she was a kid, the bike was her imaginary horse. She'd ridden it everywhere. Now she rode it for exercise.

Powering down, she headed for the outskirts of the city before the traffic kicked in. The wind she created lifted her hair off her skin as she began to sweat. She soon found herself in the countryside. Corn stood in rows, gently swaying in the fields on either side of the road.

She caught a glimpse of something moving in the ditch and sped on for another hundred feet or so, before concern made her turn around and head back the way she'd come. She got off and walked her bike back, eyes scanning the ditch until she saw something move again. She feared she'd find an animal struck by a vehicle, dying among the grasses. Instead, a child was struggling to get up.

She dropped her bike and hurried to help. Conflicted, because she knew better than to move someone who was hurt, she pushed gently on the girl's shoulders. "Please. Tell me what happened before you get up," she said to a girl of about nine or ten years.

The kid began to yell—high-pitched screams that hurt the ears.

The girl's alarm triggered her own. "Okay, okay. I'm just going to phone for help." She looked around for a place to make a call.

But the girl wasn't waiting around. Even though her face was bloody, she got to her feet and scanned the area wildly. "Where's my bike? You stole my bike." She spied Chelsea's bike and tried to take off with it, but Chelsea grabbed the handlebars.

"Let's go look for your bike," she said when the girl started screaming again.

The bicycle had jumped the ditch and lay near the cornrows, the front wheel bent. "It's broken," the child wailed. "My brother's going to kill me." Chelsea saw that it was a boy's bike.

"Look, I'm going to ride to that farmhouse there." She pointed at the white house at the end of a long drive nearby. "You stay here. I'll be back as soon as I can."

The girl gave her a baleful look but said nothing.

She was only gone ten minutes at most, immediately returning to the girl when the woman in the farmhouse said she would call for help, but already a car had parked by the side of the road.

"What's happened here?" A middle-aged woman holding a leather bag was hurrying toward them. She looked as if she'd just jumped out of bed. Could she have responded so quickly?

"Who is hurt?" she asked.

"She is." Chelsea put a hand on the girl's back. "Who are you?"

"Wanda Kloepke. I'm a first responder. I live down the road. Let me look at that wound. It needs cleaning and bandaging." She glanced at Chelsea. "The ambulance is on its way. Are you the mother?"

At the word "mother," the girl started crying—loud, gulping sobs. "I want my mom."

"I found her in the ditch," Chelsea said. "She had a bicycle accident."

In an inoffensive authoritarian way, Wanda took over. "What's your name?" she asked the child.

"Lindsey," the girl mumbled.

"I don't hear as well as I used to. You have to talk louder." Wanda gently cleaned the wound.

"Ouch. Lindsey Morgan." She batted at Wanda's hands.

"Do you know your mom's phone number, Lindsey?"

"'Course." She rattled off the number. "But I'm staying with my dad." And she gave that number.

The farmhouse woman had arrived in an old Ford pickup and stood nearby. "I'll call both numbers."

"Tell them Lindsey here had a bike accident and will be taken to AMC. We'll probably be gone before either gets here. They can meet the girl at the hospital."

The woman jumped back in the truck, raising dust as she returned to the farmhouse. An ambulance pulled up along the edge of the road, and two EMTs jumped out.

Lindsey looked frightened and Chelsea put a hand on her shoulder. The girl jerked at the touch. "I want my mom."

"She'll come to the hospital," Chelsea reassured her, but Lindsey started to cry.

The male EMT pulled a gurney out of the ambulance and placed Lindsey on it. His female partner took over from Wanda and bandaged the wound. The man found a cervical collar to put around the girl's neck. "Must have gone off head-first," he said. "Need to put this on for safety, hon." He slid the gurney into the back of the ambulance and loaded the damaged bike in behind.

"Will you go to the hospital and give a statement on what happened?" Wanda asked. "You're the primary witness."

"Sure," Chelsea said. "I'll go home and get my car."

She drove to AMC so deep in thought about what had happened that it took someone laying on the horn to startle her into the present. At the hospital she met Lindsey's parents in the emergency waiting room.

The father stepped up to her. "Thanks for rescuing our daughter. I'm Jim Morgan and this is Catherine, Cat, Lindsey's mother."

Chelsea introduced herself. The father wore a suit. His hair was graying, and his somber brown eyes spoke of his care for his daughter. The woman appeared distracted. Trim in jeans and a T-shirt, her dark hair pulled severely back into a braid, she barely looked at Chelsea.

"Thanks," she said, looking toward the door where the doctor would enter.

A woman police officer took Chelsea's statement about the accident and then left with her male partner. There was a lingering question about a ten-year-old riding alone so far from home. Chelsea decided to hang around to find out how Lindsey had fared.

The parents were quietly quarreling in a corner of the room. "Why did she run away again?" the mother asked.

"She's my daughter too," he replied. "Jay never runs away."

They stopped arguing when the doctor came into the room. To Chelsea he looked too young to be trusted. "Mr. and Mrs. Morgan?" he asked, his eyes going from the couple to Chelsea and back again.

"We are the parents," Cat Morgan said.

"Chelsea here found Lindsey," Jim added.

"I'm Dr. Toomey. Your daughter appears to have suffered a concussion, and we had to stitch the wound on her forehead. I think she should spend the night here, so we can reassess her condition in the morning."

"Will she be all right?" Cat asked.

"Yes, she will be fine. She just needs to rest right now."

"Can we see her?" Jim asked.

"Of course."

As they walked away with the doctor, Jim turned to Chelsea. "Thanks again for rescuing Lindsey. Nice of you to wait."

Chelsea went home. By then it was noon, and she made a sandwich before picking up the manuscript.

June failed to return that night. Chelsea went to bed alone and woke up at daylight, still alone.

CHAPTER SIX

1973

Secretariat won the Triple Crown, and Suzy began taking hunt seat lessons. Her life turned on horse shows. She was a good little jumper. Chelsea and her kids went with Gina and Matt to watch some of the hunter-jumper events. Chelsea asked Gina how much the lessons cost. She knew better than to even bring up the topic with Brad.

When Gina and Dan bought a big pony for Matt to ride, Chelsea and the kids went with Gina to pick up the gelding and take him to the stall she and Chelsea had hammered together in Gina and Dan's shed.

Abby begged her father for a pony of her own. When he gave in, Gina helped find a gelding suitable for Abby. The pony, Chico, came with a saddle, halter, and bridle. The two women built a stall at the end of the pole barn that housed Brad's workshop. Abby and Matt rode up and down the old railroad tracks. Dan worked out a deal with a horseman, fixing his truck and trailer in exchange for several riding lessons for the kids.

When Chelsea tried to pay for the lessons, Gina refused to take any money. "Hey, it isn't costing me anything. Why should it cost you?" Gina asked.

"Because it's not my husband's auto repair shop," Chelsea countered.

"Yeah, well, you share your mowing jobs with me." Gina and Chelsea had six mowing jobs between them and another two possibilities. They pulled the tractor and mower on a flatbed trailer Brad had bought at a farm auction.

"What do you think about taking Matt and Abby to an open horse show at the Shrine fairgrounds on Saturday?" Gina asked after the riding lessons had run their course.

Saturday was a sunny, hot day in September. The women loaded the ponies into Gina's horse trailer. They had outfitted the kids in western show clothes and cowboy hats. By now, Suzy was showing with the kids who took hunter jumper lessons. The horses were hauled to shows by a trainer. Suzy rode with her horse friends. They were also showing at the Shrine, though. It was a big show, but Gina said the ten and under classes wouldn't be all that large.

Abby spent the pre-show time running to the rented porta-potty. Matt kept telling her not to be nervous because it was just supposed to be fun, but he went two or three times too.

The two kids looked so young to Chelsea. She didn't wonder why she had let Gina talk her into doing this. She realized she had agreed because it meant she could be with Gina. She didn't want Gina's friendship to go to another horse show mother.

There were seven kids in the ten-and-under class. Some were riding horses and looked tiny on the animals. Matt got third place and as he rode out of the lineup to get his ribbon, her heart ached for her daughter. When Abby's name and number were called for fifth place, she felt a jolt of pride. The two kids who didn't place had kept their animals from running off only by hanging on to the reins for dear life. They got participation ribbons.

Gina patted both kids' legs and told them how well they'd done. Chelsea put Lizzie on the pony behind her sister. While the kids rode around the grounds, Chelsea and Gina sat in the bleachers, eating dust while waiting for Suzy's class.

When Suzy aced the course and placed second, it was late in the day. Gina and Chelsea loaded the ponies and the three kids and left. Suzy would ride home with the kids from her stable.

Her skin shriveled by the sun, Chelsea looked in the backseat and saw that all three kids had fallen asleep. She wondered if the long day and cost had been worth the bother. Yesterday, Gina had shown Chelsea how to clip the long hair under Chico's chin, in his ears, his bridle strip, and his fetlocks. They had tried to tame the pony's mane. She had been up since six the day of the show, washing Chico, while Abby held the lead rope, and wiping him down. She and Abby had sprayed and brushed him, cleaned his feet, and put hoof black on them. Then Abby had ridden him over to Gina's house, while Chelsea and Lizzie drove over.

"This way they'll be ready for 4-H horse and pony classes next summer," Gina said, as if reading Chelsea's thoughts.

Chelsea was jolted out of a stupor. "I wonder if we have enough leftovers for dinner tonight."

Gina lightly punched her on the arm. "Isn't it time we got our own horses?"

Chelsea looked at her in surprise. "I can't think further than today." Brad would not be happy about spending money on a horse. She wasn't sure she wanted a horse.

"We could leave the kids with their dads and spend Sundays riding. Wouldn't that be fun?"

"I don't think Brad is up to buying a horse. I can just hear what he'd say."

"Offer him a little loving." Gina gave her a crooked grin.

"He's not like Dan." Gina had told her that Dan was always eager, always ready.

"Want to change guys?" Gina asked, and Chelsea snorted.

She gestured with her head. "Someone might be listening back there."

"Seriously, though, think about it, Chelse. It won't be any fun riding without you."

She and the kids went with Gina as she searched for a horse. Chelsea couldn't quite believe this was actually going to happen, that Gina was going to buy a horse and maybe even ride it in shows. She wasn't ready to show. She doubted she'd ever be.

"Why can't I just be the groom or gofer? Why do I have to have a horse?" She was just a little bit afraid of the pony. Sometimes when Abby went to get him out of the field next to their house, dragging Lizzie and the dog with her, his head would swing up and he'd pin his ears. Sometimes he cow-kicked when Abby tightened the girth of her saddle, just like Rodeo Joe had done with Suzy.

In the end not only did she buy a horse, she bought one that terrified her. The small bay mare snapped at her when she brushed the animal and kicked when she tightened the girth. It swung its head and tried to bite her leg when she was riding. Gina thought the horse must have been drugged when they rode it before taking it home to the second stall she and Chelsea had banged together next to Chico's.

Boot and Bonnie went with them when they rode on the old railroad bed with the kids on their ponies, all but Suzy. Lizzie sat in front of Gina, because Chelsea's horse was so unpredictable. The mare would leap sideways as if spooked, but Chelsea was certain the animal was trying to get rid of her. Boot picked berries and ate them along the way. Matt steered his pony toward wooly bear caterpillars, and Abby yelled for him to stop. Gina finally told him to cut out the teasing. He never did squish any.

Every summer Chelsea went back to her mother and the cottage with the kids. Her father had died by then. Gina did not go with them again. She had horses to care for and yards to mow. Brad would come for a few days.

Still, she loved it there—the serenity of the water and woods, the nights lit only by the moon and stars. Things had changed, though, since she'd been a kid. There were more speedboats, some way too big for the small lake, most of them pulling skiers. Large summer homes were springing up around the water, and personal watercraft like Jet Skis and Waverunners buzzed annoyingly as they zigzagged pointlessly. At least it seemed that way to her.

She always took several books and her swimsuit. She and her mother and Boot went for long walks with the kids on state land, often next to trout streams. Her mom was a birder with a life list of birds she had spotted. They'd wear hats to ward off the flies, and her mom would stand glued to her binoculars while the rest of them waited to move on. Chelsea had a picture of her in that pose. She had realized she had too many pictures of the girls and too few of her mother and father.

At night they would play card games with the girls and Scrabble with each other while the moths and June bugs buzzed at the screens. The girls swam in the heat of the day, while Chelsea read and alternately cooled off in the water. It was a true vacation for her. Her mother did most of the cooking.

Celie usually turned up for a couple weeks with her two boys, Tom and Will. She was as boyish as they were, throwing a little football back and forth in the water. "Don't duck, Abby," Tom yelled, "and stop throwing like a girl."

"I'm not Abby. I'm Lizzie. And I am a girl. Get it straight." Lizzie's blond hair hung in wet kinky strings. She could be fierce.

"Let me show you," Will said, splashing over to his cousin. He put his right arm around her, his larger hand over hers, which held the little football, and threw a perfect pass to Abby. Jealous of Will's attention to her sister, Abby caught the football before it hit her in the face and threw it back as hard as she could.

"Hey, no fair. You're supposed to throw to Tom," Lizzie hollered as the football flew past her ear into Will's outstretched hand.

The oldest boy, Will, was two years older than Abby. With his fair hair and sky-blue eyes and his strong body, he was the better looking of the two. Shorter and punier, Tom was the smart one. He was Abby's age with the fair hair and blue eyes of his brother.

Later, as they sat for dinner, Lizzie asked Will if he rode horses. Chelsea had already told Lizzie that her aunt and cousins lived near Boulder and did not have horses, but Lizzie thought everyone out west rode whether they had a horse or not.

"Nah," the boy said. "I play football."

"We have horses," Lizzie said proudly.

"Ponies," Chelsea corrected.

"You have a horse, Mom," Abby said.

"The meanest animal on earth. She bites and kicks and tries to jump out from under me." She had meant to be funny, but no one was laughing, and her mother looked horrified.

"Why do you keep her?" Celie asked.

"I don't know," Chelsea answered after a pause.

"'Cause Gina has a horse. So, Mom can ride with her. Right, Mom," Lizzie said.

"Mmm," Chelsea murmured, her cheeks red from the sun and embarrassment.

When she returned from the cottage, Chelsea told Gina she wanted to sell the devil mare—right after she thanked her for taking care of the animals.

"I think we should take her to auction," Gina said thoughtfully. "I'd hate to sell her to some unsuspecting person."

The two of them took the mare to auction on a Saturday evening. She'd told Brad where they were going, leaving the girls with him.

She and Gina sat on the bleachers while the animals were led into the auction arena, one by one. The auctioneer's voice, so loud coming out of the speakers, and the buzz of the crowd startled the animals. They looked around wild-eyed, and Chelsea felt sorry for them. A young horse whinnied, and an answering whinny came from somewhere out of sight. A mama and baby were being separated.

"This is horrible," she whispered loudly into Gina's ear.

Gina met her gaze for a moment. "It's a horse's life," she said. "They're always being sold."

The bay mare balked before being led into the ring. Number 27 was stuck on her rump. The handler jerked on the lead, and she almost ran him over. She was a pretty mare. Maybe she wouldn't go for meat, Chelsea hoped, although sooner or later she'd end up that way. There was a big rig outside for transporting horses to slaughter. This was something Chelsea knew but didn't want to think about. She forgot how the horse had lashed out at her.

Someone paid five hundred dollars for the horse and she was led away, prancing sideways. That much money meant she hadn't gone for meat, but she would likely be back in a few weeks.

"Now we have to find you something gentle yet willing." The night was warm and clear.

Chelsea glanced at Gina. Oncoming traffic momentarily lit up her face before it plunged into shadow. Chelsea was thinking that she might have to buy a horse trailer. Dan didn't seem to mind the cost of the horse and pony. At least, she didn't think he did, but Brad thought horses were money pits. She understood why. However, showing gave the girls poise and taking care of an animal made them responsible.

CHAPTER SEVEN

Late 1989 and 1990

The good news was President George Bush had met with Soviet Union President Mikhail Gorbachev to talk about the end of the Cold War. The Berlin Wall had fallen.

The bad news was that before she left her home with Brad, she had to sell the horses. By then, they weren't the same animals she and the girls had started out with. Abby's horse was gentle and sweet and a great western pleasure horse, although a little flighty. Lizzie's gelding was a halter horse, also gentle. Liz rode him in western pleasure and often placed, not because he worked better than the other contenders but because he was better looking. She hated to sell them. It felt like a betrayal. But she couldn't leave them behind. She asked Gina to find them good homes, even if she had to sell them for less than she'd paid for them.

"I will," Gina promised, looking away from Chelsea. She dug a hole in the dirt with her toe. "I'll help you move," she said. "When do you plan to go?"

"After Christmas." The girls would be home for the holiday. She'd have to go shortly after they left—Abby to her apartment and job in Indianapolis, Lizzie also to Indy for her first year of teaching. She'd hoped Brad would make himself scarce too. She didn't think she could bear to take her things and go if he was home.

Brad had told Chelsea he would send her a maintenance check once a week, which he was required to do as long as they were still married. She thought it was only fair. They'd been married a bit over twenty-five years, and in the beginning, they'd lived on air. Sometimes there had not been enough money for a loaf of bread. She had raised the kids and worked part-time in the welding shop office, a job that hadn't paid much. Nor had the mowing jobs she'd shared with Gina. Both had helped pay for the horses' keep, though. She also had inherited money when her mother died, although it was not enough to live on without Brad's check.

As it was, it was a terrible time for her, and, she was sure, for Brad. She had to box things up and set them by the back door. The day she and Gina loaded the boxes in the rental trailer, Dash, the dog, followed them back and forth. How do you say goodbye to the family dog? She left in tears, as did Gina. Thankfully, Brad had made himself scarce.

What she wanted now, a few months later, was a part-time job, in order to sock away her inheritance. Brad would want a divorce sooner or later. She had gone to a temporary employment agency when she first moved and had picked up a couple of short-term jobs. The last one had ended a couple of weeks ago. When the phone rang, the woman who always called her from the agency was on the end of the line.

"That's odd. I was just thinking of you, Martha." Martha was a cheerful woman, more a friend than the person in charge of finding Chelsea work.

Martha laughed. "I was thinking of you too. We've a need for a half-day receptionist. It doesn't pay a heck of a whole lot, but it's the only job possibility right now, and it should last a few months."

"Thank you, thank you," Chelsea said. "If I get it, want to go out to dinner?" Martha was divorced.

"It's against company policy, you know," Martha said mildly. "When?"

"Friday. Whether or not I get the job." She needed a friend.

The next morning she drove to the address Martha had given her. Graphics Inc. was the name of the company. There was no one at the reception desk, so she rang the bell. A woman around her age hurried out of a nearby room. She had keen brown eyes and short dark hair that was turning gray.

"Hi. Were you sent by Temporary Solutions?"

"I was. I'm Chelsea Browning. Martha Sorenson sent me." She put on a friendly smile.

"Wonderful. I'm Jane Nichols, and I was asked to talk to you about the job. It's temporary, you understand. No benefits. Half days until our receptionist returns. She just had a baby. If you want it, it's yours. When can you start?"

"Right away," she said, pleased. She hadn't expected to be hired on the spot.

Jane gave her a dazzling smile. "Okay, then," she said, "let me fill you in on things." She pointed at the chair behind the desk. "Take a seat."

Jane leaned over her, one hand on the desk and one on the back of Chelsea's chair. Whatever cologne she was wearing reached Chelsea's nose and it was all Chelsea could do not to tell her how good she smelled. Once she bent so close that Chelsea's nose was practically in Jane's hair, which was thick and clean smelling.

Fortunately, it was an easy job, because she found it difficult to concentrate on anything except Jane. The hardest part was remembering which button buzzed in whose office. After a few mistakes, which everyone seemed to find funny, she got the hang of it. When she was bored with nothing to do but wait for the phone to ring, she asked Jane for any kind of work, even stuffing envelopes.

Whenever Jane came out of her office, Chelsea perked up and thought of something to ask or comment on.

That night June walked into the kitchen as Chelsea was cleaning up after eating. "Hi," June said as if she hadn't been gone for three days.

"Come for your clothes?" Chelsea asked, vigorously wiping the clean counter.

"You know, I'm not sure what I want."

"Why don't you pack enough stuff to last till you do know?" Chelsea's heart was pounding. She tossed the dishcloth in the sink and put her hands in her pockets to hide their shaking.

"You want me to leave?" June looked incredulous.

Chelsea almost laughed despite the ache that June still elicited. If June tried to coax her into bed, she wasn't sure she could resist, and that scared her. "I do."

June stomped out of the kitchen and returned about ten minutes later with an overnight bag. "I'll be at Dana's." She stared at Chelsea for a moment or two as if waiting for her to say something. When she remained mute, not even asking why June wasn't going to Karen's, she turned away. "Bitch," she muttered before leaving.

Chelsea heard the garage door go up and wondered why she hadn't heard it when June came home. She watched from the window in the computer room as June drove away.

The next morning at work as she was putting labels on advertising copy, the door opened, and Jim Morgan walked in. She later wondered if she looked as surprised as he did. For a moment she couldn't remember his name.

"How is your daughter?" she asked, hoping the name would come to her before she had to buzz someone to tell him or her who was here. "Lindsey," she said as the girl popped into her head along with his name.

"She's with her mother. I guess that's where little girls belong. Right?"

Jane came out of her office with an armful of envelopes. "Hi, Jim," she said. "Have you met our new receptionist?"

"Yes. I was about to thank Chelsea again for rescuing my daughter after she had a bicycle accident."

"Is Lindsey all right?"

"She is. Did you just start here?" he asked Chelsea.

"Yes, I'm a temp."

"Well, it's good to see you again."

"You too. Are you here to see someone?" Chelsea asked.

"Bob Van Hook."

She buzzed Mr. Van Hook and told him Jim Morgan was here to see him. Van Hook said to send Jim to his office.

Jane put the envelopes on her desk. "If you have time, will you label and put stamps on these?"

"Of course," she said.

Jane turned at her office door. "I think I read about the girl's accident in the paper and how someone came along on a bike and took care of her."

"It was nothing. Really." She waved a hand as if to dismiss the words.

"It would be a better world if we all helped others," Jane said before she disappeared into her office.

She was overwhelmed by all the attention. She'd never expected to see Jim again or for him to go on about her rescuing Lindsey. She returned to her labeling. The feisty, angry little girl came to mind. Her parents were apparently separated, and the kid had run away from her dad's place. She'd thought the mother attractive even though she'd virtually ignored Chelsea.

Chelsea might have been affronted if she hadn't known the woman had serious worries on her mind. The dad hadn't ignored her, but people reacted differently. The kid could have broken her neck. A chill raced across Chelsea's skin when she thought how she hadn't managed to keep the child on her back just in case her neck had been compromised.

Martha called on Thursday to ask where they should meet for dinner the next evening.

"I hear Mark's has a good fish fry," Chelsea said.

"Yeah, but mostly old people go there. How's the job?"

"I've got lots to tell you." With June gone Chelsea had no one with whom to share the days' happenings. She was busting to talk to someone, anyone. "I've not been to the Adler Brau Brewery and Restaurant. Want to go there?"

"I'll meet you there at six thirty. Is that enough time?" Martha asked.

"Plenty."

She ordered perch and french fries and coleslaw. And a beer, of course.

Martha had ordered the same. "Tell me about your week."

Chelsea left June out of it and told about finding Lindsey in the ditch and all that went with it, including seeing Jim Morgan at Graphics Inc.

Martha had stopped eating and was staring at Chelsea. "What a week you've had. And the job?"

"Kind of boring now that I've figured out who goes with each button. They do give me easy work to do—stuffing envelopes and putting on labels. Things like that. But hey, I'm not complaining. I'm grateful, actually." Was she? She had sent the most recent manuscript back to FemBooks with comments. She didn't need any other work that required concentration. "And what's new with you?"

Martha smiled, and her face lit up. She had dimples and shiny blue eyes and naturally curly hair. She was cute. "A guy came in. I found him a temp job that might turn full time. He's taking me out to dinner tomorrow night."

"What's he like?" Chelsea asked, thinking how her love life lay in ruins.

They talked about the guy, whose name actually was Guy—Guy Martin—and then ate silently for a few moments as conversation buzzed around them.

"I know a Catherine Morgan. Pretty woman. Long brown hair. Hazel eyes. Very slender. Could that be Lindsey's mother?"

Surprised, Chelsea looked up from her food. "Yeah. Did you find her a job?"

"I did. She makes pottery. I introduced her to The Pottery Shed people on Ebert Road. They have all sorts of art—paintings, sculptures, pottery, silk scarves, and more. We should go there sometime, just to look. It actually is an old barn. But now that she and her husband are separated, the pottery business is part-time. She works full-time at The Garden Place."

After dinner, they stood in the parking lot next to Chelsea's car and talked. The night was warm with a half moon. "It's too nice to go inside," Chelsea said. But of course, they did go home, deciding to do dinner or lunch soon.

The pain never quite left Chelsea alone. She felt it as a hard ball in her chest, impeding her breathing. She didn't feel so lonely that night, though. Martha was a friend now, maybe not someone to confide in, but someone to call and chat with.

CHAPTER EIGHT

Dana called just as she was drifting off. "Hey, do you want to go to Barb's for dinner tomorrow? I would have called you earlier, but June was here overnight. She left not long ago. Mickie is going with us. You want to pick us up at my apartment at five and I'll tell you how to get there?"

The call and invitation were totally unexpected. Dinner out two nights in a row! *Great*, she thought. "Sure," she said. "Jeans or what?" She wondered if Dana had invited June first, or worse, if June had told Dana to call Chelsea.

"No. A prom dress." Dana laughed and laughed. "Jeans, of course."

Barb lived in the upper story of a two-story house. The flat consisted of two bedrooms, a living room, and a kitchen. Chelsea sat across from Barb, who had made meatloaf, twice-baked potatoes, and a green salad. Barb was talking about one of the girls in Glee Club, who couldn't stay on key. She started singing the "Hallelujah Chorus," changing into a lower key when the notes got high.

They all laughed. In fact, they laughed all through dinner, so hard that Chelsea hurt. After dinner, they moved to the living room and listened to lesbian music that Chelsea had never heard. She hadn't known there was such music until June had introduced it to her. She went home feeling mellow.

Once she dropped Dana and Mickie off at Dana's apartment, she began to think about the two of them as a couple. She wondered if Dana had coerced Mickie into the relationship. Dana was kind of overbearing, and she had some strange ideas. She had pointed out a small, square, fenced-in field on the way to Barb's place and called it "their field," hers and Mickie's.

"We're going to build a house on that field someday, aren't we, babe?" she'd said.

Mickie had laughed.

June's Honda was in the garage. Chelsea parked next to it and turned off the engine. She listened to it tick as angst crept in to replace the mellowness. She went quietly into the house, feeling as if she were walking into danger.

"Where have you been?" June asked. She was standing in the kitchen with only the light over the stove for illumination.

"Where have *you* been?" she countered, before adding, "No, I don't care where you've been, and it's none of your business where I've been." She walked through the den toward the bedroom to get her sleep shirt.

When she turned around to leave the room, having decided to spend the night in the guest room, June was in her face. She tried to brush past her, but June put out an arm to stop her. She knew she was no match physically. "Get out of my way."

"I will when you tell me where you were."

"I had dinner at Barb's."

"With Dana and Mickie?" June's smile and voice were mocking, but Chelsea didn't take the bait.

"Now will you get out of my way?"

June laughed harshly and dropped her arm. "Have a good time?"

"Yes." She hurried into the bathroom and locked the door. She took out her contacts, washed her face, brushed her teeth, and stripped. Before pulling the too-large T-shirt over her head, she looked at her body. It wasn't bad. In fact, it was pretty shapely. She stayed in the bathroom till June pounded on the door.

"Hey, I have to go. What are you doing in there?"

She gathered her discarded clothes and slipped past June and into the guest room, closing the door behind her. She had to work the next day and so did June. Like every night after getting into bed, she opened a book. Before she'd read five pages, the door opened, and June stood in the opening dressed in an undershirt and panties.

"Why are you sleeping in here?" she asked.

Chelsea looked at her over her reading glasses. "I have to get some sleep. Don't you? I think we'll sleep better apart."

To her surprise June left, closing the door behind her without slamming it.

Did this mean their short love affair, if that's what it had been, was over? She felt someone had to finalize it by moving out. She couldn't leave, because she wasn't sure June would stay to take care of the place, and right now there wasn't a goddamn thing she could do about it. She put the book down along with her glasses and turned off the lamp on the nightstand.

On Friday she had lunch with Martha at a Thai restaurant. They were sitting in a corner, when a familiar-looking woman walked over to their table.

"Hi, Martha. How are you?"

"I'm good." Martha looked from the woman to Chelsea. "Catherine Morgan, I believe you already know Chelsea Browning."

"Call me Cat. And yes, I do. Chelsea rescued my daughter, and I don't think I properly thanked her." Cat was smiling, which changed her appearance so much that Chelsea realized she was staring at the woman.

Cat's outstretched hand was in Chelsea's face. Belatedly, she grasped the warm flesh, and Cat's fingers closed around hers tightly. She liked a firm grip, but this was over the top. She took her hand back.

"Hey, you don't have to thank me," she said. "Anyone would have done the same."

"But it was my daughter, so I do have to thank you."

"Would you like to join us?" Martha asked.

"Sure," Cat said. "Let me get my things."

"How is Lindsey?" Chelsea asked as Cat began to turn away.

"Sassy as always. She says thanks, too. See you at the buffet."

At the buffet Chelsea filled a plate with spring rolls and crabmeat rangoons, her favorites. Martha stood next to her, talking to Cat.

Chelsea went to the booth, where she waited for Martha and Cat before eating. They were chatting when they sat down opposite her. Chelsea ate with fervor, listening to the other two talk.

Cat said, "I'm at loose ends next weekend. The kids are at their dad's. Would you two go to Door County with me? It's always a great getaway."

Chelsea stopped eating. She had always been kind of cautious about committing herself. "Where would we stay?" She knew every place was probably already booked.

"At my place. It's on a little bit of beach. Won't that be fun?"

Martha and Chelsea stared at Cat. Then Martha said, "Love to. How about you, Chelsea?"

Cat pulled into her driveway at noon on Friday. It had been an unusually warm, sunny day for November. Martha was sitting in the front seat, which was a relief to Chelsea. She threw her overnight bag into the backseat and climbed in behind Martha.

"What a great day," she exclaimed, "and the weekend is supposed to be just as nice."

"Aren't we lucky," Cat said. Her thick dark hair was pulled back in a ponytail, which made her look younger—although Chelsea had no idea how old she was. Her kids were younger than Chelsea's, so she probably was too.

"We're taking the scenic route when we get to Sturgeon Bay," Cat said.

Only the evergreens held their needles. The spectacularly colored leaves of fall were on the ground. Chelsea easily saw the bay when they got north of the city of Green Bay. It glittered off to the left. *What is it about water that is so compelling?* she wondered.

At Sturgeon Bay they picked up a road along the bay. Huge ships floated at the docks of ship builders. The road wound away from Sturgeon Bay, heading north. It was hard for Chelsea to hear the conversation in the front seat, but she was content to lean back and take in the scenery.

When they arrived at Egg Harbor, Cat drove to a grocery store and parked in the lot. "I'll be back in a moment," she said.

"Oh, no," Martha said. "We're coming with you."

The grocery store turned out to be a shopping pleasure. The wine selection was large and varied. The food offerings, meat and fish and fresh vegetables, were inviting.

Martha picked up some salmon spread and crackers. Chelsea chose a couple of bottles of wine, one red and one white. Cat protested, so they let her buy the salmon, red potatoes, and salad.

Back in the car they drove through Egg Harbor and Fish Creek. At Ephraim, Cat turned into a half-circle drive and parked next to a small cottage, sandwiched between the highway and the bay.

"This is it," she said. "Nothing fancy, but it's on the water, not that we can swim or anything."

They carried in their bags and the food. The place wasn't posh, but most of the windows faced the water. The main floor consisted of a galley kitchen, one bedroom, a full bath, and a living room that looked out on the bay. A large TV took up most of one wall. A couch and sofa faced it. The kitchen had the necessary appliances behind a counter with a sink and counter space. Four tall chairs faced the counter. On the bay side was a sliding door that opened to a small deck with a table and four chairs. On the side of the sofa and chairs were steps that led up to a loft with two single beds, where Martha and Chelsea put their bags.

While there was still light, the three women took the appetizers and wine out to the sheltered deck and sat in the cold, watching the waves crash on the shore. Far out, a freighter plied the waters. The front yard was sand.

Chelsea wished it were warm enough to swim or wade. "Would it be okay if I walk along the beach for a bit?" she asked.

"Of course," Cat said. "I'll come with you."

"We'll have to spend a weekend at my cottage next summer," Chelsea said impulsively. "Although this is great," she added. Door County was an experience no one in Wisconsin should miss. The peninsula was the thumb of the state, with the bay of Green Bay on one side and Lake Michigan on the other. The small towns and villages that populated the bay's shores—Egg Harbor, Fish Creek, Ephraim, Sister Bay, Ellison Bay, and Gills Rock—were quaint. They swelled to ten times their size during the tourist season, but this was way off-season.

The women took their wine with them. They turned back when they reached the town harbor, deciding that watching the water from a shelter and downing appetizers with wine was warmer and more fun.

Dinner was salmon, which Cat fixed. Chelsea put a chunk of butter on the red potatoes and sprinkled them with seasonings before nuking them in the little microwave. Martha put together a delicious salad. They set their plates on the table near the patio door and sat down to eat. When Chelsea had finished her food, she was stuffed, but she managed to eat one of the macaroons they had bought.

That night as she crawled into the bed next to Martha's, she eyed the night sky through the window. "Have you noticed any traffic?" she asked quietly. "I mean, we're so close to the road, and I haven't heard any cars."

"Neither have I," Martha replied. "It's not exactly a touristy month, but I'll bet it's always this way with all the focus on the water."

The next morning, after showering and drinking coffee, they climbed into Cat's comfy Taurus and drove south to the White Gull in Fish Creek for breakfast.

"I hope we're going to hike today. I can feel my hips growing," Martha said.

"We'll go to Peninsula State Park just down the road and hike the Eagle Trail. That okay?" Cat asked.

"Okay with me," Chelsea said. She had hiked the trail before. It cut through the Niagara Escarpment with the cliff on one side and the water below.

She led the way. Biking had kept her in good shape. She was standing in a hollowed-out place in the cliff, looking over the water, buffeted by a cold wind when Cat reached for her hand. Chelsea looked at the hand before raising her gaze to Cat's wide gray eyes.

"I'm hanging on to Martha," Cat said.

It was just that she had not expected to see Cat look vulnerable. "Guess we'll all either walk out of here together or not," Chelsea said with a grin.

Cat grimaced, and Chelsea took her hand. "Okay. Let's go."

When they were back in the car, they made stops at the few shops that were still open, driving all the way to the tip of the peninsula at Gills Rock. They parked in the lot facing the water where the waves hit the wall. The water rose in the air and fell on the vehicle, which squatted under the onslaught.

At midafternoon they made their way back to Cat's cottage, where they snacked and read. Chelsea found herself wishing the weekend were longer. After taking Cat out to dinner, they watched a movie on TV and went to bed.

On Sunday after breakfast they crossed the peninsula, drove south on Highway 57, and turned off on the road to Cave Point County Park on Lake Michigan. A cold breeze whipped the waves against the rocks and into the underground caves. They walked the path to Whitefish Dunes State Park, watching out for the places where the water in the underground caves had worn a hole in the forest floor.

The path ended at the dunes where rolling sand spread before them. They made their way to the wet sand near Lake Michigan, where it was easier to walk. Groups of gulls ran before them, squawking and finally flying. They turned back after fifty feet or so, hurrying through the woods to Cave Point and the car. The afternoon had turned colder, more like November, and Chelsea felt the chill like a knife. She was ready to go home.

"Thanks so much for the wonderful weekend, Cat," Chelsea said, before getting out of the car. "I had such a good time. I'll see you both soon."

Inside, the house was quiet, and she felt a mix of loneliness and a relaxation that being alone can only give. She realized how tired she was when she turned on *Masterpiece Theater* and fell asleep on the couch.

CHAPTER NINE

Chelsea dreamed about Cat that night. Of course, the woman in her dreams didn't look like Cat or act like her. Sometimes she was female, sometimes male. Chelsea was terribly afraid of her, yet sexually drawn. She shook off the dream when she awoke and dressed in good slacks and a nice blouse with a cotton sweater over it.

When Chelsea arrived at Graphics Inc, there was only one car in lot. Inside, Jane Nichols greeted her.

"Cup of coffee?" Jane asked, holding a steaming mug toward Chelsea.

She took the coffee from Jane with thanks. Chelsea admired the woman, who seemed to run the office so efficiently. Jane had been unfailingly friendly and supportive. "Thanks, Jane."

"Sure. Have a good weekend? You look like you spent it outside."

"I went to Door County with friends. It was kind of cold but fun. How about you?" She sipped the coffee, almost burning her tongue. "Hot and strong, the way I like it," she murmured appreciatively.

"I stayed home and cut back the roses and finished putting the garden to bed. I should have done it weeks ago. It's good to have that done."

"I bet," Chelsea said. She glanced at Jane's hands again. There were no rings, but that didn't mean she wasn't married. She sat down at the front desk to greet those who came through the door and watched Jane walk away. She wanted to know her better and didn't know how to go about it, because she thought of her as her boss.

When she went home at noon, she saw someone throwing something at her house, throwing so hard that whoever it was came off her feet with each swing.

What the hell? she thought. She jammed the car into park and ran to stop the intruder. It was Lindsey, Cat's daughter. She had been heaving clods of mud at the windows of Chelsea's house. The girl had a small bucket of water and a pile of clay, which she was using to make mud balls,

Chelsea pinned the girl's arms and held her body against her own, while Lindsey struggled.

"Let me go, you big shit."

"Whom should I call first? The police or your parents? Hmm? Life is full of choices, Lindsey."

"I hate you, fucking bitch."

The language shocked Chelsea. "Why are you throwing mud balls at my house?" They were more like ice balls. It had turned cold overnight. She was having trouble holding the kid.

"Stay away from my mother, you lesbo."

"What?" Chelsea asked, stunned.

"My mom loves my dad. She's not queer," the girl said furiously. "Let me go."

"It's Monday. Why aren't you at school."

"Because I didn't want to go, you dummy," the girl yelled, twisting and turning.

She realized she couldn't hold the girl forever. She had to do something else. "Look. I'm going to make a deal with you. It's your honor on the line. I will let you go without telling anyone if you wash the mud off my windows."

Lindsey stopped trying to free herself. "You won't tell my dad or anyone?"

"Nope. You have to do a good job, though." She felt the girl relaxing in her arms, but she wasn't fooled into loosening her grip.

"And you will stop seeing my mom. I know you went to our cottage with her."

"She invited Martha and me. We had a lovely weekend."

"Did you sleep with my mother?" The kid stiffened in her arms.

"Of course not. Martha and I slept in the loft."

"Okay," Lindsey said, and it was as if the fight went out of her. "Give me the cleaning stuff."

"First you get rid of that pile of dirt and bucket of water. Then come inside and I'll give you a bucket of water and vinegar and rags for scrubbing."

To Chelsea's surprise, Lindsey did as she was told. When the girl came inside, Chelsea directed her to the bathroom so she could wash off her hands.

Chelsea watched the girl going out the door with the pail and rags. After a few minutes, though, she heard a rasping sound from the den, which faced the street. She went to investigate and looked at the large window in the den with dismay. It was smeared with mud, which Lindsay seemed to be spreading around instead of wiping off.

Chelsea felt a touch of anger before she realized that it was probably impossible to get the dirt off with a rag and bucket of water. She grabbed an old jacket from a hook in the mudroom and went outside. She'd put the hose away for the winter, but she carried it now to where Lindsey was futilely attempting to rub the mud off the window.

Tears were running down the girl's face. "It won't come off," she said in a small voice. "And I can't get the stuff up there." She pointed to a clod that was out of her reach.

Chelsea clamped down on her tongue. She screwed the hose onto the faucet. She had turned the outside water back on inside. She backed up about five feet and aimed the hose on the mud. She reached down and dumped the muddy bucket of water in among the shrubs and rinsed it out with the hose, then poured fresh water in the pail.

She said, "Lindsey, you wipe off the parts of the windows you can reach after I hose them down." Then she moved around the house, hosing not just the glass, but also the sills and the siding under the sills. She cursed the many windows she had always enjoyed.

By around four the damage the kid had inflicted had been minimized. The windows were still kind of smeary, but Chelsea no longer cared. In fact, she thought she would hire someone to wash them in the spring.

She rolled up the hose, draining it of water. She would once more turn the water off and drain the outside faucets for winter. She glanced at Lindsay, who had dumped the bucket in the shrubbery and was wringing out the rags. The kid was wet, her arms and chest and legs soaked. Even her hair looked bedraggled. And she was shivering.

Chelsea put the hose in the garage and told Lindsey to come inside. "Why don't you go dry off a little?" she suggested. "Would you like a cup of hot chocolate?"

The girl shook her head and said something Chelsea didn't hear. "What?" Chelsea asked.

"I have to go home," the girl called from the bathroom.

"I'll take you."

"No," Lindsey said.

"We'll put your bike in the back of the car. I won't tell anyone what happened, but how are you going to explain why you are so wet?"

The bathroom door closed behind the girl. Chelsea leaned against the doorframe to the den. If she was so tired from hosing down windows, the kid must be exhausted.

Lindsey staggered out of the bathroom and followed Chelsea into the garage. Chelsea put the girl's bike in the back of the Escort. "Get in the front," she ordered. "Are we going to your mom's house?" The girl nodded.

Chelsea felt Lindsey's warm, wet presence steaming next to her. At a stop sign she glanced at the girl and saw that she had fallen asleep wedged against the door of the car.

"Wake up, Lindsey," she said when she parked in front of Cat's two-story house on Forest Avenue.

The girl jumped.

"Look, if your mom asks what happened this afternoon, I'll have to tell her."

"You said you wouldn't."

"I'll say that I gave you a ride home, but if she asks why you are all wet, what then?"

"Tell her. I knew you would," the girl said with bravado. She grabbed the bike that Chelsea handed her and ran toward the house with it.

The porch light came on and Cat stood in the doorway, clasping her arms with her hands. She said something to Lindsey.

Chelsea slammed the hatchback and jumped into the front seat. She waved and took off with an embarrassing screech of tires.

She went to bed shortly after supper. The phone rang twice, but she didn't answer it. Off and on after taking Lindsey home, she had pondered the girl's motives. The kid had attacked her house because Chelsea was spending time with her mother. She didn't get it, but it wouldn't be a chore to give up her budding friendship with Cat.

When Chelsea returned home at noon the next day, a Taurus was parked in her driveway. She parked next to it.

Cat, who was about to knock, turned toward Chelsea. "There you are. I should have known you would just be getting home."

"What's up?" Chelsea asked as Cat moved out of the way so she could unlock the door. She invited Cat in.

"I just wanted to know what happened yesterday. That was you who brought Lindsey home, wasn't it?"

"Yeah. It was getting dark out."

"What had she been doing, do you know? Her clothes were wet and muddy."

"Did you ask her?" Chelsea looked into Cat's gray eyes. She was an attractive woman, Chelsea realized. Was Cat a lesbian, and had Lindsey found out somehow? Kids were so precocious these days. Her own kids had guessed that she was a lesbian, but they were much older.

"Yes. She said she was helping you with your windows."

Stunned by Lindsey placing the blame in her court, she stared at Cat for a moment before throwing her head back and laughing. When she could finally talk, she said, "That's some girl you've got. You'll have to take her word for it, because I promised not to tell."

It was Cat's turn to look dumbfounded. Then she shrugged. "She told me I shouldn't spend time with you, because you are a lesbian and say bad things about me."

"Now wait a minute. I never said anything bad about you. I wouldn't do that. I mean, she's your kid."

Cat was silent for a moment. She studied Chelsea's face as if she could read the truth on it. "I believe you. Lindsey doesn't hesitate to lie if she thinks it helps her case. Now tell me what happened."

"I will only tell you if you promise not to confront Lindsey with it or punish her for it. She was punished enough."

Cat put her hand over her heart. "I promise to say nothing to her."

Chelsea let out the puff of air she had been holding. "I caught her throwing mud balls at my windows." She nearly smiled at the look of disturbed surprise on Cat's face. "Listen, how about a cup of coffee to make this go down better? We can sit and talk like civilized adults."

"Okay. Sounds good." She took off her jacket and hung it on the back of a chair.

Chelsea made a fresh pot of decaf, poured them both a cup, and led the way to the sofa in the living room, which faced the backyard. The bay window was streaked from being hosed down and not wiped clean. She saw Cat looking at it.

"You have a lot of windows," Cat said.

"I do. She was punishing me for spending the weekend with you. She said I was a lesbo and you were not, that you loved her dad."

Cat blushed. "I did have an affair with a woman. It was the reason Jim and I separated. I wanted to find out who I was." Her voice dropped to a whisper.

"You don't need to be embarrassed. I loved my best friend in Indiana. I was in such denial I didn't let myself even wonder why I wanted to be with her all the time, until recently."

Chelsea looked at Cat, who smiled wryly. "Are you hungry? I'm starving. I'm going to make a grilled cheese sandwich. Want one?"

Cat nodded. "Please."

They ate at the dining room table, which was at the end of the living room, just outside the kitchen.

"Thanks. This is really good," Cat said after a few bites. "I'm sorry about Lindsey. She is so angry at me about the separation and embarrassed by the possibility that I might be different from her friends' mothers."

"How did she deal with this other woman?"

A little frown appeared between Cat's perfect eyebrows. "You mean, the woman I was with?" she stammered. When Chelsea gave a slight nod, she continued. "That ended almost as soon as it began, when she caught us together."

Chelsea swallowed. "In bed?" she asked with horror.

Again, Cat blushed. Chelsea was amused. "Yes," she said curtly. "It's not something I want to talk about. I can barely think about it."

"What did Lindsey do to that woman? Throw stones through her windows?"

"I don't know. I hope not. I suppose I should call and ask." She heaved a sigh. "I will pay to have your windows washed professionally."

"I was going to have that done in the spring. But why should you pay? You didn't do it." She was remembering how exhausted Lindsey looked after wiping down the parts she could reach. "I think your daughter is sorry she ever decided to warn me off.

She was so tired after helping me clean up her mess she could hardly stand up. Even I was exhausted." She smiled grimly in remembrance.

"It isn't amusing, Chelsea. She had no right to do such a thing, and I have to find a way to talk to her about it. I'll agree to wait till spring, but I am paying to have your windows cleaned professionally," Cat said firmly.

Chelsea decided to let her. "Okay. She's your daughter. Would you like to split another sandwich? I'll make more coffee."

"Yes, I'd love to."

Now that they had finished talking about Lindsey, they fell quiet until Chelsea switched the kitchen radio to WPR.

"That's my station too," Cat said.

"Tell me something," Chelsea said, thinking aloud. "Is it smart for us to continue to see each other since Lindsey is so against it?"

"We can't let a child tell us who we can and can't see," Cat said.

"Good. I wondered about that."

"What kind of a mother do you think I am?" Cat asked indignantly.

"I have no idea," Chelsea said cheerfully as she buttered the bread and sliced the cheese. The coffee was already dripping. The house felt cozy.

Cat laughed. "I hope I can redeem myself."

"Who am I to criticize? My two girls are so angry I almost wish I hadn't left Brad. He's a far better person than the woman I abandoned him for. Careful what you wish for," she almost whispered, suddenly wanting to cry. It was as if she'd lost all reason, but would she have stayed if she had given it more thought? She'd hardly known June.

CHAPTER TEN

She met Cat and Martha at the University Chapel for the December performance of the *Messiah*. Cat had called Chelsea early one morning saying she had an extra ticket, would Chelsea like it? Chelsea had been so surprised she thought she must have sounded stupid.

"Cat? What a surprise. Ticket for what?"

"Handel's *Messiah* at the University Chapel. Would you like to go with Martha and me?" Cat asked.

"I'd love to go. How much do I owe you?"

"It's my treat. We can meet in the lobby of the chapel at six thirty."

"Thank you," she'd said, finally managing to sound coherent. "I'll see you there."

She'd had to park blocks away. It was seven before she got to the chapel. The lobby teemed with people. She heard someone call her name as she shouldered her way through the crowd. Martha tapped her when people began to move inside.

"Here," Martha said, handing her a ticket. "Follow me."

The two seats Cat was saving were halfway to the stage. Cat stepped into the middle aisle so Chelsea and Martha could sit down. The orchestra was tuning up in the pit, but the choir was not yet on stage.

She removed her winter coat and sat down. She was dressed in black slacks and a red sweater, appropriate for the season she thought. Martha also wore black slacks and a sweater, hers with a Christmas tree embroidered on the bodice. Cat had chosen a forest-green dress for the occasion, a tasteful one-piece that was fitted on the top and flared at the waist. A gold necklace with a small bell pendant lay between her breasts. Hose and short black heels completed the outfit. Her hair was swept up in a bun. She looked elegant.

Chelsea and Martha exchanged a look. "Wow!" Chelsea breathed with a slight nod of the head toward Cat, and Martha raised her eyebrows in agreement.

A dimming of lights drew their attention to the stage as the choir and soloists took their places. The audience clapped, and the conductor bowed and acknowledged the soloists and the first violin. More clapping. Some even stood.

The performance left Chelsea glowing. *What a great way to start the season*, she thought, before being brought to her proverbial knees by thoughts of how she would be spending the holidays. She had promised to return to Indiana. She had already made plans to stay with Gina nights and spend Christmas Eve and Christmas Day at her former home with Brad and the girls. It would be heartwrenching, because, while the girls were angry, Brad had been so nice about it all. He hadn't wanted her to leave, but he had accepted it. Comparing his behavior to June's made June look really rotten and Chelsea look like a fool.

She thanked Cat again and said goodbye to her and Martha on the sidewalk outside the chapel. Martha gave her a hug. She was going to her parents' home for the holidays. Cat did not say where or how she would spend Christmas.

Chelsea walked quickly through the frigid night toward her car, which was almost as cold inside. She drove to the house, passing strings of lights on trees and houses. In the front windows of most homes stood brightly decorated trees.

She drove past Karen's truck into the garage, coming to a stop next to June's Honda Civic, and began to fume. The Christmas music that met her as she walked inside made her even angrier. She took off her coat and walked through the den to the hallway between the bedrooms where she slipped into the bathroom. As she sat on the toilet, she considered what to do.

She hated confrontations, but she could not let this go. Karen might move in if she did. She walked toward their voices, her wrath growing. This was her space, and June had allowed it to be invaded. Karen had once been her friend, but she apparently had no respect for Chelsea or she wouldn't be here.

Karen and June were hanging ornaments on a scotch pine in front of the bay window in the living room. The lights were already strung. The two women were apparently unaware of anyone else in the house. Chelsea walked up to the tree and began removing the ornaments, dropping them into the open box on the carpet.

"Hey, you're going to break them," June said, moving toward Chelsea.

Chelsea lost it and threw a glass ball at the window, where it shattered, tinkling as it fell.

June grabbed her before she could throw another. "You bitch," she said.

"No! She's right. Let her go, June. I'll leave. This is her place."

Chelsea froze on the spot. For a moment, she almost liked Karen, but Karen had taken her space. She couldn't forgive that.

June let go of Chelsea's arms and backed off. "Let's go to your place, Karen. We'll take the tree."

Chelsea watched as they carried the tree out to Karen's Chevy and tied it in the bed, lights and all. June returned for the ornament box, but Chelsea was holding it.

"Some of these are mine," she said.

"Take yours out," June growled, and Chelsea did.

After getting the owners' approval, Chelsea had set up an appointment with a locksmith to change the house locks on Wednesday of the coming week. She knew this would end any shred of a relationship with June, so she had weighed her decision carefully. Now she was glad she already had made the arrangements. She would let June get her clothes and belongings and be done with her, but she would not tell her in advance of her plans.

She watched the two vehicles drive away, feeling almost as chilled as she had when she'd walked to her car after the *Messiah*. She wiped a few tears away and went for the vacuum cleaner to suck up the needles that had fallen off the tree and the broken ornament. It was better to keep busy.

As she put the vacuum away, the phone rang. She picked it up warily. "Hello?"

"Hi. This is Barb Dunhill. You had dinner at my house," the voice said.

She barked a laugh. "How could I forget you, Barb?" she asked, thinking it odd that Barb wouldn't think she'd know her. "Thanks again for the dinner. It was such a fun evening."

"I'm glad you liked it," Barb said. "Dana and I are going out to lunch on Saturday, and we wondered if you would like to go too. If you're not too busy," she added.

"I'd love to!" she exclaimed. "Where?" She was ridiculously delighted.

"Good Company. At least, that's where Dana wants to go. Mickie can't make it, though."

That was a good thing, she thought. Four of them might seem like a date. She was just looking for friendship. "Thanks for asking me. What time?"

"How about twelve?" Barb said.

"I'll meet you there."

Barb was standing in the small lobby Saturday, her purse clutched under her arm, when Chelsea breezed through the door at a minute after noon. One of Barb's expressive eyebrows rose higher than the other.

"Dana is usually late."

"Do you want to get a table?" Chelsea asked.

"Sure."

They were seated in a booth near the bar. A waitress appeared almost immediately. "Anything to drink?" she asked.

Chelsea asked for water and Barb got a Coke. Chelsea met Barb's eyes. "How's your job?"

"Ah, my job. It is harmonious. It's the coaching that is the bane of my existence. We have one parent, a man, who stands in the bleachers and shouts at the girls during volleyball games. And then he yells at me, if the girls don't play well. The last game he came down the bleachers, huffing and puffing, his face all red, and said, "What is it with you, Dunhill? Get your act together and win a game." Chelsea listened with amused horror. "His daughter is a little bitty thing, who cringes whenever he opens his mouth. One time the refs threw him out of the gym." Barb laughed so Chelsea laughed with her.

"What do you say when he yells?"

"I say, 'Calm down, Mr. Buxley. They're doing the best they can.'"

"What does he say to that?"

"That they need another coach. That I'm not tough enough."

"And?"

I say, "Maybe they do." Her eyebrows shot up as if they had a life of their own and Chelsea laughed. She couldn't help it.

"It's true. We have one girl who falls over her feet, trying to get to the ball. I can't keep her from running all over the court, knocking the other girls down. It's pathetic. No wonder we haven't won a game. One of them even ducks when the ball comes her way."

Chelsea's laughter died when she saw Dana striding toward them. June was with her. "Uh-oh," she said.

"What?" Barb asked, turning around. "Oh no."

"Shove over," June said, standing next to Chelsea.

She moved. What else could she do without making a scene? Dana slid in next to Barb.

"You changed the locks on me." June was shaking with what Chelsea knew was rage.

She took her courage in both hands and looked June in the eyes. "I did. One of us has to leave. Let me know when you want to get your belongings."

"Give me that key, bitch," June said, grabbing for Chelsea's jacket, which lay on the other side of her.

Chelsea let her take the jacket. The key was in the pocket of her jeans.

"Do you really think you should have changed the locks without telling June, Chelsea?" Dana asked.

"She and Karen were decorating a tree when I got home from a concert, as if Karen lived there. I signed the contract with the owners, not June," Chelsea said, trying to remain calm.

"You did that, June? Took Karen to the house?" Dana asked.

"Fuck yes," June said in a raised voice. "It's my house too."

"It doesn't belong to either of us," Chelsea said, her face flushed. How was she going to let June in now? She might take Chelsea's stuff or damage something in her anger.

"Give me that fucking key," June growled, her face red with anger.

"Don't get all upset," Barb said.

"Stay the fuck out of this, bitch," she said to Barb, who looked as if she'd been slapped.

"Hey, quit saying the F word," Dana said.

"I'll say whatever the fuck I want to say," June growled.

Chelsea saw the waitress hovering nearby. "Get help," she mouthed.

A moment later a dark-haired man, dressed in black slacks and a white polo shirt, appeared next to the booth. "Is there a problem here?"

"What's it to you?" June snapped, but she looked nervous.

"Yes, there is," Chelsea said, her heart pounding so hard she could hear it in her ears. "This woman is making a scene."

"I'm the manager. I think it is best if you find another place to sit, ma'am, or perhaps you should leave." He was looking at June.

June stood up and marched for the door. "I'm coming tomorrow for my things, and you better let me in."

Chelsea's face burned. Everyone around them had stopped talking and was watching. She noticed Barb's face had turned crimson too. "I'll come with her tomorrow," Dana said. "It will be all right." She followed June.

Chelsea whispered her thanks to the manager, who nodded. "What is her name? She's not welcome here."

"June Paulson," she said, her voice unsteady.

He wrote the name down. "Enjoy your lunch, ladies. Don't let someone else spoil it." He walked off.

But it was spoiled. Chelsea looked at Barb. "Sorry," she said.

"Holy Toledo!" Barb said. "Let's get out of here."

Chelsea barked a laugh. Who said 'Holy Toledo' anymore? "Want to go somewhere else?" Chelsea asked as they walked toward their cars.

"I'm sorry. I didn't know Dana would bring June." Barb looked apologetic.

"How about Chi Chi's?"

Chelsea ordered enchiladas and Barb asked for burritos. They each had a margarita and ate chips and drank while waiting for their orders. Chelsea had finally stopped shaking. It wasn't the first time June had embarrassed her in public, but it was the worst.

Barb let out a long sigh.

"What?" Chelsea asked, looking at her.

"Just relaxing. I feel like I escaped a bomb or something."

Chelsea laughed abruptly. "It's not funny, is it?"

"I think you better have someone there to defend you when June gets her stuff."

"Yeah. I think so too. Do you want to be there, Barb?"

"No, because she'd roll right over me."

"I suppose I could ask Martha," she said. Martha might guess that she and June had been lovers. It made her realize how ashamed she was of her bad judgment. She would be embarrassed if June caused a scene, and she was pretty sure she would.

She met Barb's gaze and let out a burble of laughter. Before long they were both laughing so hard they could neither eat nor drink.

Martha showed up around noon, the agreed-upon time. She looked at Chelsea as if she were a curiosity. "You don't want to be alone with this woman?"

Chelsea felt the heat of embarrassment engulf her. "No. She's unpredictable and very angry because I changed the locks without telling her, but that was the only way I thought I could make her move out."

"I see," Martha said, looking as if she didn't see at all. "What time is she coming?"

Chelsea looked at her watch, twice. The first glance didn't register. She just hoped her nervousness didn't show too much. "Any time now." She remembered her manners. "Want a cup of coffee? I really appreciate your coming over."

"I'd love one, and I don't mind. I'm curious about this person."

"Think about where you want to go out to eat. I'm buying," Chelsea said. Just then someone pounded on the door.

"I'll get the coffee. You let her in," Martha said, unerringly heading toward the kitchen.

"None for me," she shouted after Martha. She was nervous enough. Her hands were shaking.

She looked through the glass and saw June and Dana. Unlocking the door, she let them in. They had brought boxes and two suitcases. "We don't want to have to come back," Dana said.

"I don't want June to come back," Chelsea said, as Martha walked into the room with a cup of coffee.

"You're not going to offer us a cup of joe?" June asked, her face twisting into a wry smile.

"Just get on with it," Chelsea said irritably.

Chelsea followed June and Dana from room to room. She let June take the things she and June had bought together. She didn't want them anyway. But when June put her hand on a paperweight that had been her mother's, she pulled June's hand away. "Don't take anything that's not yours," she warned. June gave her an angry look and shook her hand off.

June and Dana carried out clothes and put them in June's car. They put paintings and dishes in boxes. The linens went into one of the suitcases. In an hour they had packed all of June's belongings.

"You are such a sorry weasel," June said before she left, her face so close Chelsea could feel the heat of her breath and wondered if anger made it sour.

"Hey, back off," Martha said.

"C'mon," Dana put down a box, pulled on June's arm, and mouthed, "Sorry," to Chelsea.

When they were gone, Chelsea breathed a sigh of relief. "Thank you for coming. You're really good at this."

Martha gave her a small smile. "If you ever need a bodyguard, call me. But she is kind of threatening, isn't she?"

The unanswered question, the question too impolite to ask—why had Chelsea been living with June in the first place—remained in the air between them. That's what Chelsea was thinking, anyway. She was weak with relief when June and Dana drove away.

"I owe you, Martha."

"No, you don't. Let's go out to lunch."

"Only if you let me buy."

"Hey, I might need your moral support one of these days."

CHAPTER ELEVEN

It was already a third of the way through December, late for her to Christmas shop, but the weekend was coming up. She had asked her daughters if they had any Christmas wishes a while back.

Abby had told her point-blank she only wanted her mother to come to her senses, which meant moving back in with her dad. Liz had said with a bitterness that was unlike her that Christmas would be more like a funeral, since it would probably be the last time they were all together for the holiday.

She called Brad with trepidation, not because she was afraid of what he might say, but because it always made her terribly sad to talk to him. He tried so hard to sound upbeat. She cringed as she recalled a trip to visit Abby in Michigan where Abby had been working on her master's degree at the University of Michigan. On the way home Brad had rested his right hand on the shift lever. The pop tune, "I'll Always Love You," wailed on the radio. Why that station was on, she couldn't recall. Maybe it had been the only one that came in clearly. In the past she would have put her hand over Brad's because it was true. She would always love him.

But she hadn't wanted to give him false hope. She'd already told him she was moving out after Christmas. She had not yet informed the girls. Brad had guessed she was a lesbian. How could he not have? June's visit to their home and Chelsea's frequent drives up north on weekends were dead giveaways.

She shook her head. He actually had told her he could overlook her affairs with women. She couldn't, though. It had been as if she were possessed. She hadn't been able to stay away from June once they became intimate. She'd fantasized about sex endlessly, and it wasn't even good sex. She'd had better sex with Brad.

Although she and Gina had remained best of friends, they no longer saw each other several days a week. Their kids were grown and had gone separate ways. Gina's work at the auto repair business and her involvement in the horse world occupied her time.

Now, a year later, Chelsea remembered with keen shame how she had behaved when she'd been so enthralled with June. She wanted to tell Brad how sorry she was, but that might make him think she wanted to move back home. And that would be unfair to both of them. When mulling over her life-changing infatuation, she decided June had been a catalyst—the thing enabling her to leave her marriage. Even though she was ashamed of her behavior, she realized leaving Brad had been the best choice.

She had been holding the receiver, not even hearing the dial tone. Now she put it back on the handset. She would browse until she found gifts for Brad and her girls.

She wandered through crowded aisles, looking for gifts for her daughters. She had no wish list, so she bought things that she thought were pretty—a silk scarf for each of them that seemed to her to suit their personalities. Earth tones for Abby and bright colors for Liz. She purchased a gift certificate to The Gap and another to Victoria's Secret for each of them. For Brad she bought a tie, a belt, and socks. She had always bought his ties. Then she had gone hunting for something for Gina and found a small bronze statue of a horse and rider. Surprisingly, the rider was a woman.

Early on December 24 she set out for Indiana. She was grateful it wasn't snowing or sleeting, although in open spaces she could feel the brunt of the wind slamming against the Escort. She had driven these roads so often, though, that they were boring.

In midafternoon she drove into Gina's driveway. As she opened the car door, Gina flew out of the barn and ran to her. To her chagrin Chelsea found herself crying into Gina's smelly barn jacket.

"What is it, Chelse?" Gina asked when she held Chelsea at arm's length. "Did you miss me that much?"

Chelsea's smile wavered as she futilely swiped at her eyes. "Yes. I did." She felt foolish, but she couldn't stop the tears.

Gina hugged her close again. "I miss you more than I thought possible too." She barked a sound. A laugh or a sob? "Come inside. It's damn cold out here."

Chelsea grabbed her bag and hurried after Gina into the warm house. When she looked around and saw that nothing had changed, she almost cried again. It could have been any afternoon. She could still be with Brad.

"What is it, Chelse?" Gina asked again.

She couldn't tell Gina what a nightmare her life had become, because she'd never told Gina she'd been in love with a woman. She'd given up a comfortable life with Brad and her close friendship with Gina and for what? Her daughters and sister were estranged, and she was lonely, even desolate.

"Is it that bad?" Gina asked.

She pulled her ragged pride around her. "It just didn't turn out the way I thought it would." There was that be careful what you wish for thing again. "I dread tomorrow. The girls are furious with me. Brad is sad. I feel as if I might have jumped the gun."

Gina leaned toward her. "Do you want to come back? I'd help. I miss you so much."

"I would if I could, but I can't." She looked away from Gina's shining eyes. "If I came back, I'd never be able to leave."

"Was it so bad here for you?"

"You made it bearable." Out of the corner of her eye she saw Suzy about to join them.

"Chelsea! I thought that was you!" Suzy said. Then Suzy's arms were around her. "You have to see my new horse. He's gorgeous and moves like a dream."

"I'd love to." She took Suzy by the arms and smiled at her. The young woman was the spitting image of her mother. "You're looking good."

"When are you coming home?" Suzy asked. "Mom misses you."

Chelsea's eyes jumped to Gina, who looked pained. "I miss her too." She missed the way they'd been almost inseparable when the kids were young.

"Come out to the barn before you go anywhere else," Suzy said before leaving.

"Where is Matt?" Chelsea asked.

"He works for Dan," Gina told her. "Do the girls know you're here?"

"They can see my car from the house. They are so angry."

"I talked to them," Gina said in a rush, her brown eyes worried. "Don't be upset, Chelse. I can imagine how difficult it must be…"

Chelsea stared at her friend as worry coursed through her. "Talked to them about what?"

"I guessed. They guessed. They want you to tell them, you know, why you really left." Gina looked so nervous that Chelsea was silenced. "I can understand why you didn't tell them, but why not me?"

"You?" she asked. "How could I? It was you I…" She couldn't finish. She chewed on her upper lip and tried to tamp down the flush.

"You should have trusted me," Gina murmured. She stood up abruptly. "Would you like some water or iced tea?"

"I'd like a real drink," she said, knowing Gina wouldn't have any liquor in the house. She didn't drink.

"Wish I could help you." Gina reached across the table and patted Chelsea's hand.

Chelsea jumped at the unexpected touch, causing Gina to flinch.

"Come on, Chelse. Can't we just be who we were before you left?" Gina almost sounded angry.

Chelsea laughed. "I wish."

"I do too," Gina said. "Fervently. I loved who we were."

"When the kids were little, you mean? Before they all went their separate ways and we did too?" she asked with a trace of bitterness.

"That's not why you left," Gina said accusingly.

"No." But it came to her that it was part of the reason. They stared at each other as Chelsea recalled telling Gina she was leaving. She'd seen the shock on Gina's face, seen her eyes widen, her mouth drop open a little. With her heart racing she'd waited for Gina to ask why. Chelsea had quickly covered her tracks, saying she missed Wisconsin. The kids were grown. If she didn't leave now, she would never leave. It had all been true, of course, but she'd left out any mention of June and the bit about her love for Gina and the growing gulf between them.

"Well, you're here now. Let's make the most of it. You can put your suitcase in the guest room. You know where it is."

She did. The window looked out on the side lawn and the woods beyond. She dropped her small bag next to the bed and hurried out to where Gina waited. They were going to the barn to see Suzy's horse.

Chelsea was glad she had brought her old goose down jacket, the one she'd worn when taking care of her horses in the winter. She'd known she'd end up looking at horses in a cold barn.

When she headed to Brad's house for dinner, Dan and Matt were still not home. Her heart was in her throat. Gina had said the girls missed her, that they had told Gina they couldn't wait to see her. But she knew her mere presence set off sparks of anger in them.

Boot was long dead. She was met by Dash, the dog the girls had brought home as a puppy from a horse show. He was so glad to see her that she began to cry. She dropped to her knees and wrapped her arms around him as the dog tried to climb into her lap.

She was wiping her nose and eyes as the door opened and Lizzie looked down at them. "Mom? I didn't see you at first," her daughter said in a high voice. "Why don't you both come in?"

She smelled the roast in the oven and saw the Christmas tree standing, as always, in front of the bay window in the living room. The *Messiah* was playing. She carried her bag full of presents into the living room and emptied it under the scotch pine.

With a nervous smile she turned to hug her daughters. She felt Abby's muscles tense under her touch and released her. Lizzie fell into her arms as if she belonged there. When she turned to Brad, she gave him a quick hug.

Her daughters had changed over the years. Abby's now thick auburn hair was pulled back in a messy ponytail. She was almost too slender, and her blue eyes glared at Chelsea. Liz's full head of hair had darkened to a dishwater blond. She was taller and bigger-boned than her sister, and her blue gaze was sad. Chelsea knew she had hurt them, but with life came change. The knowledge failed to make her feel any better.

Dash was leaning against her leg, looking up at her with adoring eyes. Why couldn't people be more like dogs? More forgiving. But how boring they would be then. She had expected her family's anger.

"It smells wonderful. Who is the cook?"

"I am," Brad said. "These two are my sous chefs."

"I'll be glad to be a sous chef too," she said.

"Would you like a drink?" Brad asked.

"That would be nice," she said gratefully, almost adding, "Make it strong." Of course, she said no such thing.

"Why don't you sit down?" he asked as he handed her a vodka and tonic.

The girls brought in a tray of snacks and set it on the dining room table. When Chelsea didn't get up and make a plate for herself, Lizzie brought her one.

"I didn't know what you wanted, so I just put everything on it."

"Thanks, Lizzie," she said, realizing she was hungry. Dash was sitting on her feet. Now he watched her eat, begging with his eyes.

"Lie down, Dash," Brad said.

Dash collapsed where he was, his head still craned toward Chelsea and the plate of snacks. She looked at Brad. "Can I give him a bite?"

"If you want him in your lap," he said. Brad looked older to her. He seemed heavier and his hair appeared thinner, but maybe that was because she hadn't seen him in a while. He was still a good-looking man, though.

She laughed and stroked Dash's head, which was now lying in her lap, his eyes trained on her plate. In some ways it had been hardest to leave the dog. She hadn't been able to tell him she wasn't coming back, that he was better off here where he could be outside without being leashed.

"How is Gina? I haven't seen her in a long time," Brad asked.

"She's working fulltime at the auto shop. So is Matt."

"We thought we'd go to a movie tonight, if that's okay with you, Mom," Lizzie said. "*Christmas Vacation.*"

Thank God, she thought. She'd wondered what they would do all evening. "Sounds like fun."

"It's a comedy," Lizzie said.

"Even better," Chelsea added.

"We need one," Abby said.

When they sat down to dinner—beef burgundy, mashed potatoes, and baby lima beans—Chelsea exclaimed over the food. "It tastes delicious. Thank you so much."

"We'll have dessert when we get home," Brad said when they cleared the table. The dog was still following Chelsea around. She had given him a bit of meat.

They put the leftovers away and quickly cleaned up the dishes. She couldn't recall them working together like this. She felt mildly insulted, as if her leaving had made them a team.

The movie was funny. Perhaps their laughter was a bit over the top, but it felt good. Back at the house, though, she became a guest again. No matter how good it was to see her daughters, she was relieved to get into her car and drive to Gina's.

One light had been left on for her. The family had gone to Dan's sister's home for the evening. Chelsea buried herself in the guest room bed and never heard them come home.

She woke in the morning when Gina sat on the edge of the bed and handed her a cup of coffee. She pushed herself up against the pillows, took the steaming cup, and smiled.

"How was it?" Gina asked.

"Hard. Awkward." She pictured Dash's adoring gaze. Did she feel so bad about the dog because he would never understand why she left? She asked Gina, but her voice broke and she began sobbing.

Gina took the hot cup from her and set it on the floor next to her own before wrapping Chelsea in a hug. "Shhh," she said softly.

"One night June left with her girlfriend to spend a weekend with another couple," she said between sobs, "and I wondered how I would meet people like me. I was never so lonely." She brushed at the tears. They were on Gina and Gina's tears were on her. "You're crying!" she exclaimed.

"For you. Stay, Chelsea. No one knows."

"I can't." She met Gina's gaze. "I do have friends now." She thought of Martha and Barb and Cat. "Not friends like you, though." No one could take Gina's place. She tried to smile. "I have to go to Brad's and put on a good show."

"Move over," Gina said, handing Chelsea her coffee and holding her own. She put her feet up and leaned against the pillows next to Chelsea. They drank their coffee in silence until they heard Gina's family getting up.

The day went better than Chelsea thought possible. It was as if they all decided to enjoy this holiday. She helped stuff the turkey and put it in the oven. She was consulted about the side dishes, because the girls wanted the food to be the same as it always had been.

The girls gave her gift certificates as did Brad, and each of them seriously thanked her for their gifts. She had bought the dog a rawhide bone, and he lay on her feet and chewed it whenever she sat down.

"Mom, why don't you stay here tonight?" Lizzie asked as she was gathering her things to go. "You can have my bed. I'll sleep in Abby's room. Don't go."

She looked at her daughter's pleading blue eyes, at the once-blond hair that had darkened with the years and now hung in a thick French braid. Impulsively, she hugged her. "It will be just as hard to leave in the morning, Lizzie."

"Why don't you come over for breakfast, Chelsea?" Brad said.

She felt as if he had just thrown her a lifeline. "Thanks. What time?" She saw Abby, standing nearby with her arms crossed, and understood her pain. In Abby's eyes, she had abandoned all of them.

Chelsea put her arms around her older daughter. "Come visit me."

Abby leaned into her before pulling away. "At the cottage?"

"That will be next summer. Come any time. My home is your home."

"This is my home," Abby said.

Lizzie looked stricken.

She looked at Brad as if for help. His arms were crossed over his chest and his smile was wry.

On the drive home, she cried so hard that it was difficult to see. She shouldn't have come. She should have handled it differently. How could she not have come back? What should she have done differently?

She'd asked Gina before leaving. Gina had given her a sad smile and shook her head.

CHAPTER TWELVE

The sun had left a smudge of yellow on the horizon when she carried her bag into the quiet house. She turned up the heat before taking off her jacket. The last fifty miles or so she had engaged in a mental struggle to keep her spirits from taking a nosedive. Going home to a cold empty house made her feel cold and empty as well. She turned on public radio and hurried from room to room flipping on light switches.

After tearing up lettuce for a salad, she sat down with it and the rotisserie chicken she had stopped to buy. The radio was so loud she failed to hear the knocking on the door until it turned into pounding.

Martha looked back at her through the small rectangular window. Chelsea jerked the door open, glad to see her, not even wondering why she was there. "Hey, come on in. I hope you haven't eaten. I'll make another salad."

Martha shook the light snow off her coat and removed her boots. "I thought you were coming home today and here you are."

"Yes." She hung Martha's coat next to her jacket on the hooks in the small mudroom. "Your feet are going to be cold."

"I brought slippers." She pulled them on. "I carry them everywhere in the winter. How was the trip?" She followed Chelsea into the kitchen, wiping the steam off her glasses with her shirt. "Forget the salad, but I wouldn't mind a bite of chicken."

Chelsea put another plate and flatware on the table and filled a glass with water. It only then occurred to her to ask why Martha was there. "Is something wrong, Martha?"

Martha cut off a slice of white meat and put it on her plate. "Nothing is wrong. I was at loose ends after spending so much time with family. Kind of lonesome when I got back home, you know?"

"Well, I'm awfully glad you came. I was dreading coming home to an empty house." She already missed Gina terribly.

"How were your daughters?" Martha looked at her with interest, a forkful of chicken halfway to her mouth.

"It was hard." Children wanted their parents together at the home where they grew up. "Hard for them and difficult for me. I understand their anger, but I can't talk about it with them." *Or you*, she thought. She felt like crying when she even thought about why she had left Brad. She only had to think how much she must have hurt him to shed tears.

"What are you going to wear to Cat's New Year's Eve party?" Martha asked between bites.

"What party?" Chelsea asked, feeling the uncertainty of being left out.

"Have you listened to your messages or looked at your mail?" Martha asked.

"I scanned the mail. Nothing from Cat there," she said, talking between chewing and swallowing.

"Listen to your messages. Now. I know she invited you."

Wondering if Cat might have overlooked her, Chelsea pushed the flashing numbers on the answering machine. The first two messages were nonprofits, looking for money.

"Call me when you get home," Cat said. "I'm having a New Year's Eve party. Bring your jammies in case you can't drive home."

Martha picked her up at eight on New Year's Eve. They wore slacks and blouses under winter coats. Snow was falling, covering the streets. When Martha stepped on the gas, the car skidded and hit the curb.

"Whoa!" Chelsea said, grabbing the dashboard.

"Maybe we should stay at your house," Martha said as she clutched the steering wheel. "Nah. It's New Year's Eve. Let's go celebrate," she added in the next breath.

"Slower," Chelsea cautioned.

The tires whirred as the snow whorled toward the windshield, a vortex of white. Until they neared Cat's house, they were the only vehicle on the roads. Martha skidded to a stop behind a car parked a block away.

"Guess we'll have to walk," she said.

Chelsea opened the door and stepped out into snow up to her boot tops. Muffled voices came from others exiting their vehicles. It was eerie and beautiful and wet. She waded through a foot-deep drift to reach the sidewalk.

She and Martha hung on to each other when they climbed the slippery, snowy steps to Cat's front porch. "God, why did I bother to dress up? I look like I went for a polar plunge," Martha said.

"Me too. Should we go back and change?" Chelsea asked, laughing nervously. She didn't want to fall.

Cat stood inside the door, looking elegant in tight black pants that traced her lower body and a brilliant green blouse with a plunging neckline made of some silky material. She wore low heels. "Sorry about the steps. We keep shoveling."

Sexy, that's how she looked, Chelsea thought as she and Martha said their greetings and presented Cat with a wine bottle apiece.

"Thank you, ladies, but this is my party. Hide them somewhere and take them home when you leave."

Properly chastened, they headed for the bathroom, their slacks dripping on the hardwood floors. "Nobody else is all wet," Martha whispered.

"I don't know how they got here. Let's blow ourselves dry," Chelsea said, thinking wearing a skirt or dress would have been mad.

Their rippling slacks made them both laugh. Martha began dancing before the mirror, and Chelsea turned off the dryer. Someone was knocking. Chelsea opened the door a crack.

"Cat," she said as if surprised to see her. "We're drying off a bit."

"I followed the water trail," Cat said.

"We'll clean up the floors," Chelsea said.

"It's already done," Cat replied. "Why don't you come out and join the party?"

The two women followed Cat into the crowd, where she introduced them to her friends. When Cat began to introduce them to Jane Nichols, Chelsea took Jane's hand in both of hers.

"We know each other. Jane hired me."

"One of my best decisions. Hi, Martha. Martha sent Chelsea to our office."

"Oh, come on. I'm a receptionist. I answer the phone and label envelopes," Chelsea said, thinking Jane looked fantastic. She was dressed in a flowing top and bottom and wore short black heels, her gray hair shone, and her brown eyes were alight with pleasure.

"And you do it well," Jane said and laughed. "It's just so nice to have someone to talk to. You're the only other woman there." She paused. "I'm going to get a drink. Want to come with me, you two? I know Cat has to socialize."

The bar was in the corner of the dining room. The three women sat on stools and each ordered a glass of wine. Martha and Chelsea smiled at each other.

"How do I look?" Martha asked.

Chelsea burst into laughter, nearly spitting the red wine.

"That bad?" Martha looked dismayed.

"Hey, you both look terrific." This was from Jane.

"Why didn't you get all wet on your way here?" Chelsea asked.

"I wore jeans and changed here," Jane said, smiling.

Chelsea loved her smile.

Martha hit her forehead with the palm of her hand. "Why didn't we think of that?"

"Oh well, it can't be undone," Chelsea said, smiling.

"I'm going to make the rounds," Martha said, leaving Chelsea alone with Jane.

"Do you know Cat well?" Chelsea asked. She'd never seen the two together.

"Only through Jim, and I know him only through work. And you?"

"I met her through her daughter, Lindsey."

"I've heard that the child is difficult."

"Really?" Chelsea said and laughed.

"I saw from your résumé that you lived in Indiana for many years."

"My married years."

The conversation took flight. They exchanged details of their past and present lives—nothing too personal—but Chelsea learned with surprise that Jane had never married.

"I didn't want to be a housewife and raise children, although I like other people's kids—my nieces and nephews, for instance. Cooking, cleaning, and PTA meetings are not my things."

Chelsea studied Jane's face, the keen brown eyes and high cheekbones, the dark-toned clear skin. "Kids do hamper a career." But she would rather have her girls than a high-paying career, she thought, no matter how they were behaving right now.

Martha returned. "It's almost midnight in New York. Everyone is gathering around the TV. The ball is about to drop."

The three women walked to where the others stood. When the ball dropped, they all began to sing "Auld Lang Syne." Chelsea was in full song when Jim Morgan kissed her. His tongue snuck in her mouth, and she pushed him away. He went on to kiss Martha, but when he turned to Jane, Jane shook her head.

"I like you, Jim, but not that much," Jane said. "I'm going home now." She said goodbye to Chelsea and Martha and went to thank Cat.

Chelsea walked to a window and peered out. The streetlamp was shrouded in a halo of snow.

"I think we should take Cat up on her offer and sleep here," Martha said.

Chelsea wondered how Jane was going to make it home. She saw her drinking a glass of champagne with Cat.

Someone handed her a glass of champagne and she raised it and drank.

People began to leave shortly after midnight. Cat told Martha and Chelsea they should stay. Not much later she showed the two friends to two small bedrooms on the third floor. Chelsea turned off the light, wrapped the blankets around her, and fell asleep in her wrinkled clothes.

She got up once to pee and quickly returned to the twin bed. Light shone through the small window. It looked like the snow had stopped. She closed her eyes and was drifting off when she thought she heard a click. The bedsprings creaked, and her eyes snapped open.

Stretched out, facing her, lay Cat. "I didn't get this wrong, did I?" she asked, the pupils of her eyes almost blacking out the color. Cat wriggled under the blankets, took Chelsea in her arms, and gently kissed her face. "I've wanted you since the first time I laid eyes on you," she murmured.

"Then why were you so rude to me after Lindsey's accident?" Chelsea asked, wide-awake and totally confused.

"I'm not good at being grateful."

When Cat began removing Chelsea's clothes, a very awkward process, Chelsea did not resist, but she didn't help either. Her heart was pounding too hard. Zippers stuck, and buttons refused to unbutton. The outfit Chelsea had so carefully chosen soon lay in a heap on the floor, along with Cat's clothes. She took a peek at Cat's naked body. For being so slender, she had surprisingly large breasts. Emboldened, Chelsea traced the tan that outlined swimwear, feeling only bones.

She felt Cat's probing tongue, hands that were all over her. When Cat started to make her way down Chelsea's body, Chelsea pulled her back. "We don't know each other well enough," she protested.

Cat climbed on top of her, and Chelsea shifted her weight to accommodate her. When Cat kissed her now, instead of being surprised, she wondered what it would be like with Jane.

"God almighty, woman," Cat exploded, "what does it take to get your attention?"

"A hand in the right place for starters," she said.

Cat's fingers felt warm, and Chelsea moved against them ever so slowly. She reached between Cat's thighs and stroked her. Cat strained toward her touch.

"Easy," Chelsea whispered. "Relax and enjoy." The act was short as is.

When Cat threw back her head and began moaning loudly, Chelsea quickly put a hand over her mouth.

"Shh. Martha's in the next room."

"I know. I put her there," Cat said, removing the hand. "We may as well stop, if you're so disinterested."

"I'm not disinterested," Chelsea protested. "I like quiet sex. Somebody might hear you and come to the rescue." She giggled.

Cat pushed away from her. "You think it's so funny, you can go fuck yourself." She began jerking on her clothes.

"Hey, no fair. You get me all worked up and then you leave." Another giggle escaped, and she knew she wasn't going to be able to stop.

"Go fly a kite," Cat said.

Chelsea began to howl, rocking back and forth on the bed, her face screwed up as if in pain instead of laughter. "G..go fly a..a kite," she repeated, her belly aching. It was just that she'd expected to hear the word "fuck," not "fly."

The door slammed shut and still she laughed. Had Martha heard? The thought made her laugh harder.

CHAPTER THIRTEEN

She awoke in the morning to someone knocking on the door. She was naked and desperate to pee. "Who is it?" she asked, hurriedly pulling her clothes on without the underwear.

"Me. Martha."

"Come in, but I've got to go."

Martha opened the door, took one look at Chelsea, and started to laugh. "Your top is on backward." She snorted.

"I'll be right back," Chelsea said and ran for the john. After peeing, she flushed the toilet and looked in the small mirror over the sink. A woman with black around her eyes and wild hair looked back at her. "I would have laughed at me too," she muttered.

She and Martha crept downstairs. The only person up was the kid, Lindsey, who eyed them with hostility.

"Where's your mom?" Martha asked.

The girl shrugged. She had lined up glasses on the coffee table and was drinking the leftover liquid.

"Tell her thanks for us," Chelsea said. "Go easy with that stuff. It'll make you sick."

"I drink it all the time," the girl said. She was dressed in tights and a too-big sweater.

"It will rot your brains," Chelsea warned.

"Happy New Year," Martha said. "Tell your mom I'll call. I'm Martha."

She and Chelsea found their coats and went out into the cold day. Chelsea pulled her collar together, and the two women pushed through the wind toward Martha's car. Miraculously, someone had shoveled the sidewalks and the streets had been plowed and salted.

At home alone, Chelsea opened an envelope she had put aside. There was no return address. She read the first sentence and her gaze dropped to the signature. It was that of Mimi Kincaid, the author whose manuscript, *Fire Works*, she had read. Mimi thanked her for being her first reader and for writing such a nice letter. She wanted to be friends. Mimi thought they should meet, so that she could run by Chelsea the ideas she had for her next book, which was already in progress. She wanted to know what Chelsea thought.

"Would that be appropriate?" Mimi asked. "I live in the Twin Cities. It's not too far a drive." She ended with her street address and phone number.

No author had ever asked to meet her, but the request put her out of sorts. She didn't want to drive to Minneapolis.

On the phone she discussed the letter with Martha, giving voice to her concerns.

"What are you afraid of?" Martha asked.

The question stopped her in her mental tracks. "I don't know," she said after a few moments of silence.

"I mean, she's an author. Right up your alley. You can talk books. You could invite her for a weekend and have a welcoming party," she said, warming to the idea. "You could invite me and Cat and anyone else you want."

"I'd keep it small." If she had a party. If she even invited Mimi to visit.

The party was to take place the last Saturday in January, the day Mimi arrived. That morning Chelsea arose before dawn to finish the appetizers. She had awakened at 1:15, 3, and 4:30. At 5:45 she had given up and got up. The party was scheduled to start at 1. By 8:30 everything she could prepare in advance was ready. She showered and dressed before sitting down on the sofa with a cup of coffee to read a bit—and promptly fell asleep. She was awakened by a knock on the door. She ran her fingers through her hair and straightened her sweater after standing unsteadily. She looked at her watch. It was 11.

Hurrying through the den to the front door, she peered through the small glass pane there and found herself eye to eye with someone. She opened the door with caution. A slender woman with large hazel eyes peering out from behind wire-rimmed glasses shot out her hand, very nearly punching Chelsea in the belly.

"Oops, sorry," she said. "I'm Mimi Kincaid."

Chelsea shook the hand. It was cold. "Welcome. Come in." She looked around for a vehicle and saw a Chevy Nova parked at the curb across the street. "Is that your car over there?" Mimi nodded. "Why don't you park it in the garage?"

Mimi gave her an apologetic smile. "I'm going back to Point tonight." *That's right*, Chelsea thought. Mimi had told her she was spending Friday and Saturday nights with a friend in Stevens Point.

"You're welcome to stay over," she said anyway, "but we can talk about that later." She hung Mimi's jacket on the coatrack. She refilled her cup of coffee and poured one for Mimi. They sat at either end of the sofa.

"Good coffee. Thanks. I needed a pick-me-up."

Chelsea looked at the other woman and was met with an impish smile. "Tell me about your new book," she said.

Mimi started talking, using her hands for emphasis.

After ten minutes or so, Chelsea was overcome by drowsiness. She tried to stay awake. She knew how embarrassed she would be and how hurt Mimi might feel. But it was no use. She heard Mimi's voice fading away.

This time it was the doorbell that awakened her. Disoriented, she opened her eyes and heard voices. Mimi was no longer sitting on the sofa. She got up and walked toward the voices. One she recognized as Martha's. How long had she been asleep? Martha was supposed to arrive at 12:30, and Mimi had been here since 11. She glanced at her watch—11:25.

"Martha. You're early," she said. "Really early."

Martha and Mimi glanced at each other and giggled.

"I'm sorry, Mimi," Chelsea said, her face reddening, "I fall asleep at meetings and movies, don't I, Martha? I was awake much of the night. Mimi was telling me about the book she is working on."

"She does fall asleep at lectures and meetings and movies. I can attest to that," Martha said.

Mimi startled them both with a full-throated laugh. "Here I am, prattling on about my writing, and I look up and see that my audience has fallen asleep." She giggled again. "This will make a great story when I give readings."

"Please don't tell anyone," Chelsea pleaded.

"I won't use your name," Mimi promised.

Later, when others began to arrive, she heard Mimi retelling the story, her laughter pealing through the house.

Cat had arrived with Lindsey in tow. "I can't leave her alone," she said, her eyes pleading with Chelsea.

Chelsea was momentarily speechless. She looked at Lindsey with a slight frown between her eyes.

Lindsey stuck her tongue out and retracted it with such speed Chelsea thought maybe it hadn't happened.

She met Cat's eyes and shrugged. "Come on in." She knew Cat could tell she didn't want Lindsey there. She also knew that because Cat had brought Lindsey to the door, Chelsea wouldn't send them away in front of the girl.

When Lindsey and Cat went in the house, Chelsea went out and stomped around the sidewalk until she cooled off. She was about to go inside when Barb drove up.

"Hey, lady. Aren't you the hostess? What are you doing out here?"

Chelsea gave her a little history on Lindsey. "I can't trust her."

"I'll keep track of her," Barb offered.

"That's not fair to you," Chelsea said.

"I want to."

Inside, Chelsea introduced Barb to the guests who stood around the punch bowl talking to Mimi and each other. Chelsea had invited Dana and Mickie, because she had so few friends. She had forgiven Dana for June's tantrum at the restaurant. After all, she was June's friend first, and she'd said she was sorry.

"Are you a big reader, Lindsey?" she heard Barb ask.

"Why?" the girl answered.

"Because this is a party for an author."

"I didn't ask to come," Lindsey said and wandered away.

Barb followed. Cat shot Chelsea a questioning look.

Mimi was talking about how thrilled she was when FemBooks accepted her manuscript.

Dana had her arm around Mickie, who looked disturbingly young. Chelsea wondered if the girl was even close to eighteen. She'd have to ask Barb, who had just now joined the group with Lindsey.

Lindsey pulled on her mother's sleeve and said in a faux whisper, "Can we go home now?"

Cat moved away from the group and spoke quietly to her, but the girl raised her voice. "I'm bored. I can walk home."

Cat argued quietly with her daughter before rejoining the group. Lindsey went to the sofa where Chelsea could see her kicking her shoes against the fabric. Chelsea looked at Cat, but Cat wasn't where she could see her daughter.

Barb walked over and sat next to the girl and shortly after, Lindsey stopped the kicking.

In her peripheral vision she saw Dana run her fingers through Mickie's hair. She noticed Martha throwing puzzled glances their way and felt the heat of embarrassment.

"Mickie is a budding writer," Dana said out of the blue.

"I'm not either." Mickie blushed as eyes fell on her. "I just dabble."

"I did too at your age," Mimi said with enthusiasm. She had a wide mouth full of rather large white teeth and showed them all when she smiled—as she did now. "It's good to have such a supportive mother."

Chelsea's brain froze. She looked with horror at Dana, imagining how insulted she would be.

"I'm her lover, not her mother." Dana enunciated every word, her voice icy.

Mimi laughed. "God, I'm sorry. I never learn. The other day I asked a woman in the checkout lane when her baby was due and guess what? She wasn't pregnant." She laughed again.

The others laughed too, and Mickie turned a bright red. Chelsea also felt heat on her face.

"You're lesbians?" Lindsey asked. Unnoticed, she had rejoined the others.

Dana frowned at the girl as if wondering how to respond.

What a disaster, Chelsea thought.

"Well, at least you're open about it," Jane said, and Chelsea released the breath she had been holding.

"I think if everyone who is gay came out of the closet, people would wonder what all the hullaballoo had been about. They'd realize they're just like everybody else," Martha added.

"Are you a lesbian?" Lindsey asked, looking up at Martha.

"I believe everybody has a little same sex love in them, especially for our close friends."

Lindsey turned her gaze on Chelsea. "I knew she was a lesbian," she said.

Chelsea threw an angry look at Cat, who met her glance with a helpless shrug. "Come on, Lindsey. You wanted to go home."

After that, everyone seemed to relax. At least Chelsea thought so.

CHAPTER FOURTEEN

Mimi left shortly before five. Chelsea had again invited her to stay, but Mimi said she had promised her friend in Stevens Point that she would return that night.

"Sorry if I spoiled the party," she said as she stood next to her car.

"You didn't spoil anything. At least no one was bored, except Lindsey." They both laughed.

She went back in the house to find Martha and Barb cleaning up. "Hey, you don't have to do that."

"We want to. We were just talking about what Mimi said to Dana." Martha snorted a laugh.

"I couldn't believe my ears," Barb said, also laughing.

"*You* couldn't believe your ears. I hoped I had misheard."

"Maybe Dana will think twice about what she's doing with someone so young," Barb said.

"How young is Mickie?" Chelsea asked.

"Not eighteen yet, and Dana just turned forty."

"She could be her mother," Martha said.

The next day Chelsea woke up to a phone ringing in her dreams. She fumbled for the receiver and heard Lizzie's voice.

"Mom, is that you?"

She always called her daughters Sunday evening, even though Abby unfailingly said something rude and Lizzie was always aloof. "Is something wrong?" she asked, instantly awake.

"No, Mom. We're going out tonight, Abby and me. Do you remember Keith Davis?"

Keith, the son of friends, was the same age as Lizzie. "He was a nice boy. What about him?"

"He's my boyfriend, but he's not a boy anymore."

"Really?" She sat up and swallowed a yawn. "Are the two of you serious?" God, how would she handle a wedding?

"Yes, and Abby is serious about Jeff Livingston. You remember him?"

"I do." She recalled them as boys, loud and unruly, but unfailingly polite to her. Her throat thickened.

"We're talking about having a double ceremony."

"When?" her mother asked.

"Dad says we should wait a year. I'm not sure why."

Lizzie had not spoken so openly to her mother since she'd separated from Brad. She was thrilled by this sharing and relieved that it would be at least a year before any weddings.

"Is Abby willing to wait that long?" She fell back on the pillow.

"She said she was."

"Is she there?"

"No. She went out to breakfast with Dad."

Chelsea's heart contracted. "You didn't go with them?"

"I wanted to call you."

She didn't know what this meant. Couldn't Lizzie talk to her around Abby and her dad? But she felt she shouldn't ask. "I love that you called," she said instead.

"I have to go now," Lizzie said.

"Keep me up to date on your plans, yours and Abby's. Will you do that?"

"I will. 'Bye, Mom."

"Goodbye, sweetie. I love you."

"Me too." And she was gone.

She was feeling a little panicky as she pulled on sweats and went to make coffee. She could well imagine what a wedding would be like. What would she say to those who had been acquaintances of hers and Brad's, to Brad's relatives and her own?

She pushed away the unpleasant thoughts and considered what she would do today. She had two manuscripts to read, but Martha had mentioned cross-country skiing and asked Barb to come along. She'd said she'd call Cat too. The sun was shining, and High Cliff was not far away.

She would never admit it, but she wasn't very fond of cross-country skiing. It was better than downhill, though. She and her girls had gone on weekend trips, and although she loved being with her daughters, she hated to be cold and wet and out of control on the steeper downhill runs.

The four women and their gear crowded into Cat's Taurus in early afternoon and headed out of town. Chelsea had positioned herself to be in the middle backseat. Sitting close to Cat had made her uncomfortable since that unsuccessful romp in bed on New Year's Eve.

Cat parked up top in the tower parking lot. The skis were on the roof. Barb's were rentals, and Chelsea helped her snap her rental boots into the bindings. They started out along the bluff overlooking Lake Winnebago. Chelsea felt off-balance from the get-go. A wind that hadn't been noticeable at the bottom of the cliff burned her cheeks. She noticed that Barb appeared to be even more off-balance than she was.

As they shushed along, she and Barb fell further and further behind the other two women. When the trail crossed a tiny creek, creating a small dip and turn, Barb stopped in her tracks.

Chelsea looked at the small dip. "I'll go first." she said and then eased off without waiting for an answer. Her arms waved in the air as her balance wavered. One ski came off the ground, but then she regained her stability and poled herself up to flat ground.

Barb laughed and pushed off. Arms and poles pinioning, she made it to the other side without falling as well. "Whew," she said. "Onward, brave woman."

And they set off again. Both had cheeks bright red from the cold wind. Stopping for long was unbearable.

They braved every dip and hill, each falling twice in the process. They only caught up with Cat and Martha in the tower parking lot, where the two women were warming up in the car.

"What was holding you up?" Cat asked. She and Martha got out of the vehicle to help.

"The hills," Barb said.

"What hills?" Martha looked puzzled.

"Hey, this was my first time on skis," Barb protested.

"And I was staying with her," Chelsea said, hiding her shame at being so unathletic and cowardly.

She should ask Barb out, she thought. It would be a blast.

Chelsea began looking for signs of spring on the first day of March. In Indiana crocuses often poked their heads above ground in February. On warm nights, spring peepers could be heard through an open window. Not here, though.

Jane had invited her out to eat on Friday, and Chelsea was waiting for her to show up. Friday evenings every restaurant offered a fish fry, a popular holdover from when the only meat Catholics could eat on Friday was fish. The fish were deep-fried and served with french fries and coleslaw. As a rule, no reservations were taken. Customers might wait an hour or more to be seated.

It was the first time Jane had asked her to go out, and Chelsea wanted to know her better. She wasn't sure why. She hoped she wasn't falling for another straight woman like Gina. She did remind her of Gina, but only because of her friendliness. During the week, she arrived at Graphics Inc. early and made coffee. Chelsea got there shortly after. They talked about anything and everything—their lives, politics, dreams, and families. Although Chelsea tried to keep her former life under wraps, Jane asked probing questions like, "What was it like for you, being married?"

Chelsea had to think about that one. "Well, you can't do whatever you want. You have to consult with your husband or maybe share is a better word, unless he's not around. Brad worked nearly every day. I had a good friend with kids the same ages as mine. We spent our days together. She saved me from boredom." What would she have done without Gina?

"If you could do it over, would you get married?" Jane poured more coffee into Chelsea's cup. They had about ten minutes before opening the doors.

"I was pregnant with Abby. I thought I had no other choice." But she could have gotten certified to teach or applied for other jobs in her field. She had a degree but not a career. She wasn't sure she was ready to raise a child alone. And she was ashamed to have let herself get pregnant.

Jane met her eyes with a puzzled look. "You always have choices."

"All right," she said, annoyed. "It was the easy way."

"How did you meet Brad and end up in Indiana?"

"We went to university together."

"But I thought he was a welder."

"He loves to weld, and his dad owned a welding shop. His dad wanted him to take his place when he retired. Instead, his dad died before he retired, and Brad took over." He also had taken the easy way, she realized.

Jane unlocked the doors and made more coffee as the others who worked there began drifting in, greeting the two women as they poured a cup and took it to their desks. Before Jane went to her office, she gave Chelsea's shoulder a squeeze. By then they were alone again. "I shouldn't be so curious. I'm sorry."

"It's okay," Chelsea said, putting her hand over Jane's. A warm feeling flooded her.

After work, as she was looking at the fresh fruit at Woodman's, she wondered what Jane did at night. Did she go home to an empty house too? Did she watch TV or read a good book? How nice it would be to have dinner with her that night.

At home, she unloaded her groceries and was putting them away when the phone rang.

"Hi. How are you?" June's voice floated into her ear. She had expected anyone but.

"I don't want to talk to you," Chelsea said and hung up. Her legs had gone weak. When the phone rang again, she walked away from it. She heard June yell "Fucking bitch" into the answering machine as she had so many times, but this time the words were punctuated by sobs.

She stopped in her tracks, uncertain whether she should or shouldn't have picked it up. Her hand hovered over the receiver, and then she went into the computer room and shut the door.

Later, before she cleared off the message, she listened to the sobbing for what seemed a long time before deleting it.

Just as she was getting ready for bed, the doorbell rang. She pulled her sweats back on and peered out the little window on the front door. Dana stood outside, her breath generating clouds. Chelsea opened the door a few inches.

"Is something wrong, Dana?" It was after nine.

The door crashed inward, hitting Chelsea on the nose and slamming her body into the wall.

"Hey, you said you just wanted to talk," Dana protested. "Don't smash her."

Head reeling, Chelsea touched her nose and looked at her fingers. No blood, thank God. Someone shut the door and she took a few steps away. "What the hell," she said. "I'm calling 911."

"No, you're not," June said. "You're going to listen to me."

"Why did you bring her here?" Chelsea asked Dana.

"She told me she was going to kill herself. I didn't know she was going to act like a maniac."

"And how many times has she told you that?"

"Couple of times. Maybe three," Dana said.

"And you still believe her?" she asked.

"I guess not."

"Well, don't bring her here again."

"I won't. I'm sorry," Dana said.

"You hung up on me without hearing me out," June said.

"And you left me for Karen. Remember? Now get out of here." She worried that June would start breaking things that belonged to the owners.

"It was a stupid thing to do. I wanted to tell you I was sorry. I want to come back."

Chelsea stared at June in disbelief. "I don't want you back. Go away."

"I thought you cared for me."

"Not anymore." She turned to Dana. "Get her out of here, will you?"

"Come on, June. Let's go." Dana took June's arm.

June jerked away. "I won't give you another chance."

"Good. I don't want one," Chelsea said.

As soon as they were out the door, Chelsea shut and locked it with shaking hands. How could she have misjudged someone so badly? June wasn't at all who she thought she was—fun, caring, understanding, reasonable. And neither was Dana. She must be just plain stupid to listen to June.

CHAPTER FIFTEEN

On Friday Chelsea looked out the windows, waiting for Jane to show up. She had said she'd be there by five. Otherwise they might wait an hour or more to eat.

At five Jane parked her Honda Accord in the driveway, and Chelsea hurriedly put on her coat and gloves and went out the side door. It was March, but it felt more like January.

"There's no rush," Jane said.

"I didn't want you to have to get out of your car."

"Spring will come, I promise. We usually have a snowstorm or two in April."

Warmed by Jane's grin, Chelsea settled into the passenger seat. "At least your car is warm. Where are we going?"

"I thought we could try Mark's. I've had good fish there. What do you think?"

"Fine with me. Martha and I went to Adler Brau Brewery and Restaurant, and it was good. I haven't been to many fish fries since I came back."

"We can go there if you want." Jane was looking at her, one hand on the gear stick.

"No, Mark's is good." That's where all the old people went.

Mark's was a babble of voices as the hostess seated them in a corner booth. They would have to talk loudly, and there were things she wanted to ask Jane that shouldn't be said in a shout.

"I'd forgotten how noisy it is in here," Jane said. "We could go somewhere else." She raised her eyebrows in question. "But most restaurants are noisy."

"No. Let's stay put. So how was the rest of your day?" Chelsea asked.

Jane shrugged. "Nothing happened worth mentioning. How about yours?"

"The same." Any personal talk would have to wait. "I did make brownies this afternoon." She'd baked them as an afterthought because she had a box mix on hand.

"For our dessert?" Jane asked.

Chelsea nodded.

"Good idea."

She was comfortably full when they got back in Jane's car, closing the door against a cold wind.

"You know, I used to love winter," Jane said.

"What did you love about it?" Chelsea asked.

"The snow. I even liked to shovel, and I loved to ski."

"I did too, but I've always loved summer best. I like it hot enough to sweat at night."

Jane laughed. "So, how do you like living here?"

The wind was blowing snow across the road in front of them. "I grew up here, you know. It's sometimes lonely now, not like it was when I was young. I guess I'm used to living with someone. What do you do in the evenings?" In the passing streetlights Chelsea could see Jane smile.

"What everybody else does, I suppose. Watch TV. Read. Sometimes I go for a walk. Sometimes a friend comes over."

"Don't you miss having someone to go places with you, to talk to, to just have around?"

Jane shot her an indecipherable look. "Sometimes. Then I call a friend." She parked in the driveway and they hurried inside.

Chelsea was glad she didn't have to go out again that night. She turned on lights that led to the living room and went into the kitchen to get the brownies.

"Want ice cream with your brownie?" she asked.

"I'm just warming up," Jane said from outside the kitchen door.

"Sorry. Didn't mean to holler at you."

"It's okay. We've been doing that most of the evening."

Chelsea laughed. "Well, not in the car." She carried out two small plates with a brownie on each. Then she went back for the two cups of decaf.

"Thanks. This is nice, having dessert here where it's quiet." Jane took a bite of her brownie. "I love brownies. Why did you move back here, Chelsea?"

Chelsea burned her mouth on the coffee. "Careful. It's hot."

"You don't have to tell me anything, you know."

She glanced at Jane, met her eyes, and quickly looked down at the coffee. She felt teary and hot and foolish. Would she feel this way had things turned out better with June? If they had, she wouldn't be with Jane tonight. "For the wrong reasons," she finally said.

The pause couldn't have been more than a moment or two, yet it seemed much longer. "Well, I'm glad you did," Jane said. "I never would have known you. So much of life is chance."

Was Jane talking to give her time to recover? Chelsea thought so. She took a deep breath and lifted her head.

Jane met her eyes, and her gaze softened. "I should go home before it gets any colder out."

"No, don't go. It's too cold already." Chelsea couldn't let Jane leave until they cleared some things up.

Jane's hair shone under the overhead light. "I have to go sometime," she said with a friendly smile.

"No, you don't. There is plenty of room. I have a new toothbrush, a sleep shirt you can use, and another bedroom."

Jane looked at her with those keen brown eyes until Chelsea looked away. "Good planning," Jane said. "I have no wish to go out in the cold."

"Would you like another brownie?" She was heartened. She hadn't expected Jane to stay.

"Yes, but no. I'm pretty full."

Chelsea jumped up and put the plates in the sink. They were finishing off the coffee on the sofa. She asked Jane if she'd like to watch a movie, but there was nothing on TV worth watching.

Jane started looking through the bookcase next to the TV and came back to the davenport with *Other Women*. "I absolutely loved this book. May I take it to bed with me?"

"Of course. It is one of my favorites." Chelsea smiled, the first easy smile since Jane had asked her why she'd moved back and she'd given that stupid answer. "In fact, that book is the reason I moved here."

"That powerful, huh?" Jane asked with a warm smile.

Chelsea could only nod. That too was not quite the truth. "Well, one of the reasons." If Jane had asked her the other reasons, she would have told her, but Jane didn't ask.

"I put the toothbrush on the bathroom counter and the sleep shirt on the bed in the guest bedroom," she said when she came out of the bathroom a while later.

"Sorry," Jane said, closing the book. "We should start a book club. I've never discussed this book with anyone."

"We should," Chelsea agreed. She could ask Martha and Cat and Barb. "And start with *Other Women*."

"I forgot you edit books."

"I'm a reader, not an editor. I tell the publisher whether I think a book is worth the effort and cost of publishing."

Jane was smiling as if amused.

"I talk too much," she said.

"No, you don't." Jane's expression changed to concern. "I enjoy having someone to talk to." She leaned toward Chelsea.

Chelsea's hair rose on the back of her neck. She knew Jane was going to kiss her and worried about the lights being on and blinds open for anyone to see.

"Don't worry. I know there might be eyes out there," Jane said, and the moment passed. "I should go to bed."

"Me too," Chelsea said, disappointed. She had a fleeting memory of the aggressiveness of Cat, the fumbling of June. What would Jane be like, if she even was a lesbian. If she hadn't meant to kiss Chelsea, why would she have said what she had about there being eyes watching them?

"Come on. I'll show you to your room."

At the bedroom doorway as Chelsea reached to turn on the light, Jane put a hand on her arm. "Not yet," she said. She buried her fingers in Chelsea's hair and kissed her, long and sweet. "Goodnight," she said with a mischievous smile and stepped past Chelsea into the room.

Stunned, Chelsea stood stock-still for a moment before flipping the switch. The room erupted in light and she wished she had turned on the bed lamp earlier, but then the kiss might not have happened because the blinds were open.

Jane closed the blinds and turned on the bedside light, and Chelsea turned off the overhead light. "That's better," Jane said.

"That was nice," Chelsea said. She wanted another kiss and took a step toward Jane.

"I shouldn't be so impulsive," Jane said.

Chelsea took it to mean Jane was sorry. "It's okay." Her throat closed when she tried to say how much okay it was.

Jane lifted her shoulders. "I guess I'll go to bed then."

"See you in the morning." Chelsea moved into the hallway. Inside she was screaming, *No, no, no. Go to bed with me.* She quietly closed the door, while telling herself she was a goddamn coward. She deserved to sleep alone. She wondered how she could have chased June and was unable to do the same with Jane.

She was sitting up in bed, reading the same sentences over and over, when she looked up to see Jane standing in the open doorway. A slow smile stretched across her face.

"Do you want company?" Jane asked.

"I haven't changed the sheets for over a week." Why the hell was that the first thing out of her mouth? "But if you don't mind, yes."

"I don't mind," Jane said with a grin. "I brought *Other Women* with me. We can read in bed together." She walked around the end of the queen-size bed and climbed in. If one of them stretched out an arm, she could touch the other.

They might as well have been on the davenport, Chelsea thought as they each lifted their books and appeared to be reading. But she couldn't read. She continued to go over the same sentences, trying to absorb the words.

"That book made me admit who I was, what I was," she said.

"It made me feel as if it was all right to be who I was," Jane said.

"I'll never sleep tonight." Chelsea lay back on her pillows and sighed.

"Nor will I. Let's do something about it," Jane said.

Chelsea looked into Jane's brown eyes, now filled with what Chelsea thought was lust. They edged sideways across the bed until they met in the middle.

CHAPTER SIXTEEN

Their shoulders and thighs touched. Chelsea's heartbeat went crazy but when Jane turned toward her, all she could think about was if her breath smelled. Would Jane be offended? She was stiff with worry when Jane kissed her again.

Jane slid down, taking Chelsea with her till only their heads were on the pillows. They stretched out face-to-face, the heat from their bodies flowing between them. Chelsea's worry was rapidly overwhelmed by desire. She tugged at Jane's T-shirt and pulled her own off as she watched Jane do the same. When Jane was close enough to feel her breasts and pelvis against her own, she began to move, ever so slightly.

They kissed gently, slowly—lips, chins, eyelids, and cheeks. Their tongues touched. The heat between them grew and Chelsea spread Jane's legs with her knee. Her hand moved slowly over her body—her breasts, her abdomen, the inside of her thighs—before covering the crisp, curly hair. There she lingered, her fingers stroking the silken wet folds before plunging inside.

Jane's breath caught and she rose to meet the touch. Her hand traveled over Chelsea in the same way, and Chelsea tensed, waiting for the teasing touch that would end in climax.

They rocked against each other, making indecipherable sounds of pleasure until Jane began to spasm, her body arching against Chelsea, her fingers stilled during the nearly unbearable moment of pleasure.

After, Chelsea felt the stroking begin again and she came quickly. A moment or two later, she rolled onto her back. Touch was now unbearable.

Jane kissed Chelsea's breasts, her abdomen, and the insides of her thighs. Chelsea closed her legs and pulled Jane's body close. "Let me hold you," she said, and Jane stayed her touch.

Entwined, they fell asleep.

Chelsea woke up with her bladder uncomfortably full. She was surprised to see how little time had passed since they'd had sex. She freed herself gently from Jane's embrace and padded to the bathroom. When she came back, she backed up to Jane who pulled her close and, spoonlike, they slept again.

When long slivers of daylight crept through the closed blinds, Chelsea opened her eyes. She was on her back, and Jane was looking at her. Slightly embarrassed, Chelsea studied Jane's expression—the faint smile, the nearly black eyes. Was Jane pleased? She couldn't tell.

"Wow!" Jane said, and Chelsea smiled.

They began kissing, which led to touching. This time they could see. Chelsea kissed Jane's neck, ran a hand intimately over her soft skin, and when Jane arched her back, she slithered down her body to taste her. Jane went wild.

Reaching for Chelsea's hips, Jane pulled her down. When Chelsea felt the warm tongue, the probing fingers, she came quickly.

Afterward, they lay stunned. Finally, Chelsea broke the silence. "How about some coffee?" It seemed like such a mundane thing to say after ecstatic sex. They both burst out in embarrassed laughter, which went on too long.

"Come on." Jane pulled Chelsea toward the edge of the bed.

Chelsea understood. If they didn't get up now, they might start over again. They needed sustenance.

"You're a wonderful lover," Jane said over coffee while Chelsea fried eggs.

She was flattered. No one had ever told her that. Of course, she'd had only three lovers, including Jane and leaving out a few one-night stands. "You are too."

"Will you wash my back?" Jane asked when they had finished breakfast.

"Just your back?" Chelsea flushed a little.

"You can wash anything you like, and I'll do the same. How does that sound?"

Chelsea put the dishes in the dishwasher and followed Jane into the bathroom. It was the first time they had seen each other totally naked. When they had first made love, it was dark. The second time they were partially covered. Now they stood in front of each other, trying not to be obviously curious, neither wanting to bend over and turn the water on. Since it was Chelsea's house, she climbed into the tub and squatted in front of the faucet.

"I'm not looking," Jane said, laughing.

"Good. You better not be." She didn't want to bare her ass to her newly found lover. "Are you my boss? You did hire me."

"I was doing someone else's bidding, and I wouldn't be the one to fire you," Jane said.

"Good. I was feeling a little vulnerable." She turned to face Jane as the water washed over them.

Jane slowly looked her up and down. "You are a beautiful sight."

"You are too, you silly thing. Turn your back and I'll wash it."

Instead, Jane walked into her arms. "I hate to leave," she said.

"Don't then," Chelsea said, kissing her wet face. "We have the whole weekend."

"I don't. I have to run some errands."

"Will you come back tonight? I'll fix dinner."

"I'd love to. I'll bring wine. Red or white?"

"I like either or both."

They washed each other's hair and bodies.

"Let's wait till I get back," Jane said. "It will be sweeter."

"Why?" She held Jane's face between her hands.

"Because waiting is a tease."

Jane was hardly out the door when the phone rang. Expecting the caller to be Martha or Barb, she was floored to hear Lizzie's voice.

"Hi Mom, you want company next weekend?"

"Are you coming here?" She must have sounded astonished.

"Abby and I thought we would. It has been nearly three months. Why are you so surprised?"

"Well, I got the impression that Abby, at least, didn't want to see me."

"Could we go to the lake?"

"It's cold and dismal there this time of year. It's as if the cottage is waiting for summer, like I am. Why don't you come here?" She was thinking she wouldn't be able to see Jane and wondered if Jane would understand.

"I'll talk to Abby and call you back."

"How are you, Lizzie? Is everything all right?" she asked.

"I'm good, Mom. And you?"

"Fine." What was her boyfriend's name? Keith, right? "How is Keith?"

"He's okay. Dad has a girlfriend." Lizzie's voice cracked.

"That's good. He has to get on with it, Lizzie," she said gently, although she was surprised.

"I know." Lizzie was crying.

"Do you like her?" She tried not to sound curious, but she was. She wanted to know her name and what she looked like and how old she was.

Lizzie sniffed. "She's okay."

"Aw, sweetie. Don't cry. It's a good thing."

"He'd never have looked, if you hadn't left." Now she was accusing.

"I know, and I'm sorry you are taking it so hard." She had been feeling so good before Lizzie called.

"Yeah. So am I. I'll call you back in a couple days. I can't talk right now."

"All right, sweetie. I love you."

Lizzie mumbled something that sounded like, "Me too," and hung up.

Guilt was strangling her. She wouldn't be spending next weekend in bed with Jane, which was more disappointing than she expected. She could hardly wait to see her again. Should she introduce the girls to her? Would they embarrass her? Probably. Anyway, if they came, it would be better not to see her. It wouldn't be fair to anyone to involve Jane in the family fray. She was ashamed that she felt torn.

She wanted to see her girls, of course she did, but she also wanted to see Jane. She hadn't realized how much she'd missed making love. Well, she didn't know if she'd been making love or just having sex.

When Jane returned, knocking on the door, Chelsea had dinner ready. The phone rang twice during dinner, but Chelsea didn't answer either call. She had made barbecued chicken and mashed potatoes and thrown together a salad. For dessert they could eat the brownies from the other night.

Jane thanked her for the delicious food and proved it by taking seconds. "Want to go to bed?" she asked after they'd cleaned up.

"Yes."

Lizzie called the next day late in the morning, when she and Jane were drinking coffee and reading the paper in bed. She picked up without thinking.

"Mom, Abby definitely wants to come next weekend. Will that be okay? We'll arrive kind of late. We're okay with just sitting around and reading. We hardly get to do that."

"I'm thrilled, honey," she said.

"Is anyone else going to be there, Mom?"

"No, sweetie."

"If we talk about Dad, we don't want to criticize him."

"I would never do that."

"I know, Mom."

"Well, we'll have lots of time to talk next weekend."

"Okay. We need directions, though. I've got a pen and paper here."

"Of course, you do." She gave directions from Highway 41 to the house before Lizzie ended the call.

"Your daughter?" Jane asked.

"Lizzie, yes. She and Abby are coming next weekend." There was a pause while she wondered how to say the next thing. "Things are so iffy between us and they're not ready to share me. I'm sorry."

"I understand. I'll miss you, though." And Jane pounced on her. "We best make the most of the time we have before then."

"I never would have guessed this of you from how you are at work." She laughed.

"Guessed what?"

"That you'd be so sexy."

"Get used to it," Jane said and kissed her.

"I already am. I love it."

CHAPTER SEVENTEEN

Her girls arrived around midnight on Friday. Abby felt stiff in her arms, and she remembered how this daughter had clung to her as a baby and toddler. The same was true of Lizzie, though. She felt reserve in her hug too, just not as much.

She asked if they had eaten, as she hungrily took them in with her eyes.

"We ate at McDonald's in Oshkosh, but if there is any dessert, I'll have a bite." This came from Lizzie, the one with a sweet tooth.

"I've got some leftover brownies that need eating before we get to the lemon cheesecake."

"Cheesecake, Mom, please," Lizzie begged.

"The cheesecake is still setting up. You'll have to settle for brownies and ice cream if you want it. Maybe I'll have a brownie. How about you, Abby? Can I talk you into a brownie or ice cream or both?"

"No thanks. Just tell me where the bed is. I want to hit the sack."

The next morning at breakfast, the girls ate the scrambled eggs and fried potatoes and toast she made for them.

"So, how is everything at home?" Chelsea ventured.

The young women lifted their heads and exchanged a glance. "Okay," Abby said. "Jeff has a job with an engineering company that works with the state—Engineering for the Future. I've been thinking about going back to law school."

"You don't like what you're doing?" her mother asked.

"No, Mom. Sometimes I feel like a glorified clerk." Abby had taken a year of law school before taking a job as a paralegal.

"What do you do?" Chelsea asked.

"Wills and probate." Abby made a face, then went back to eating.

"It sounds interesting to me," her mother said.

"Sometimes." Abby shrugged.

"I love my job," Lizzie put in. "The kids are so cute, and they love their teacher—me." She grinned, showing off the straight white teeth that Chelsea and Brad had paid an orthodontist to make perfect.

"Did you go downhill or cross-country skiing this winter?" Abby asked.

"I cross-country skied at a state park nearby with friends." She wondered if Jane skied. Perhaps the two of them could do a weekend up north. "Maybe we can plan a trip together next winter," she said cautiously.

"We already have with Jeff and Keith," Abby said. "We're going to Colorado."

"You could come with us," Lizzie said.

"We'll see," her mother replied, knowing it wouldn't happen.

"Mom, Dad broke up with that woman I was telling you about. You could come home again, you know. Hardly anyone knows you left," Lizzie said impulsively.

She smiled to take the edge off her reply. "I can't, sweetie."

"Why? You said you love Dad?" Lizzie's sky-blue eyes implored her to change her mind.

"I do love your dad, but I love him like a friend."

"You slept with that woman—June?" Abby asked, making a face.

"Did you, Mom?" Lizzie asked and covered her mouth with her hand as if to take back the words.

How could she ever explain her sexual orientation to them when they didn't share it? "Yes," she admitted and quickly changed the subject. "Don't you have any gay friends?" she asked. "What about Sam Snyder, Lizzie?"

"He's been my friend forever," Lizzie admitted. She and Sam had playdates at each other's houses when they were little.

"Have you never asked him why he's attracted to men?"

"Yes," Lizzie admitted in a small voice.

"What did he say?"

"That he's always been that way, but you were married to Dad for over twenty-five years."

"How could you leave him?" Abby asked.

She sighed. "It wasn't easy. I'd buried who I was all those years. A lot of people marry, thinking their gay feelings will go away. It's called denial."

"You never told us," Abby said.

"I know." She looked at her older daughter and saw the resentment in her flashing eyes. "I didn't tell anyone, not even Gina. I was afraid I'd lose you." Her voice quavered, and she knew she was close to tears.

"Gina knows," Abby said.

"Yeah, she talked to us."

"I know. She told me. Let's clean up the dishes and get dressed," she said, taking hold of the situation. "We have all weekend to talk."

The day was warming up, and around ten they went for a short walk. Chelsea lived near the river, which had a much-used trail. They got back just after eleven. Abby had been looking at her watch and speeding up their pace.

"I have to go somewhere. I'll be back by twelve thirty. Can you wait lunch for me?" she asked, heading for the car she and Lizzie had driven.

"What? Where are you going?" her mother asked, but Abby was already backing out of the driveway.

"I think I want another cup of coffee," Lizzie said. "Is there any left?" She slid her arm under her mom's and hurried her into the house. "Even warm isn't really warm when there is a breeze, is it?"

"It's all relative. I'm sure it's warmer in Indiana," Chelsea said, thinking the hyacinths and jonquils would already be pushing out of the ground.

"It was supposed to get into the high sixties there today," Lizzie said. She filled a cup with leftover coffee and put it in the microwave. "Do you want some, Mom?" Her mother had made two pots that morning.

"Sure. Where did Abby go in such a hurry?" Chelsea asked.

Lizzie looked at her and laughed. "Don't look so worried, Mom. She'll be home before you know it."

Though consumed with curiosity, she knew Lizzie wasn't going to tell her. She took the cribbage board and a deck of cards from a kitchen drawer and sat down with her coffee. "Want to play?"

They were still playing when Abby pulled into the driveway. When she heard more than one voice, Chelsea rose out of her chair. She thought she recognized Celie. Her sister visited the cottage in the summer, but it wasn't summer.

"Celie?" Chelsea said, astonished when her daughter and sister came through the side door. "What brings you here?"

"Hi, sis." Celie threw her arms around Chelsea and hugged her as if she wasn't going to let go.

Chelsea felt Celie's softness yield against her. She had always envied those big boobs of hers. Hadn't every girl in high school? But Celie was also shorter and had always had to fight the fat. Chelsea didn't envy her that. "You look great," she said. "What a surprise!" But she quickly realized why Celie was here. "How long can you stay?"

"Till Monday. What's for lunch?"

"Sandwiches and soup. Why was it such a secret, your coming?" Chelsea looked from one face to another. "And why have you come so far and are only staying a couple days?"

"I wanted to talk to you, Chelse. I think leaving Brad is a huge mistake—emotionally and financially."

"Can we sit down and talk about something else first? I haven't seen you for months. How are the kids?"

Celie briefly smiled. "Busy with work. Obsessed with sports. Skiing on weekends. I think they've grown up to be dummies."

Chelsea laughed. "In other words, normal." Then she gave each of them a hard stare. "You're not going to change me, if that's why you're here. Let's just have a good time."

Abby looked at the ceiling as if for help.

"Mom, you can't do this," Lizzie wailed.

Celie got up and began rummaging around the kitchen. "Coffee," she murmured. "I need coffee."

Chelsea took over and made coffee, put tomato soup on to heat, and took the bread and sandwich meat out of the fridge. "Who wants cheese with their turkey sandwich?"

When they sat down together, everyone began talking at once and ended up laughing.

"What do you want to do this afternoon?" Chelsea asked.

"Hang out," Lizzie said, and that's what they did—they read and talked, listened to music, and played cards.

After dinner, they watched a movie. Only twice did someone bring up Chelsea's reasons for leaving her marriage. She silenced them with a look. Later when she shared her bed with Celie, it became impossible not to discuss it.

Celie rested on an elbow. "I traveled a long way to talk about this, and you have to let me have my say. You won't find a better man than Brad. Any woman would be glad to snap him up."

Chelsea let out a huge sigh. "I hope some lucky woman does, but you're missing the point."

"I'm just telling you what you're throwing away."

Chelsea flashed back to the first time Gina showed up with her kids and rescued her from loneliness. "I know Brad is a great guy, but that's the problem. He's a man." She nearly choked on the words, but she needed to say them. She took a deep breath. "I tried marriage. Now I want something else." She glanced at Celie, admiring the way her breasts embraced each other. Why wasn't she built like her sister?

"Quit looking at my boobs," Celie said.

Chelsea laughed. "Just wondering why you got so much and I got so little."

"Yeah well, you're the slender one. Nothing is ever fair."

"Turn off that light. I'm exhausted. You're not going to change my mind." A few minutes passed with only a streetlight penetrating the darkness. "I wish you had come just to see me," Chelsea murmured.

"I came because I love you and want to keep you from making a terrible decision," Celie said.

"I think what pisses me off is how everyone seems to think they know what is best for me. It may be best for them, but it's not best for me."

CHAPTER EIGHTEEN

Chelsea could hardly wait to see Jane. She wanted desperately to get a nonjudgmental opinion on the weekend. Her emotions had exhausted her. She knew she hadn't convinced her daughters or her sister of her need to be with a woman. The inability to make them understand had just plain tired her out.

She realized most kids failed to see their parents as individuals with lives of their own, that they thought their parents should stay together where they had always been—at the family home, with all the childhood baggage they'd left behind. Actually, she figured she was doing them a favor—giving them free rein to follow their dreams, not what they thought their parents wanted for them. If she could go her own way, so could they. They would always have a big piece of her heart.

She hadn't slept well all weekend, disturbed by her family's disapproval. They had no way to know how incredibly difficult it had been for her to pack up and leave. And of course, they had no inkling of how disappointing and disheartening her first lesbian relationship had been. She had felt lonely and cut off, as if she'd made a huge mistake, when June took up with Karen. She'd had no idea how to meet other lesbians.

There it was again, that warning—"Careful what you wish for." If you heeded that, though, you might never take any chances. Not only had she made friends, but Jane was in her life and her bed.

These last thoughts cheered her so that by the time she got to work, early as usual, she felt upbeat. The parking lot was empty, and she worried something might have happened over the weekend. But, if so, why wouldn't Jane have called? Chelsea sat in her car, listening to NPR, until a black BMW parked next to her vehicle. Bob Van Hook smiled and nodded at her before unfolding his tall frame and getting out of the car. He unlocked the front door and gestured for her to come in.

A jaunty beret covered the bald spot on his head so that only a fringe of white, curly hair was visible. "You're early," he said as she followed him inside. "Let me know when the coffee is ready." And he disappeared into his office.

When it was ready, she carried a cup to his desk.

He didn't look up, but he did thank her, adding, "I make lousy coffee." He took a sip. "This is as good as Jane's. Where is she anyway?"

"I don't know," she said. "She's usually here before I am."

Jane arrived about the same time everyone else did. She was talking to Jason Erickson and never glanced at Chelsea as she poured a cup of coffee and disappeared into her office.

Chelsea watched her go, her mouth slightly open. She could only guess that Jane was upset about being shut out over the weekend. What else could it be? The morning passed slowly and just as slowly her sadness turned into anger.

Jane came out of her office when Chelsea was getting ready to leave. She poured another cup of coffee and watched without comment as Chelsea put on her coat and grabbed her purse. Neither spoke and Chelsea walked out the door.

Instead of going home, she went for a drive. The temperatures had risen into the fifties. She rolled her window down to smell the air and earth and to hear snatches of birdsong. She hadn't figured there would be a problem because Jane had seemed all right with Chelsea's daughters not wanting anyone else at the house. If Jane couldn't handle being left out the first time Chelsea's kids came to town, then there was no hope for the two of them. But her heart ached like it had when June had gone off with Karen.

At home a message from Martha asked if she wanted to go out for fish Friday night. She phoned Martha at work.

"What time and where?" she asked.

Martha laughed. "Adler Brau, shortly after five? That all right? We'll beat the crowd. How was the weekend with the kids?"

"I'll tell you on Friday," she said, thinking she needed to make more of an effort to keep her friends. Today had been a reminder that she shouldn't and couldn't count on one person. She'd have to give Barb a call too, and Cat.

She spent the early evening on the phone, catching up on Barb's life, laughing at her student stories. One of Barb's students, who often skipped school, had dropped to the floor and pulled herself toward the door with her elbows, military-style, as if no one could see her.

"Did you say anything to her?"

"I asked her where she was going. She said 'Damn, I wanted to see if that worked.'"

"What did you do about it?" She was laughing.

"I sent her back to her seat. The kids laughed their heads off, of course."

After, she phoned Cat and her daughter answered. "This is Chelsea. How are you, Lindsey?"

"Mom's not here."

"Would you tell her Chelsea called?"

"'Okay," Lindsey said and hung up before Chelsea could say anything else.

She hadn't made a dent in improving her relationship with Lindsey.

When the phone rang at ten, Chelsea was in bed, too tired to talk to anyone. Even so, she lay awake staring at the overhead fan, finally picking up her book and reading till she fell asleep. In the morning she checked the answering machine, but whoever had called had left no message.

The next day, she arrived at work at eight, exactly on time. The coffee was already made, but she didn't pour herself any. She'd drunk two big cups at home. It would be enough to keep her awake. She never saw Jane and assumed she was in her office.

When she left work, the day was so fine that she drove to High Cliff and sat in her car at the marina, watching a sailboarder zip across the water. He was wearing a wetsuit. The water had to be icy. Then she drove to the top of the cliff and set out on a trail high above the huge lake. A few older people were hiking the trails, some with dogs. She passed one mother pushing a stroller with two little kids in it. A soft wind lifted her hair, and she was filled with pleasure by her surroundings.

On Friday, she was waiting outside Adler Brau at five, missing her mother. She often missed her mother, who had died two years ago in the spring of the year. She wanted someone to tell her why she had waited to come out till after her mother died. She wanted to believe that if her mother were alive today, she'd understand why she'd left Brad. She'd been a tolerant, loving woman, but Chelsea also knew her mother had loved Brad. She'd had no one to talk to about this, except her deceased mother, whom she talked to often when no one was around. She was sure it would sound crazy to anyone else.

Startled when Martha came up behind her and said something, she spun toward her, hand on her chest.

"You're jumpy tonight," Martha said with a smile. "Who did you think I was?"

"I was deep in thought."

"Care to share?" Martha asked as they headed toward the door.

She wasn't sure Martha knew she was a lesbian and short of asking she could think of no other way to find out.

They walked down the stairs to the basement restaurant and took the same booth they'd had before.

"So, any news?" Martha asked as they studied the menu, even though they were both going to order the fish fry.

"I talked to Barb last night. She told me a funny story about one of her students, but I'm no good at telling stories. Not like she is, anyway. I tried to talk to Cat, but I got Lindsey and she cut me off pretty quick. And you?"

"I had a date with Guy last weekend. Guy Martin?"

"And?" Chelsea asked.

"It's a piss-poor dating market for women my age. Guy is a jerk. He kept eyeing all the younger women and asked me to repeat myself about a hundred times, because his attention was wandering along with his eyes." She shrugged. "I'm not interested in someone who's not interested in what I have to say."

Chelsea sympathized. It seemed there weren't many available lesbians around her age either. "How many guys are out there?"

"Not many," Martha said, "and they're either divorced or gay. You're lucky to have found Jane. Wait a minute. Why aren't you with her?"

Stunned, Chelsea was torn between denying her sexual orientation and asking how Martha knew.

Martha smiled and put a hand over Chelsea's. "Come on, woman, you may fool others, but I've had a lot of gay friends. It's okay. I don't care one way or the other. Now tell me, where is Jane?"

"I don't have a clue. She gave me the cold shoulder all week. Last weekend the kids wanted me to themselves. Actually, my sister showed up too—all three trying to change my mind. The thing is Jane seemed to be all right about not being included. She said as much and then she ignored me the entire workweek."

"Ouch," Martha said as if punched. "She didn't strike me as the jealous kind, but you never know."

Chelsea took a swig of her vodka and tonic.

"Here I was envying you. It seemed so easy."

"Nothing is easy. First, I have to defend my choices from my kids and sister, and then Jane blames me for not having her over. At least, I think that's why she's ignoring me. I feel like going into hiding."

"Give them time to get used to it. Your daughters and your sister will forgive you. I don't know what to think about Jane. Your husband's not giving you any guff, is he?"

"No. He dated a woman recently, and guess what? I was relieved and a little jealous."

"That's probably pretty normal."

Their food arrived, and they began to eat.

"It's good to be able to talk to someone." She had thought she could do that with Jane. She didn't like how she felt now. She had been blindsided by Jane's behavior and didn't understand why it wasn't easier for her to shrug it off. After all, they hardly knew each other. She flashed back to their night in bed and shivered at the memory, wondering if Jane's apparent pleasure had been faked. Hers had been real—thrilling, in fact.

"So, have you any advice for me?" Martha asked. "I should have toughed it out with my ex. We married young, just out of high school. We both went to college, working our way through, which was hard. I finished. He dropped out. When I made more money than he did, he moved out. That was bizarre, because men almost always make more than women."

"I have no more idea how to meet guys than I know how to meet women. We could go to some bars together."

"Gay or straight bars?" Martha's eyebrows peaked.

"Are there gay bars here?"

"Well, there is one," Martha said with a determined nod. "Let's do it."

"Okay," she said nervously. "When?"

"Tonight."

"Can we start with a straight bar?" she asked.

Martha grinned. "Scared?"

"I don't know whether I'm more afraid of being found out or finding someone. I don't really want a one-night stand."

"Aw, come on," Martha said teasingly.

CHAPTER NINETEEN

They started with Bad Badger Sports Bar, driving there in Martha's car. Although the days were warming, the nights were still cold. Chelsea hunched into her collar as they walked from a nearby parking lot to the bar across the street. The space between the outside and inside doors reeked of cigarette smoke. She held her breath.

Inside, all the men were sitting at the bar, drinking and smoking and watching basketball on the TVs. Chelsea followed Martha to one of the booths.

A waiter came over and put a bowl of popcorn on their table.

"Oh, you lovely man. Thank you," Martha said in a sultry voice.

Chelsea shot her a surprised look.

The waiter gave a little bow. "Compliments of the house. My name is Seth. Can I get you ladies anything else?" He was kind of cute, slender with dark brown eyes and curly brown hair with blond tips.

"A glass of red wine, please," Chelsea said.

"A Blatz for me." Martha smiled coyly.

Chelsea put a finger down her throat when Seth turned away. "No one is *that* cute."

"Come on," Martha hissed. "I'm on the prowl."

The volume on the TVs was so loud they had to lean forward and read each other's lips.

Seth returned with the drinks and sat down next to Martha. "So, what are your names?"

Chelsea took a sip. The wine tasted bitter. "I'm Chelsea and this is Martha."

"Do you like basketball?"

Chelsea choked back a laugh, which turned into a snort, and pretended to be chastened when Martha threw her a dirty look.

"Do you?" Martha asked Seth.

"Oh, yeah. I love all sports. That's why I like working here."

"Well, we stopped in to see how the game was going," Martha said.

Chelsea excused herself and went in search of the john. When she returned, Seth was back behind the bar.

"Sorry," she said. "I didn't know you were a basketball fan." She glanced at the TV and saw the Milwaukee Bucks were playing Detroit.

Martha lifted a shoulder. "You're supposed to be helping me. Remember?"

Chelsea nodded slowly. "Sorry. Do you like him?"

At the end of the evening, Seth asked Martha if he could take her out to dinner Monday night. It was his night off.

The two women hurried through the cold night to the car. Thin clouds covered the night sky. "You'd never guess tomorrow will be April," Chelsea commented.

"Hey, thanks for going with me," Martha said as she started the engine. Cold air rushed out of the vents. She turned the fan off. "It will warm up in a minute or so."

"Seth only has one night a week off? Right?" Martha nodded. "You won't see much of him, unless you hang around the bar."

"Maybe one date will be all I want with him."

"Then we'll have to do this all over again," Chelsea teased.

"Next Friday we go to the gay bar. Remember?"

A chill raced through Chelsea. "I'll drive," she said when Martha took her back to her car. "But we should eat at the bar. It will give us something to do besides drink. We can hang around longer. I'm sorry I behaved like an ass," Chelsea added. "I don't know why."

"Maybe because I was behaving like one too." Martha's eyebrows peaked in question.

"I didn't recognize that coy person." Chelsea shot her a wry smile. "Why do women turn into someone else when a man is around?"

"We don't always. Let's see how you behave around the cute ladies." Martha laughed.

"Ah. That's the difference between women and women and women and men."

"We'll see," Martha said.

They decided to wait till eight to go to The Pivot, the gay bar. Even so, that was really early. Bar life started after nine, Martha pointed out, and Chelsea remembered her girls leaving for the bars near their cottage about the time she and Brad and her parents were heading for bed.

"Well?" Chelsea asked when she picked Martha up Friday evening.

"Well, what?"

"You said you'd tell me all about your date with Seth when you saw me."

"Oh. Well, it was kind of disappointing. No. It was really awful. He took me to another sports bar. I didn't realize the college finals in men's basketball were going on. He couldn't keep his eyes off the TVs, which were so loud we couldn't hear each other—that is, if he'd wanted to talk, which he didn't. He shushed me every time I said something.

"And then he had the nerve to ask me if he could come in when he took me home. I said no, of course."

"Good for you." She resisted the urge to remind Martha that Seth worked in a sports bar because he loved sports.

When Chelsea turned into the parking lot at The Pivot, only a red Dodge pickup was there. "No one's here. What's the point of going inside?"

"What do you suggest we do? Shop?"

"What a great idea," Chelsea said. "We can go to the mall, have a cup of coffee, and then do some window-shopping."

"I was joking," Martha said.

"No, it's a good idea." Chelsea turned around and drove to the mall.

At eight fifty-five they parked outside the gay bar. The lot was nearly full. Chelsea didn't know what to expect. She kept telling herself it was just another bar.

No dream woman was at the bar, only guys. Chelsea studied the men. Some she would have tagged as gay, but others looked like her neighbors' husbands.

Martha pulled at the sleeve of Chelsea's denim jacket. "Let's get a booth and eat."

The booths were crowded with women, talking and laughing loudly. Chelsea tried to look casual while taking in the scene. She stuffed her hands into the pockets of her jacket and looked about for someplace to sit down. At the end of the bar were two empty stools.

Martha pushed Chelsea toward them, and they found themselves sitting next to a middle-aged man. When the bartender got to them, they ordered fish and fries and coleslaw.

"There is just enough for two plates. You're new, aren't you?"

"We came earlier, but no one else was here."

"Hey, welcome. The food has been sitting for a couple hours. Hope you don't mind."

"We don't care," Martha said. "We're really hungry."

"I'm Jimmy," the bartender said and gave them a big, white-toothed grin. "Are you thirsty too?"

"We are. I'm Chelsea," she said, "and this is Martha, and I'd like a vodka and tonic."

Martha ordered draft beer.

By the time Jimmy brought the food, they were each on their second drink, and Chelsea was feeling good. She asked Martha if she was going out with Seth again.

"You're kidding, right? What a bore." She jerked her head. "Isn't that Cat?" Dressed in skintight jeans and heels, Cat tottered toward them.

"Hello, girls." Cat put a thin arm around each of their shoulders. She smelled of beer and cigarettes, and once again Chelsea was reminded of their failed attempt at lovemaking. "Come meet my friends."

"After we eat, Cat," Martha said. "Okay?"

Cat began dancing to the music as she walked toward a booth. She pulled a woman out of her seat and swung her so hard, she went flying into a man at a table.

He was more boy than man. "Hey," he said, catching her. "I didn't know you women were so strong."

Cat showed off her skinny bicep muscles. Jimmy came out from behind the bar and spoke softly in her ear. He steered her back to the booth, and a woman's arms reached for her. The woman she'd thrown into the man joined them.

Martha and Chelsea ate while Cat made her little scene. They pushed their plates away when done.

"I'll take those," Jimmy said. "Want a refill?" He nodded at their glasses.

"Have you got any root beer?" Martha asked.

"Sure do." When he blinked, his lashes were the same color as the thick dark hair on his head. He had stunning blue eyes and a mischievous smile.

"I'll have a glass too," Chelsea chimed.

"Do you think he's gay?" Martha asked wistfully when he went off to fill their order.

"Probably. Why else would he work here?" She leaned in. "You like those bartenders, don't you?"

"He's gorgeous. Look at him. Wonderful smile, eyes to die for, and hair I'd love to run my fingers through."

Chelsea did look. "Want me to ask him?"

Martha's head snapped toward her. "Don't you dare! Anyway, we're here for you. How about Cat?" She grinned.

"Tried it. No mutual attraction." She blushed.

Martha looked interested. "At the party? What a shame!"

Chelsea kept quiet.

"Well, the least we can do is let her introduce us to her friends."

"Save our places?" Chelsea asked the man sitting next to her.

"You kidding? First come, first served." He guffawed. He'd seemed so dour until then.

"Honey, I'll save your places. Your root beer is here," Jimmy said with a beautiful grin.

"I think I'll stay here," Martha said, gazing at him.

"Oh no. You're coming with me." Chelsea dragged her off the stool and over to the booth, where Cat was sitting on the lap of a woman—the one she'd flung into the guy.

CHAPTER TWENTY

Cat grabbed Chelsea's arm and held on tightly. "This is my good friend, Chelsea. We're not compatible, but she'd be a real good catch."

Chelsea tried to pull away, but Cat's grip was surprisingly strong.

"Get your drinks and join us," said a woman sitting across the table from Cat.

"Where?" Chelsea asked. The booth was packed, three on a side.

"We'll pull up a couple chairs."

Martha grabbed their root beers and returned, her gaze lingering on Jimmy. She tripped over someone's feet and nearly went flying. Cat let go of Chelsea and caught the glasses.

"He's gay, honey," Cat said.

"But he's so beautiful," Martha protested.

"The young ones always are," another woman said with a sage nod. "I'm Sarah with an h, by the way."

"Oh well, we didn't come here looking for men." Martha smiled at Chelsea, who looked away.

"Sarah is single right now." A woman with a beautiful smile winked at Sarah.

Chelsea blushed and snuck another look at Sarah, at what she could see of her slender figure, her crinkled white hair, and sparkling brown eyes behind wire-rimmed glasses. Chelsea thought she could do worse.

"I'm just looking for friends is all," she said.

"I'm Jeanine and this is my lover, Nan." A heavyset woman reached out to shake her hand as did Nan, who was also "big."

"And I am Sue," said the woman who was holding Cat, "and this is my other half, Pat." Pat was sitting at the end of the booth, across from Sue and Cat. She gave Chelsea and Martha a little wave.

"Is this the woman who rescued your daughter, Cat?" Sarah asked.

There had been an article in the local paper. Chelsea smiled wryly. "Lindsey would say she hadn't needed rescuing."

"She is so ungrateful," Cat said.

Martha and Chelsea sat down in the chairs Jimmy brought over, and Cat told Sue to "Shove over" and slid in next to her.

Jimmy stood with hands on hips between Martha and Chelsea. "Can I get you ladies anything?"

"Not yet," they chorused.

Sarah leaned forward. "Chelsea, is it?"

At least that's what Chelsea heard over the loud music and talking. She smiled and nodded.

"How long have you been here?" Sarah shouted.

Chelsea laughed. "Not even a year and it seems like a lifetime."

"Where did you live and why did you choose to move here?" Sarah asked. She'd exchanged places with Cat and now was face-to-face with Chelsea. Her eyes danced with curiosity.

"I lived in Indiana, but I grew up here."

"You married someone and moved where he lived. Women are always doing that. I did. Only I stayed here, and he left."

Chelsea nodded, but she couldn't help thinking about all she'd left behind. Her kids, Gina, even Brad and the animals.

"Nasty divorces can tear a person up."

"We're not divorced yet, but it won't be nasty," she said, looking into the inquisitive brown eyes.

"That's even harder. We won't talk about it. What would you like to talk about?"

Chelsea felt the tears crowding. She was suddenly terribly sad.

"I'll talk," Sarah said. "My husband was abusive. I left him the first time he hit our son, instead of me, as he was fond of doing. He found us and told us he would kill us both if we left again. And then what did he do but run off with a younger woman. I feel very, very sorry for her." She paused as if waiting for a comment, but Chelsea was shocked into silence.

"He was a charmer," Sarah continued. "I was young and stupid and thought this handsome man loved me too much to share me with anyone. He tried to keep me away from family and friends. That should have been a warning, but I mistook controlling and possessiveness for love." She smiled sadly.

Chelsea thought of Brad and how he how loved his daughters. And her. "I'm sorry," she said. "You have a son then. I have two girls. Lizzie is twenty-two and Abby twenty-five. How old is your son?"

"Scott is twenty-nine. He recently married a lovely girl— Denise. I'll be a grandma soon, I suppose." She looked Chelsea in the eyes. "I tell my story to everyone. I don't want it to happen to anyone else, but the thing is, people, especially women, don't believe it will happen to them—even when the warning signs are all there, even while it's happening."

"It wasn't that way with my husband, Sarah. Brad is a good guy." She was unwilling to let Sarah think Brad was controlling or abusive. If anything, he was inattentive. "I did him an injustice, and my girls aren't ready to forgive me."

Sarah leaned toward Chelsea. "And your injustice was being a lesbian?"

"No. I lied to him and to the girls and to my sister, who also is angry with me. I was too much of a coward to be honest."

Sarah smiled. "A small error in the scheme of things. Think how we've all been brainwashed into believing homosexuality is a perversion."

Chelsea grimaced. She still believed something was wrong with her. After all, there were so many more who were straight. "Thanks for trying to cure me of my guilt. I even lusted after Brad's best friend's wife." She wondered what Gina was doing in her free time. Had she found another best friend?

"Lusting isn't a crime. Don't we all do it at some time?"

"Hey, Sarah, get off the soapbox," Nan said, thumping her glass on the table. A redhead, fair-skinned and freckled, she had been quiet until then. "This is supposed to be a fun night."

"All right, all right," Sarah said agreeably. She patted Chelsea's hand and turned back to the group.

Chelsea took a deep breath and turned when Martha poked her.

"Anytime you are," Martha mouthed, causing Chelsea to surreptitiously glance at her watch.

She could hardly believe it was after ten thirty. "Okay," she said and stood up. "We have to go. Martha's dog is crossing his legs." Why had she said that? Martha didn't have a dog.

"You can't go until you give us your phone numbers," Sarah said.

"Cat has them," Chelsea replied, but she wrote hers down on a napkin anyway, and Sarah did the same.

"You too, Martha," Sarah insisted.

All but Cat obligingly exchanged information. "Promise to come next Friday," Sarah said.

"We have to go somewhere else that night," Chelsea said, feeling a little overwhelmed by all this insistence to stay in touch.

"Come to the lesbian potluck next Saturday at five at our house." Tall and athletic, Sue wrapped her long fingers around her ponytail and studied Chelsea and Martha.

"Are you together?" she asked.

"We're good friends," Martha said.

"That's a beginning," Sarah insisted.

Cat cleared up the confusion. "Martha is straight."

"We alternate Friday nights between straight and gay bars," Martha explained with a crooked smile.

"Come to the potluck," Pat, Sue's partner, insisted. "It's fun." She handed Chelsea the address Sue had scribbled on a napkin.

After a moment's pause to see if anyone had anything to say about the straight and gay bars, they left. "They must think we're ridiculous," Chelsea said as she started the engine.

"Perhaps," Martha said. "I thought they were amused, though. Do you want to go there next week alone, and I'll go to Seth's bar?"

"I thought you didn't like him?"

"He can be a friend, who will introduce me to others."

"You know, I've been thinking. Maybe bars aren't the best place to meet someone."

"Yeah, you're probably right. Whose stupid idea was that anyway?" She laughed until Chelsea joined in.

"Don't," Chelsea said, snorting and struggling to breathe as she curled around the wheel in a fit of mirth. "I can't laugh and drive."

By the time she parked in front of Martha's place, she had sobered. "Can you find me another job? I can't work with Jane popping up all the time. We got a little too cozy. You know?"

"You mean…?"

"Yeah. I mean."

"Okay. Give notice. I know someone who'd make a good replacement for you. And there is another job available, but it's about as different from reading for a publishing company as anything could be."

"Doing what?" she asked, curious. The streetlight shone on their faces, which looked younger and more earnest in the dim illumination.

"I'll tell you Monday if the position is still open."

Chelsea wrote her resignation Sunday and handed it to Jane Monday morning. She watched Jane's face for clues, but when Jane caught her gaze, she turned quickly away.

"Are you sure?" Jane asked.

"It's…awkward." She stumbled over the words.

"Yes…yes, it is. I'm…sorry."

"What happened?" she blurted.

Jane looked around. "Not here. Will you hold off on this till we talk?"

"When will that be?" she asked, sitting down to answer the phone. After forwarding the call, she threw Jane a questioning look.

"Do you want to meet somewhere after work?" Jane asked.

"Like a bar, you mean?"

"Someplace where we can get a bite to eat, like Chi Chi's. Say five thirty?"

Only because she was curious did she agree. "Okay."

Jane disappeared into her office.

Chelsea left home at ten minutes after five that evening. She didn't want to appear eager and arrive early. The sky was gray with just a hint of sun. *April should be warmer than this*, she thought as she backed her car out of the garage.

Chi Chi's was at the mall. She was drinking a margarita when Jane arrived.

"I'll have one of those too," Jane told the hostess, nodding at Chelsea's drink. "It was one of those days."

When Jane's drink arrived, she took a sip and said, "Look. I'm sorry. My ex showed up the weekend your kids came…" She took another swallow. "She was waiting for me after work. It's her house too, and she wants to start over."

Chelsea felt a flame of fury. "Why didn't you just tell me, instead of letting me think I'd done something to sabotage things?" She stood up and grabbed her jacket. "I'm not hungry."

Jane did not follow her.

CHAPTER TWENTY-ONE

Barb picked up Chelsea in her Oldsmobile Cutlass. The windows were open a crack and she heard Cris Williamson and Tret Fure's voices intertwined in a duet. She heard this tape when she'd been at Barb's flat.

Barb turned the music down. "Where are we going?"

Chelsea looked at the napkin and gave Barb the directions she had found on a map in the phone book. "Turn right here, then left at the stop sign…" They parked behind a line of cars a block away.

Chelsea had ended up baking cookies, because she'd had so little time. Her new job, as a shuttle driver for a Ford dealership, was keeping her busier than she'd thought it would. She thought she'd keep it till Martha found her another.

"Who are these women?"

She looked at Barb and tripped over a place where the sidewalk had heaved during the spring thaw. It took several running steps for her to regain her balance, during which the cookies flew off the plate.

While trying to keep Chelsea from falling, Barb lost control of the cream bars she had made, and they too hit the ground.

They went down on their knees to gather the dessert scattered on the sidewalk before someone came along. Glancing around furtively, they caught each other's eyes and began to laugh. The few giggles quickly turned into guffaws. Miraculously, no one saw them, and they rearranged the dessert plates and knocked on the door.

Chelsea introduced Barb to Sue, who set the dessert plates on the kitchen counter with others. Before she followed Sue, Chelsea picked a tiny piece of grass off her plate of cookies.

Barb leaned forward and whispered in her ear. "Shouldn't we confess?"

Chelsea shook her head and they entered a room full of women—seven sitting on chairs, five on a couch, and more on the floor. Chelsea felt a painful jolt when she spied Jane, tucked in a corner with her arm around another woman. She looked away and spotted June in a chair and Karen on an ottoman, leaning back between June's legs.

Sue was introducing them, but when she caught sight of Chelsea's expression, she pointed at a table in the next room. "There are name tags over there. Fill one out and put it on. Then we'll remember who you are." She patted Barb on the back and gave Chelsea a little push in the right direction.

"You look like someone slapped you in the face," Barb whispered as women headed toward the table where the food was crowded.

"Dessert is in the kitchen," Sue hollered over the many conversations.

Barb raised her eyebrows at Chelsea. "Can't wait to taste those cookies," Barb said.

Chelsea was so distracted by Jane's and June's presence that it took a few seconds for her to catch on. She laughed. "Me too. Listen, would you mind terribly if we got out of here after eating?"

"Because of June? You're going to let her get to you?" Barb asked.

"Not just June. Jane's here too. I'm not having much luck with my love life. Maybe I wasn't meant to be a lesbian." She was whispering.

"What fools they are."

Chelsea smiled at Barb's rosy, smiling face and felt bad about leaving early. She took her plate, followed Barb into the packed living room, and sat on the piano stool with her.

Neither Jane nor June would meet her eyes. Their gazes slithered away from hers, but their partners' eyes followed her every move. She felt pinned to the wall. "Let's go see if there's any place to sit in the other room."

Always easygoing, Barb got up and left with her. They sat on the dining room chairs against the wall and finished eating.

Sue sat nearby. "Where's Martha tonight?"

"Out with a guy." She hoped that some sport on TV hadn't come between Seth and her again.

"How often do you have these potlucks?" Barb asked.

"Once a month. Next time it's at Sarah's." She wrote down the address on the back of two envelopes and handed them to Chelsea and Barb.

Chelsea took note of Sarah's last name—Thompson. "Isn't Memorial Day weekend a month from now? I'll be at the cottage. Sarah's not here tonight, is she?"

"No. She became a grandma. She flew out to Oregon to help her daughter-in-law and the new baby."

"Martha and I met Sarah, Sue, Pat, Jeanine, and Nan at The Pivot last Saturday," Chelsea told Barb. "Next time maybe you and I should go."

"Was that the straight bar/gay bar thing?" Barb asked, her eyebrows going up and down.

"We decided it was stupid." She looked at Barb's lively blue eyes. Why hadn't she asked her? Probably because Barb lived thirty miles away.

Barb guffawed. "I'd go with you."

"You'd have to come all the way here to go there, but you could stay overnight at my place."

"That's okay. It takes me less than an hour to get to home from here."

When they said their thanks and stepped out into the night, a voice called Chelsea by name. Chelsea nearly dropped the empty plate. "What?"

"Can we be friends?" June asked, stepping into the light with Karen at her side.

Chelsea's heartbeat dropped to near normal. "Don't sneak up on us."

"Hi, Barb. Are you the new girlfriend?" June asked.

"I am a girl first and a friend second, so I guess I could be considered a girlfriend, but wait. I'm a woman. Woman friend is more appropriate." Barb stepped toward Karen. "I'm Barb Dunhill and you are Karen?"

Karen lost the struggle not to laugh. "Karen Manford," she brayed, spittle spraying.

Barb jumped back and looked at her clothes.

"I'm sorry," Karen said. She put a hand out as if to touch Barb's shirt.

"Please," Barb warned.

"Do you coach girls' volleyball? You do, don't you? I've seen you at the meeting in the fall and at some of the tournaments. I work for the State Athletic Association."

"You want my job? You can have it," Barb said, raising her hands in surrender.

Karen barked a laugh. "I don't coach anymore."

"I'd take my funny friend and go home, except she's driving," Chelsea said, smiling at Barb.

"You haven't answered my question," June said.

She remembered the chaos that had defined their time together. How nasty June could be when she no longer wanted Chelsea. "No, we can't be friends, I'm afraid. Too much has happened."

Others were coming out of Sue and Pat's front door, streaming toward their cars while talking to each other. Chelsea didn't want to meet up with Jane. She already felt fragile and defensive. "Let's go," she said to Barb.

"You don't want to be friends anymore either, Barb?" June asked.

Barb walked faster, joining the flow of women, heading toward their vehicles—as if she hadn't heard.

The ride home was quiet. It was Chelsea who broke the silence. "Maybe I could have handled one of them, but not both. Sorry, Barb, I didn't make it easy for you to meet anyone."

Barb smiled at her. "I heard what June asked me, and I was too much of a coward to say no, we couldn't be friends."

"Well, I wouldn't worry about that. She doesn't make a very good friend."

"I made a choice."

"Thanks, but I won't dump you, if you want to be her friend too."

"But she would."

CHAPTER TWENTY-TWO

Chelsea's new job felt more like a vacation than work. She had always liked to drive. She worked thirty hours a week. She knew this was so the company wouldn't have to pay health insurance, just like Graphics Inc. That was something she'd have to get serious about. She was still on Brad's insurance, but that would last only until they divorced.

She quickly learned the streets in the city and the neighboring towns. She was at work at seven a.m. and left at one when someone came in to take her place. Sometimes the people she picked up or took home talked, sometimes they were silent. At times there was only one person in the shuttle, but more often there were two or more to drop off or pick up.

It was June 30 and she was thinking about what to take to the cottage Friday afternoon. The day was hot, and she hoped it stayed that way over the weekend and through the next week, which she had taken off. It was shortly after seven and she was looking for an address two blocks over from her own. The customer's name was Daphne Grayling. The address belonged to a small house on a sharp curve above a woody ravine. She pulled into the driveway, got out, rang the doorbell, and went back to the car—a new Taurus.

The door opened and a woman about her age, lean and athletic-looking with short dishwater-blond hair, emerged. She locked the door and got into the backseat of the Taurus.

"I see they have women drivers now. It's about time," she said after closing the car door.

Chelsea looked at her in the rearview mirror. "I'm the only one so far." She backed out of the driveway and headed for the bridge.

"I suppose you consider yourself lucky," the woman said.

They were always supposed to get along with the people they ferried about. "I like it."

"Because you're the only woman?"

She looked again and saw a slight smile on her passenger's face. "No, Ms. Grayling, because I like to drive and meet people. It's easy."

"I'm not Ms. Grayling. Call me Grayling or Daff."

"Ooo-kay," Chelsea said. She laughed at the nickname, Daff, thinking it must be a joke.

"What's so funny?" the woman asked.

"You're a feminist. I am too." She smiled into the mirror, but Daff looked annoyed.

"I suppose I am. I'm for equality anyway."

"Aren't we all?" Chelsea asked.

"Unfortunately, we are not. That is the problem. And they call me Daff, because that's what I call myself. It's spelled D A P H. Thanks for the ride." She got out and strode toward the building before Chelsea had even killed the motor.

Chelsea was fascinated. Daph lived right around the corner, and she had never seen her out walking or driving or working in her yard.

Chelsea went to the service department, but Daph wasn't there. She supposed she was in the oil change department. She took the sheet with names of customers awaiting rides and continued on to the waiting room. There were only two, their eyes locked on to the TV.

She was backing the shuttle out of the parking space when a Mustang convertible shot past her and braked briefly at the access road. Daph was behind the wheel. Chelsea was stricken with envy and annoyed at the painful adrenaline surging through her after the near miss.

"That lady nearly ran into you," yelped the woman sitting in the passenger seat.

"Women are the most reckless drivers," the man in the back stated.

She jerked forward before slamming on the brakes at the access road, twice throwing her passengers off balance.

"Hey," the man in the backseat protested, while the woman in front grasped the door handle.

That evening she took a walk on the street where Daph lived. The Mustang was in the driveway, jazzy music sounded from an open window, but Daph was nowhere to be seen.

She wished she had the nerve to knock on the woman's door. She wanted to know her well enough to do just that—ring her doorbell or call her on the phone. She had copied her address and phone number in a notepad she carried around to keep track of gas mileage.

She continued around the block and returned home, trying to work up the nerve to call Daph. What would she say to her anyway? "You fascinate me? I want to know you better?" She'd never have the nerve to say either of those things, although they were the truth.

The next morning, she went to the grocery store to shop for the coming weekend. As she was gently squeezing the avocados, she felt eyes on her and looked up to see Daph on the other side of the bin.

A smile crept across her face. "Hey. How's your car?"

"It was just an oil change, but there was a strange noise, so I left it overnight." Daph shrugged strong shoulders. Swimmer's shoulders? She was wearing a shirt with spaghetti straps.

"Did they find out what the noise was?"

"A loose belt." Daph studied the avocados.

"Nice car, though. I always wanted a sports car. Does it handle well?"

Daph didn't look at her or smile. "Well enough."

Chelsea tossed four avocados in a bag. "Want to go for a walk tonight?"

Laughter rippled nearby. "Sure," said a male voice, but Chelsea ignored the guy.

"Okay," Daph said. "A short one starting at seven at my place."

"Why don't you ask her out for dinner?" the same male voice asked.

She turned toward the man. "Mind your own business," she said, and polite applause came from the woman at his side. She smiled to herself and resumed her shopping.

Just before seven, while the sun was still high in the sky, she walked to Daphne's house. The air smelled of cut grass. When she knocked on the door, she heard footsteps, a lock clicked, and the door swung toward her. A woman stood in the opening—a petite redhead with freckles and a great figure.

"Hi," she said, shaking Chelsea's hand. "I'm Sally, Daph's roommate. Care to come in?"

"Sure," she stammered. It took a minute for her eyes to adjust to the darker interior. She was standing in a small living room with a large window looking out at the woody ravine. On the adjoining wall was a fireplace, and she thought how nice winter evenings would be here, reading in front of a fire. Of course, she had a fireplace too, but no one to read with her. She hadn't thought the house was big enough for more than one person.

"Want to sit down?" Sally asked. "Can I get you a cup of decaf?"

"No thanks." Coffee would make her pee, and she and Daph were going for a walk. Were they? Where was Daph?

"I hear you're a driver for the Ford dealership?"

"I just started, and I love it. What do you do?" Her eyes roamed the place for a sign of Daph. There weren't too many places to hide.

"Liking what you spend hours doing is so important. I'm a graphic artist." Sally's face lit up with a smile.

"It's not my life's passion, and I only work there thirty hours a week. I worked at Graphics Inc. until the end of March."

Sally nearly jumped up and down. "I started there this week. It's so exciting and the people are so nice."

"I'm glad you like it," she said, feeling a touch of jealousy, wondering if maybe Jane would befriend Sally, and pushed it away. Where the hell was Daphne? Then she heard a door open in another room and Daph was standing in the doorway, dressed in dirty jeans and a sweatshirt.

"I've been cutting down buckthorn trees. Is it already seven?"

Chelsea jumped to her feet. "I don't want to stop you. Buckthorns are invasive. I'll just go ahead."

"I'll go with you," Sally said, also getting to her feet.

"Sorry," Daphne said, not seeming sorry at all.

"Let me grab a sweatshirt," Sally said, and soon she and Chelsea were walking toward the path that led along the river.

It had cooled off, and Sally was talking. "I think summer is really here, and then it's not. What did you do at Graphics Inc.?"

"I was the receptionist, half days. A pretty boring job, but I only wanted part-time." She was out of sorts. She stuffed her hands in her sweatshirt pockets and looked at the sidewalk.

"What do you do when you're not working?" Sally asked.

"Read manuscripts." She had one waiting at home.

"How exciting!" Sally exclaimed. "Are you an author too?"

"No. Just a reader." She glanced at Sally and smiled. The kid was so easily thrilled. She did look a lot younger than Daphne or herself.

"I wish I could write, but I run out of words after about three sentences."

"It's not so easy." She knew, because she had tried. It was the muddling in the middle that was so difficult. She glanced at Sally again. Her cheeks were red and she bounced off her toes when she walked. Chelsea had questions, like what was her relationship with Daphne and how did she happen to be living with her, but she didn't know how to start.

They reached the end of the trail as the sky clouded over. A brisk wind picked up. They walked fast toward home. "Looks like rain," Chelsea said.

"It's supposed to rain," Sally said.

"Oh, I didn't know that. I forgot to watch the weather."

"It's always good to get a walk in every day, don't you think? I sit most of the day."

"So do I." Behind the wheel of a Taurus or with a manuscript. She hoped next week at the lake would be warmer.

By the time they got back to Sally and Daphne's house, rain was spitting. Chelsea hurried home, glad to be there. She went to bed before dark and read as thunder rumbled and roared and lightning lit up the sky.

An image of Daph in her dirty jeans and sweatshirt kept interfering with her concentration. She wondered how she could capture Daph's interest as Daph had caught hers. She laughed then, wondering why she should bother.

CHAPTER TWENTY-THREE

She turned onto the winding, sand driveway and parked behind the cottage. Whenever she arrived, she thanked her grandparents and her parents—her grandparents for building the place and her parents for buying her uncle's share. They had taken over a place further down the lake.

She carried in the groceries and her luggage, put away the food, and opened windows—allowing the smell of pines to replace the musty odor inside. She made a pot of coffee and took a cup outside to drink while overlooking the lake.

Boats were already whizzing past, pulling water skiers in their wakes. Jet Skis turned circles on the choppy water. She remembered when the lake was free of these annoyances. She liked to think of herself as a silent sports person, paddling the kayak when no-wake hours took effect or sailing or swimming. Her uncle and his family had a speedboat and water-skied. Her girls often joined their cousins and would wave when they passed her as she read on the shore or pier.

She heard the car and rounded the house to meet her girls. She had thought they were bringing their boyfriends, but only

Abby and Liz got out of the car and stretched. Then she was nearly knocked over by the joyous dog. She dropped to her knees and embraced Dash, turning her face away from his tongue.

"I forgot about the dog," she said.

"He always comes with us," Lizzie said, giving Chelsea a hug and kiss.

Seeming to forget their differences, Abby did the same. "God, it's great to be here," she said. "It's the only place where I leave everything behind."

Maybe the healing would begin here, Chelsea hoped. "I thought the guys were coming with you," she said, realizing how much she wanted this time alone with her kids.

"Nope." Abby said with a glance at her sister. "Liz told them not to come."

"Well, good." The words slipped out of her mouth, a surprise.

Abby took immediate umbrage. "You told Liz to tell them that, didn't you?"

"No, I never thought of it, but it's nice to have some time with you two. Your aunt's coming, though."

The girls looked interested. "Are Will and Tom coming too?"

"I don't think so. They both work with your uncle, and he's too busy to take a vacation. Farming is a full-time job." She looked around for the dog, realizing his warm, furry head was no longer against her leg. "Where's Dash?"

"He's probably gone for a swim," Abby said and called the dog's name.

Dash came running around the side of the cottage.

"I guess we better get our suits on. Can I carry something?" Chelsea asked. She couldn't stop smiling. "It's so good to be here with you two. How is your father?"

She grabbed a bag and carried it to the house, holding the door open for the others. It was a reasonable question, and she wanted to know.

"He's dating again." This was from Abby.

She felt a stab of jealousy. "Have you met her?"

"Yeah," Liz said. "She's nice enough and pretty."

"Dad can't do enough for her. He mows her lawn, fixes things around her house. He even put in flower beds for her."

"That's how he met her, Abby. That doesn't count."

Chelsea thought about how she had done all the mowing and planting, how things around the house had gone unfixed because Brad was too busy. "Isn't he landscaping anymore?"

"Not really. He runs the welding shop now that Grandpa died. He wouldn't have time to see her if he was working seven days a week."

Like he did when we were married, she thought. They had needed the money then. He probably had plenty of money now. Still, it was annoying. She had lived through the poor years, raising the kids and making do. *Wait a minute*, she thought. She didn't want to depend on some man to take care of her. For some reason, she thought of Daph. She guessed no one took care of her, nor would she let anyone.

"Dash wants to swim," Chelsea said, eyeing the animal standing by the door. "We're holding him up."

They put on their suits, grabbed towels and books, and went down to the lake. Talking, her daughters ran down the steps in front of her. They had each other, Chelsea thought. They didn't need her anymore. But isn't that what she wanted, for them to be independent? And friends?

"Last one in is a chicken," Abby said as the dog jumped off the pier.

"You too, Mom," Lizzie called.

Chelsea ran the length of the pier and dove. She emerged gasping at the cold water. Her two daughters were still teetering at the end of the dock.

"Come on, you two chicks. Cluck, cluck, cluck," she said. Dash began circling her, lapping water with a big grin on his face.

The girls dove and also came up gasping. Chelsea picked up a tennis ball. "How about a game of catch?" She threw the ball to Lizzie. "Heads up."

It splashed Liz as she grabbed it before Dash did. "Geez, Mom." She sent it speeding toward her mother.

Chelsea reached up and caught it with one hand and threw it to Abby, who also caught it. For about fifteen minutes they threw the ball. Then worried about Dash doggy paddling between the throwers and catchers in a hopeless quest, she called it quits. "Play catch with Dash for a while," she said and walked out onto the sandy shore, wrapped up in a towel, and sat in a beach chair with a book.

When the girls stopped throwing for the dog, Chelsea called Dash out of the water and he plopped down next to her. "Good dog," she said and buried her fingers in his wet coat. His tail flopped tiredly on the sand.

"Hey, Mum, we're going to swim down to Sarah and Cathy's." Their second cousins, whose family owned a place four cottages further down the shore. The girls chummed around with them when they were on the lake too.

The girls returned a while later, saying no one was at the other cottage. They floated around on a couple of old inner tubes, talking, before coming in and lying on the pier.

Their mother wondered if they ever ran out of conversation. "Better put more suntan lotion on," she called.

Dinner was quiet, everyone tired from an afternoon of sun and water.

"Are you going out tonight?" Chelsea asked, forking a small red potato doused in butter and popping it in her mouth. Dinner had been a joint affair—charcoal-broiled steak, tender enough to cut with a fork, boiled potatoes, and a green salad with peppers and onions.

"I'm beat," Lizzie said, looking at her sister.

"Maybe tomorrow," Abby said, "just to catch up with a few old friends."

"When is Aunt Celie coming?" Liz asked.

"Day after tomorrow," her mom said. "She's flying into Milwaukee and renting a car."

The next two days with her daughters were iffy. She guessed it had been too much to hope to heal their differences with her so soon. They had confronted her with her lesbian affair again.

She had turned redder than her sunburn and said that June was a catalyst.

"So you didn't love her?" Lizzie had asked.

"Or live with her?" Abby had questioned.

"For a short time, but not any longer." She remembered those first heady months, when they made up any differences between them with sex before the relationship turned into a nightmare. How could she ever explain what she knew they didn't want to hear?

"Then why don't you come home?" Liz had asked. Poor, hopeful Lizzie. She was not one to give up easily.

"I can't keep leaving your dad. It's too hard to do twice."

"You love Dad. Why would you leave again?"

"I love him as a friend. Besides, there would always be another June." She hadn't meant to be so blunt, but she was frustrated. Lizzie seemed bent on not understanding.

Abby had jumped to her feet, called Dash, and gone out for a long walk.

"Look, honey," she had said to Lizzie, "I can't change who I am. I can't pretend anymore that I'm straight." Once out of the closet, it was impossible to go back in.

Lizzie had nodded sadly and gone for a walk too.

They had returned around noon, bug-bitten and hungry. After a lunch of peanut butter and jam sandwiches, they all went down to the lake. They seemed intent now on ignoring what had happened. They asked no more questions, but they went out that night around nine. Chelsea never heard them return.

When Celie arrived, Chelsea had feared a repeat of the questioning and more stubborn refusals to understand. Celie should be able to put two and two together. She knew how close Chelsea had been with her best friend in high school. Celie had had more than one fight with those who called Chelsea a dyke because they thought Patsy was one. Patsy the mansie, the boys had chanted under their breaths in the cafeteria. Pat had given them the finger.

She smiled at the remembrance. The last year of high school she and Pat had rubbed against each other and kissed when alone in either one's bedroom. And still she had convinced herself she wasn't gay. She wondered what had happened to Pat, who had gone to the U of Minnesota. She was no doubt with a woman. She hoped Pat's relationships had gone better than her own.

Now she gave Celie a huge hug and grabbed her sister's backpack to carry it inside.

"Can't wait to get into the water," Celie said. "You look tan and happy."

Chelsea had a beach towel wrapped around her waist. "I am."

"Are the girls downstairs?"

"They're coming up for lunch. Are you hungry?" She tightened the towel.

"I have to talk to you. I have to talk to someone or I'll go crazy."

"What?" She dropped her sister's backpack on the bed in the smaller bedroom.

"Can't we sleep together in that huge bed?" Celie asked.

"I didn't think you'd want to," she said. "Of course, we can. We can put your stuff in here, though."

The door slammed shut and the girls gathered around with the dog. Chelsea forgot Celie's comment about having to talk. Everyone was still talking about anything and everything when they sat down to eat.

CHAPTER TWENTY-FOUR

In bed that night, Celie whispered. "I know how you feel, Chelsea. I've met someone."

Chelsea, who had been about to fall asleep, jerked to attention. "What? Who?"

"His name is Ted, and he doesn't spend all his time working. He's handsome and smart and fun."

"Mac works to earn a living for you," she said a little louder than intended. "Ted probably won't be so much fun if you move in with him. Nobody is when you see him day in and out—snoring at night, dropping his socks and underwear on the floor, slurping his coffee."

Celie giggled. "Shh. Mac doesn't even see me anymore. Did Brad know you were there? Was that the problem?" Celie sounded indignant.

Chelsea was up on her elbows. "I'm gay. That was the problem. Brad works his butt off, or at least he did," she said, remembering he was no longer landscaping or selling wood or plowing snow now that he ran the welding shop. "How can you think of cheating on him, Celie?"

"I'm thinking of leaving him," her sister said. "If you can do it, I can too."

"Is that why you came? To tell me you're leaving Mac? I think that's nuts. Let me tell you what happened when I left Brad." So she did. As she talked, she felt as if she was sinking into the mattress. The shame of it.

Celie was so quiet Chelsea thought she had fallen asleep. She supposed her story was boring to someone else, but she was hyped up by the time she finished talking about June. She fell back on the bed and felt Celie's arm under her.

Celie wrapped her in a hug, and Chelsea began to cry. "Don't leave Mac, Celie."

"Shh, Chelse. I had no idea."

"June was my catalyst, though. She got me to leave."

"That's a good thing?" Celie asked.

Frustration dried up her tears. "Yes, Celie. I keep telling you—I'm gay."

"Can't you be gay and not leave?"

"No. It's not fair to Brad or me. You're not, though, and Mac is a good man. Tell him how you feel."

"Maybe I should write Mac while I'm here. I can't tell him face-to-face. Anyway, if I put it on paper, it'll give him time to think about it." Celie released her sister. "I'm sorry. You must have felt so alone."

"Exactly. Let's go to sleep, Celie."

The next morning a warm wind blew out of the south, promising to turn hot. At breakfast Chelsea suggested a kayak ride to her sister.

"Hey, I was going to ask Abby if she wanted to go," Lizzie said. There were only two kayaks.

"You can go after us," her mother said.

"But there is still coffee," Celie said.

"It will be here when we get back. Come on. It'll be good for you."

"You forget that I get lots of exercise at the farm, but I'll go."

They went down to the lake without even brushing their hair. Chelsea loved hot, breezy days. She thought that later they should drag the old sailboat out of the boathouse and sail among the speedboats.

They pulled the kayaks into the lake, which was empty of motorboats, since it was still no-wake time. They paddled away from the shore and the rising sun, although they'd have to face it on the way back. Not even a fishing boat in sight.

A kingfisher flew low between them, looking for small fish for its family nesting in a burrow in the bank. Every year Chelsea saw them, flying between and over boats, diving and then zipping to shore to feed their young.

They passed cottages and huge second homes, standing like sentinels over the lake. Their paddles broke the ripples the breeze stirred up. Chelsea followed the contour of the lake, checking the shore for birds. Once she had seen a bittern, its long beak pointed skyward in a motionless disguise to blend in with its surroundings. She'd never seen one since, but she kept looking, knowing that the addition of more summer places with their people and dogs made it unlikely.

Celie came abreast of her. "Remember when there were so many frogs you had to watch where you stepped? We were always catching them and turtles and snakes. I haven't seen anything except that kingfisher."

"Some fungus is killing the frogs and the bats. We do see turtles, though. They sun on the log down the beach. Most of these property owners are only interested in tubing and skiing. I hope their kids have a chance to swim too. Kids should know how to entertain themselves." Chelsea spoke in a regular voice, knowing how sound carried over the water but not caring if anyone heard. She put her head back and sniffed. "God, it smells good. How do you live away from water, Celie?"

"We're on the east side of the mountains. It's pretty dry, but we have a pool to cool off in at the end of the day."

Chelsea had been out there. They'd had cocktails in the above-ground pool after they'd worked all day in the heat of the sun. It had been fun, talking after the day's work with a vodka and tonic or beer in hand, then going inside and rounding up food for dinner.

"I remember," she said, "but don't you miss the lake?"

"You know I do, but we have the mountains instead."

To each her own, she thought. She wasn't going to argue with Celie, who had followed Mac out west. After all, she'd lived in Brad's Indiana until their kids grew up. It was what women did back then. After they married, they moved to where their husbands had a job—usually where he'd grown up.

The sun had cleared the trees and was pouring heat on them. Despite her sunglasses, Chelsea was squinting, at times totally blinded. She nearly crashed into a fishing boat near the shore as they headed toward their cottage.

"Watch out!" someone yelled.

Chelsea saw the aluminum boat and motor in time to avoid contact. She looked up at the fishermen, a woman and a boy— both standing. She felt stupid.

"Sorry. The sun was in my eyes." She thought she recognized the woman. They were both wearing shorts and T-shirts and ball caps. "Don't you have a place on the lake?"

"Yep. That green one just down the shore there." She pointed at an A-frame sandwiched between two other small cottages near the shore. "Name's Dawn and this is my nephew, Phil. Where are you from?"

"The other side of the lake." She pointed. "The log boathouse over there. I'm Chelsea and this is my sister, Celie." Celie was floating next to her.

"You want a tow home?" Dawn asked.

"Oh no, but thanks," she said. "Good luck fishing."

"Thanks," Dawn said. "We're about to go in. Aren't we, boy?" She turned and pulled the bill of his cap down.

Chelsea and her sister paddled fast toward their place, staying out far enough to avoid rafts and piers. Abby and Liz were waiting at the end of the pier with the dog. The girls were swinging their feet in the water. When the kayaks got close, Dash jumped in the water and swam toward them and then around them, panting and smiling.

The girls grabbed the kayaks and climbed in as soon as their mother and aunt got out.

"Watch out for boats. Your mom almost ran into one. That sun is fierce."

"Let's get another coffee," Chelsea said.

Later in the day, Chelsea and Celie hauled the sailboat out of the boathouse. They rinsed it clean of dust and cobwebs in the lake and put the mast and sail on, along with the rudder and centerboard.

The boat traffic had slowed down when they climbed into the Sunflower and sped away from the pier. Celie let out a screech and scrambled to balance the boat as it listed toward the lee side, the hot wind pushing the sail. It was too late, though, and they capsized. Coming up gasping, they righted the boat and slithered back inside as the wind again caught the sail.

After an hour of being dumped into the lake, they made their way back to the beach and gave the boat to Chelsea's daughters. She and Celie went upstairs, made cocktails, and returned to the beach. Sitting in chairs on the beach, they could hear the girls screaming as they went overboard.

"Couldn't ask for a more perfect day," Chelsea said.

"One to remember," Celie agreed.

On the last night, a Saturday, after they'd all spent the early part of the day cleaning up—changing sheets, washing and vacuuming floors, Chelsea asked her sister if she'd written to Mac.

"I haven't had time. What I've had is one fun-filled day after another. I won't leave Mac, not yet. He needs me. But if I leave, I might come back here."

Chelsea had never thought that was a possibility. Could they share the place? They both owned it. "What about Ted?"

"Oh, he's just a flash in the pan." Celie laughed. "Don't look so panicked. It won't happen now, but be prepared."

The girls left before Celie did, taking Dash with them. Chelsea and her sister stood in the drive, waving. Chelsea felt that familiar ache that occurred when someone left. She wasn't losing them, she told herself. If anything, she thought she and her daughters had begun to close the distance between them. But there was that empty feeling nevertheless.

Celie put her arm around her sister. "You feel the way I'm going to feel when my boys leave."

"Why haven't they left?" Chelsea asked.

"They're working for Mac and me this summer. Will goes to graduate school in the fall. Tom may stay for good. I wouldn't be surprised. He majored in Ag."

Celie gave her sister a big hug. "I'll come back if you take another week off. I haven't had so much fun since I was here last."

"I might hold you to it later in July." She could always come over for weekends, but if Celie was going to come such a distance, she'd want her around for more than a weekend.

"Hey, what can beat sailing in a hot wind or sharing a drink while the sun sets over the water, or laughing over cards with you and my lovely nieces while moths bang against the screens?"

"Skiing in the mountains, watching the sun set over the Pacific on a beach in Mexico. Need I go on?" Chelsea said.

"None of that measures up to this week. Let's do it again. Soon." They hugged, and Celie slid into her rented car and drove off, beeping the horn.

Bereft, Chelsea loaded her vehicle with everything except groceries and went down to the beach for one more swim. How lonely the place felt without the girls and Celie. She'd have to invite her friends.

She paid little attention to the boat or person fishing off the neighbor's beach. She dove off the end of the pier and when she came up, the boat was in her face.

"So this is your place? Pretty fancy." It was the woman in the ball cap, and she was alone.

Chelsea shoved the hair off her face and wiped it free of water with her hand. She recognized the voice. "It's not fancy, Dawn. Do you fish down this way often?" She was treading water a couple feet away.

"Often enough. Would you like to go fishing after supper?" Dawn's face was round and sunburned, her eyes slate gray under the bill of the cap. She had reeled her line in and set the pole down in the boat.

"I have to go home today. Maybe I'll see you next Saturday afternoon, but I don't fish. I have a friend who does, though. She might come with me."

"Yeah? Well, I'll stop by if I can."

"She's a Packer fan too. Of course, we all are. Right?" Chelsea nodded at the cap.

Dawn motored across the lake. Chelsea watched her go. She'd like to take the smell of water and pines home. She dried off in the sun and went up the steps to change clothes, finish loading, and lock up. Half an hour later she drove toward home.

CHAPTER TWENTY-FIVE

She was thinking she would invite Cat and Martha and Barb for a weekend. She owed Cat, who had shared her Door County place with Martha and her. She would ask her friends to join her the first Saturday morning she didn't have to drive the shuttle.

She worried about the loneliness that had consumed her lately, especially at the lake. She might be alone the rest of her life, something she had never thought about when she'd left Brad. It no longer occurred to her to go back to Indiana, though, or even to think she'd made a mistake, not anymore.

There were good things about being alone. No one to tell her what to do, no one to watch programs on TV that she disliked, no one except herself to cook for, no one to pick up after, no one to mess up the house. So, maybe she didn't want to live with someone else. It would be nice to have a partner to go places with, though, and to share her bed.

She considered her friends. Martha was straight. And Barb was too good a friend and her day-to-day life was miles away. The two of them went to movies and had lunch together, but neither made a move toward a relationship. Cat she'd already tried, and Jane was out of the picture. The memory of her one weekend with Jane was tinged with sadness and anger. She thought of Daph, standing in the doorway, her clothes and hands filthy, asking if it was already seven. She didn't even know if the woman was gay. And Sally, nice as she was, was not much more than a child.

Having sex with oneself had its advantages, she mused. She always came and felt no need to please anyone else. Or, as in Cat's case, no worry that she hurt someone's feelings. But she missed the feel of skin on skin, of soft curves under her hands and warm lips on hers.

A horn honking shot adrenaline through her. She'd almost moved into the other lane. Now she stepped on the brakes and drifted back where she belonged. She turned all her attention to the road in front of her and the lane next to her. She had to be alive to have sex, and she didn't have the time or money to have her car fixed.

Safely home, she was cleaning up the kitchen after dinner when the doorbell rang. Standing on the other side of the screen was Daph, one of the last people Chelsea expected to see. At first glance she thought she was Dawn. The gray eyes, maybe.

"Hi, remember me—Daphne Grayling?" the woman said. "I thought we could go for a walk. It's a nice evening and it's seven o'clock."

Chelsea cleared her throat. "I just got back into town, and I haven't had time to put stuff away. Want to come in?" She stepped back and opened the door wider.

"You look just fine. No need to change." Daph stood just inside the door, looking around nervously.

"I just have to finish up here and I'll be ready." She moved fast, sure that Daph would leave if she took long.

While she was washing the few things that didn't go in the dishwasher, Daphne was looking out a front window.

"You do the mowing?"

"Yep. I'm house sitting for a couple who are in England."

"House sitting," Daph repeated. "Is that like baby sitting?"

"Yeah. You take care of the house while the owner's gone."

"How much money is involved?" Her gray eyes were unnerving.

"None. I get a free place to live. They pay for all maintenance, of course."

"Do you need a free place to live?" Daph had moved to within a couple feet of Chelsea.

"Well, it certainly is a financial boon. I can put money away every month, and I have plenty of time to look for a place to live once they're back." She felt as if she was on the hot seat.

"How long will that be?" Daph asked. She was a little taller than Chelsea.

"I don't know. Let's go for that walk." They went out the front door, and Chelsea locked it behind them. "The river trail?"

"Sure. I didn't mean to be nosy. Sally says I shouldn't ask a lot of questions, but I like to know things."

Chelsea caught up with her stride and pushed herself to stay abreast. "It's okay. I don't mind. Tell me about yourself."

"I do odd jobs. Did you notice the sign in the yard?"

She hadn't. "What kinds of odd jobs?"

"I paint. I mow yards. I fix things, not cars and stuff like that, but just about anything that's wrong with a building."

"Do you wash windows?" Maybe she could throw business her way.

"I do, and clean out gutters, build fences, patch driveways."

"You must be in great demand."

"Word gets around."

"What got you into this business?" They were at the beginning of the trail. Chelsea had been on it so many times, it should have been boring, but there were always the white pelicans and mallards with babies and golden eyes and cormorants. And, of course, eagles nested along the river too. Then there were the combinations of people and their dogs. Bikes whizzed by on either side.

"My plan is to get enough jobs so I can hire someone to work for me and build from there. What do you do besides drive a shuttle?"

"Read manuscripts."

Daph looked at her with narrowed eyes. "Well, that kills that idea."

"What idea?"

"That you might want to work for me." She walked faster.

"How about Sally?"

Daph laughed. "She's my niece. She goes to college here and her mother pays board. Those people should be charging you board."

She took umbrage. "I take care of their house and yard and plants."

"Aw, I don't have time to take walks," Daph said as they passed the hill behind the Congregational Church. "Sorry…"

"Chelsea," she supplied her name, which Daph had apparently forgotten. "There are steps here. They'll take you up to River Road."

"Thanks. I'll see you around." Daph bounded up the stairs and disappeared in the brush.

She laughed, not sure whether to be amused or annoyed. She turned back toward the house and picked up her pace.

Mondays were always busy at work. She took people to work and to their homes as soon as she arrived at the Ford dealership. Within an hour she was picking up different owners to take them to their vehicles. At noon she left for home.

She had a book to work on from FemBooks, and it was hot. There wasn't much of a story, but there was plenty of sex. She thought of Daph and laughed, imagining what an awful lover she would be. She pictured Daph telling her she could make money this way.

She called Martha. "Are you busy?"

"I've got a few minutes. How was your week at the lake?"

"Loved it. I have to work this weekend, but why don't you come for the following weekend? Hell, you can come for both, but this coming weekend will be short."

"The weekend after works for me. Want to go out for fish Friday?"

"I do."

She phoned Cat and Barb next and invited them for the weekend after. They both accepted.

The days seemed long after the week at the cottage with the kids. She rode her bike to work most days and avoided Daph's house. In the afternoons she worked on manuscripts. It all kept her busy.

Martha looked tan and relaxed when she met her for fish Friday evening. They sat in a corner booth in the rear of the room and ordered drinks.

"You look good. Still seeing Seth?" Chelsea asked.

"No. He's such a jerk."

"What have you been doing? Where did you get that tan?"

"It's only been a couple weeks, Chelsea. I've been outside, playing tennis after work, walking over my lunch hour. Nothing exciting. Now tell me about your week at the lake with the girls."

"My sister was there too. We had the best time. Hot, windy days for sailing and swimming. Early-morning and after-supper kayaks. Drinks on the beach before sunset. Warm nights on the porch, playing cards. It doesn't sound like much, but it was heavenly, and I think my daughters have begun to forgive me."

"I can't wait to go," Martha said.

"Then go with me tomorrow when I get off work. You can go again next weekend when Cat and Barb come. It's lonely when I'm by myself."

"Hey, you don't have to beg. I'll come if you let me kayak and teach me how to sail."

"It's a promise," Chelsea said, so pleased.

It seemed as if she'd hardly been gone at all. She and Martha opened windows. Speedboats pulling skiers swept past on the lake at the bottom of the hill. The hot weather had continued, but there wasn't much of a breeze.

She showed Martha the bedroom she would share with Cat next weekend. There was a smaller one for Barb, who had said she couldn't come if she had to sleep with someone. They changed into swimsuits, grabbed towels, books, and sunscreen, and clambered down to the lake.

Chelsea got chairs out of the boathouse. The two of them carried out the kayaks and dragged out the sailboat. "Let's wait for the boat traffic to slow down before we go out in the boats. Okay? You don't want to get run over."

As soon as the lake began to clear out, they put the sailboat together and pushed off. The wind was barely strong enough to push the little boat, so Chelsea let Martha handle the rudder and sail. She draped herself across the bow. Actually, the Sunflower was a yellow tub. Their legs stuck out over one side and their heads and shoulders over the other. They were becalmed in the middle of the lake. Chelsea told Martha to move the rudder till she found a breeze, but there was none. They lay in the boat, waiting for it to end up close enough to shore to swim it back to the beach.

An aluminum boat came aside them almost soundlessly. Dawn must have cut the motor and drifted close. "Looks like you need a tow."

I know that voice, Chelsea told herself and opened her eyes to the sun, which framed the woman in the other boat. "Hey, Dawn."

"Looks like you lost the wind," Dawn said, staring at Martha. Chelsea had to keep herself from doing the same when she first saw Martha in a swimsuit. Martha's breasts were eye-catching. Chelsea was envious.

"Can I get you a beer?" Chelsea asked, after Dawn towed them back to Chelsea's pier.

"Is this the friend who fishes?" Dawn asked, eyeing Martha.

"Do you fish, Martha?"

"No. Sorry. I only eat them."

"I could bring you a mess of them," Dawn offered.

"Thanks. Maybe another time. How about that beer?" Chelsea watched Dawn eye Martha as if she were a prize catch. Maybe she only admired Martha's breasts, too, or maybe she wanted more.

"No. No, thanks. I have to go back to the cabin. See you later."

Martha stood with her hands on her hips. She didn't bulge out of her suit, but it was easy to see her cleavage and she had a cute butt. How could Chelsea have missed noticing? Martha turned and caught her looking.

"We have three choices—kayak around the lake, have a drink on the beach, or go for a swim," Chelsea said.

"Is there something wrong with my swimsuit?" Martha asked.

"No. It's just that you look damn hot in it."

Martha started for her, and Chelsea ran for the water, diving when she was waist deep. They came up laughing and swam to the next pier and back three times.

"That's enough exercise for me," Martha said. "How about that beer you promised, goggle eyes."

"Okay. We can kayak after dinner." They'd picked up some deli for supper.

CHAPTER TWENTY-SIX

Martha, Cat, and Barb joined her at the lake on weekends throughout the summer, weather permitting, unless her daughters were coming or Celie. Lindsey came with her mother when her father couldn't take her. The girl swam and paddled one of the kayaks, but mostly she seemed bored. Too many women around her mother, Chelsea thought, and nobody her age.

Still, Chelsea found herself with time on her hands after the morning shuttle runs and between readings. One Saturday while waiting for Martha, Cat, and Barb to show up, she wrote a letter to her contact at FemBooks.

Dear Joan—

I am at the lake waiting for friends to show up. One of my friends has a little girl, who is a terror. I found her in a ditch after a bicycle accident a while ago, and she's never forgiven me for it. I came home to find her throwing mud at my windows one day after I and another friend visited her mom's summer place in Door County on

Lake Michigan. She thought I was having an affair with her mother, but I wasn't. I should have said her parents are separated because her mother did have an affair with a woman.

What must it be like for a kid to find out a parent is having an affair and be able to do nothing about it? Something worth writing about?

She signed her name, stuck it in an envelope, and addressed it to Joan Gordon.

She heard car doors slamming and went outside. They were all talking, and she grabbed a box of food and carried it up the back steps and inside.

"I told you I had ribs and corn," she reminded.

"These are dessert and breakfast and lunch makings," Martha said.

"You can't buy everything," Cat added.

"Or we'll just have to move here and let you support us," Barb put in.

Martha now slept on the enclosed porch with Chelsea in the other twin bed. Chelsea suspected Cat had made overtures to Martha and been rebuffed, but she wasn't certain and she sure wasn't going to ask.

All but Barb changed into their suits before going down to the lake. The day was sunny and windless. They clustered their chairs under a willow near the boathouse.

"I've been looking forward to this all week," Martha said with a satisfied sigh. "It's been crazy at work. Jobs popping up one after another at places like Walmart and McDonald's. You know, the cheap ones that pay so little you have to go on food stamps if you have kids? It's hard finding people who want to work for them."

"Why do you send people there?" Cat asked.

Martha shrugged. "When desperate, some people will take anything. I've never met anyone who wants to go through the shit to be on welfare. Of course, the people I see come to find work."

"I worked at the Pancake House when I was in college," Barb said. "I ate leftover pancakes and greasy bacon for dinner. Haven't liked either since."

"You stayed with your parents, though," Cat said. "No rent. Right?"

"Nah, I stayed in a dorm, worked my ass off, and buried my head in books. But it paid off," Barb said brightly.

"What about you, Chelsea? You hardly say anything about when you were young."

"I went to a small university in Indiana, met Brad, did a lot of necking and bridge playing, and went to classes. The girls always had to wear skirts or dresses on campus or else cover their pants with raincoats. We also had to be in the dorm by ten, while the guys could be out till midnight. How I resented those double rules."

"But I thought..." Cat said.

"And you would be right, but I didn't know it at the time. Hey, there's our friend, Dawn." Dawn was heading toward their beach.

"Whose friend?" Martha asked as she put her towel over her shoulders, effectively hiding her breasts.

Chelsea laughed and said, "I told her I had a friend who liked to fish. Just a warning, Barb, and an apology. I shouldn't have said anything."

"Why do I think I'm not going to want to go fishing with this person?" Barb asked.

"You like to fish. Give it a try," Cat said.

"I didn't bring my fishing gear. Besides, why would I want to go fishing with a stranger?"

"You don't want to swim," Cat said.

Barb wore shorts and a T-shirt. She would wade but not go out beyond her knees. "So? You don't want to fish. Everyone's different."

"Yeah, yeah," Cat remarked.

Dawn cut the engine and grabbed a pier post. "Anyone want to go for a ride?"

"No thanks," they chorused. "We're going to swim and read." Martha held up her book.

"But maybe Barb wants to go for a ride," Cat wickedly suggested. "She doesn't swim or have a book."

Barb threw Cat a filthy look, but she had no excuses. "I was going to observe," she said lamely.

"Come on, Barb. I'll show you the lake. I've even got a life jacket for you." Dawn smiled. The smile was a bare pull back of lips from teeth.

Barb gave Chelsea a look that said, "Help me," but Chelsea didn't know how to get her out of this. She and Martha should be going too. Dawn had rescued them. But she didn't want to encourage Dawn to hang around. None of them wanted Dawn as a friend. Was that a bad thing?

Dawn throttled slowly away from the dock and drove east near the shore. She'd said she was going to give Barb an intimate view of all the cottages and docks and boats and water toys around the lake. The ride would take a while.

"That was mean, Cat," Chelsea said. "You knew Barb didn't want to go."

"But why not?" Cat said innocently. "It's a beautiful day for a ride."

"Then you should have gone," Martha said sharply.

"Besides, Dawn is perfect for Barb. They both like to fish. Dawn has a boat. They're both a little different. You know, sort of loners."

Martha and Chelsea jumped on her words. "No one, especially Barb, asked you to play matchmaker," Martha said.

"Barb is no more different than you," Chelsea added fiercely.

"Okay. I'm sorry. I thought I was doing her a favor."

Chelsea backed off, although she didn't believe the part about "doing her a favor." But it was too nice a day to spoil it.

By the time Barb returned, the others had swum twice and come out dripping to dry in the sun.

"Sure no one wants a ride?" Dawn asked.

Barb looked at the questioning faces once Dawn had driven away. She said, "I'm not telling you anything. Some friends."

She dragged her chair back into the shade, sat down, and pulled the bill of her Packer cap down over her sunglasses. Wearing ball caps was something else she and Dawn had in common.

After fifteen minutes, Chelsea moved her chair close to Barb's. "I want to apologize for not thinking of any reason to keep you off that boat."

Barb smiled, her blue eyes friendly. "It's okay. It's probably the only way I'd ever see the whole lake. Hot out there, though."

"How about a wade to cool you off?"

When Chelsea and Barb started down the shore, Chelsea swimming and Barb wading, the others joined them—swimming with Chelsea. They went past several piers that Barb climbed over, tossing comments back and forth, before heading back.

Barb refused to say a word about what she and Dawn had said to each other, even after they downed a few drinks.

Sunday always went quickly. Before Chelsea thought possible it was time to go home.

A week from Monday Joan's response to her book proposal was waiting for her. She read it three times, both excited at the challenge and worried that she wouldn't be up to the task.

Dear Chelsea,
Why not? Sounds like a good idea, but remember you have to send a synopsis to Ella before you send the ms in. Good luck.

The story started out about Lindsey, or a girl like Lindsey, but eventually the woman who rescued Lindsey turned into someone like herself and Lindsey resembled younger versions of Abby and Liz. The story flashed back to her kids' childhood and the years with Brad. Gina emerged as an important character and Gina's kids became part of the book too.

She fabricated events and places and names and made the characters' lives livelier. She also disguised her characters by changing their looks and temperaments. Every time she sat down at the old computer Brad had given her when the welding shop bought a new one she reread what she had written in the previous chapter. While she was enjoying herself immensely, when she wrote about Gina, she cringed at the thought of Gina reading the book. Would it be an eye-opener, making Gina think, "Duh, how could I have been so stupid?" And Brad? What would he make of it? She hoped he would be in love with someone else by then. And she told herself again and again that she would never write anything worth reading if she worried about the reaction it elicited from anyone.

Weekends were spent with friends and family at the lake. She and her friends basked and swam in the sun, sailed, and kayaked, and raucously played cards at night. Her kids enjoyed the lake, the boats, the swimming. They kept close to each other and tolerated their mother. The book was always in her thoughts when they were around, though, worrying her.

When Celie showed up, she told her she was writing a book. "It's my turn to write rather than read someone else's work."

"What is this book about?" Celie asked.

Chelsea felt transparent. She fought a smile. "Well, it started out about Lindsey, the little girl I found in the ditch after she crashed her bike."

"And who did Lindsey turn into?" Celie asked, unpacking her swimsuit and putting it on.

"More like my kids but different."

"Do you think your daughters love you too much to kill you?" her sister asked.

"I'll let you read it before I submit it," Chelsea said. "Now let's just enjoy the lake and being together."

They mixed a couple of drinks and went down to the beach where they swam before settling down in their chairs to sip their drinks and talk.

"Did you have that conversation with Mac?"

"Sort of. He isn't the best listener. All he talks about is the farm."

"You stopped seeing Ted, didn't you?"

"I've tried. He follows me around."

"How does he do that when you're at the farm?"

"He works there. Didn't I tell you that?"

Chelsea sat up straight, righteous anger for Mac coursing through her. "You've been having an affair right under Mac's nose? I hope he kills this guy."

"Are you nuts? We kissed a few times is all. He has a great body," Celie said. "Mac might kiss me if he found out." She sighed loudly, a sound of regret. "I told Ted I loved Mac, and we had to quit sneaking around. But he still follows me, looking hangdog. Drives me wild. I'm caught in a conundrum. I can't very well tell Mac, and that's the only way to get rid of Ted."

Chelsea was doubtful about the few kisses. She thought there must have been more but wasn't sure she wanted to know. "How old is this Ted?" she asked, zeroing in on the "great body."

"Thirty-two." Celie winced. "Now before you jump all over me, I was having a midlife crisis—bored and at loose ends."

"Oh, Celie," Chelsea said, feeling rather ill.

"Let's not talk about it, Chelse. Okay? I learned my lesson."

"And what was that?"

"Don't get involved with anyone under forty." She shot a look at her sister. "Stay true to Mac."

Chelsea laughed and called a truce. After all, was what she had done any better? But Celie had no future with Ted. Then again, she had no future with June either. Did stupidity run in the family?

CHAPTER TWENTY-SEVEN

Chelsea sent the manuscript to Celie to read first, as promised. Celie called to say she'd stayed up all night, unable to put it down. She said she couldn't even guess how Abby and Lizzie might react. Or Brad. Or Gina. Or this kid who trashed her bike. And was that how Chelsea had sex? She didn't know what Chelsea's kids would think of those scenes. Hot. But kids don't like to think of their parent having sex.

Chelsea interrupted. "Pretend I didn't write it and tell me what you think of it."

"It's good, sister. I can't wait to read the second one."

"I'm thinking about it," Chelsea said. And she was.

"Can you come out in December? We'll ski and talk."

"I should be able to." She sure wouldn't be going to Indiana for Christmas. Brad's girlfriend would be there.

She hadn't seen Gina since last Christmas. One of her horses had gotten deathly ill with colic when she was supposed to come to the lake in September. The mare had lived. She was due to foal in January. Gina felt she had to stay nearby to watch the animal. So she hadn't visited.

Now it was near the end of October and she was ready to send the manuscript to Ella, who took care of the submissions. She had sent in a synopsis long ago and the jacket copy and cover had been agreed upon. The book was titled *Misadventures*. Publication date was September of the following year. After she made changes during the edit, the book would be out of her hands. When she took the box with the manuscript to the post office and sent it off, it felt as if she was mailing her baby.

Should she tell her daughters or try to slip the book under their radar? She didn't know whether to tell Gina or not. Would it seem a betrayal if she kept her first book a secret from her family and her best friend? Was she going to be cowardly again? Getting a book published was an achievement, not a source of shame.

Her daughters were coming to her for Christmas. Brad's girlfriend was spending the holiday at the house with him. In fact, she was moving in the day after. Abby's boyfriend was going with family to Ohio, where his uncle's wife and kids lived. She was invited, but she told her mother she would feel odd being the only non-relative. Lizzie's boyfriend would be skiing with his family. She wasn't invited, which pissed her off no end.

They arrived already unhappy with how their holidays had worked out. Neither acted as if she wanted to be there. Chelsea tried to be understanding.

"If you hadn't left home, Dad's girlfriend wouldn't be moving in," was one of Abby's first comments.

"Merry Christmas to you too. Did you bring your ski clothes, like I told you to do?"

"Where is there to ski around here?" Lizzie asked.

There were ski hills, of course, just no mountains.

Then she told them about her Christmas present. "We're flying to Colorado tomorrow."

"What?" they said in unison.

"Do you have any money? If you do, you can ski. If not, you can hang out with your aunt's family. It can't be any worse than hanging out here."

It was an early flight on Christmas Eve. Celie met them at the airport and drove them home, talking nonstop.

"Where's the snow?" Lizzie asked, looking out the window.

"In the mountains," Celie said. "We'll go up there. At least, you won't have to pay to ski, only for rentals. We have family passes."

"Aunt Celie, do you go out and cut a Christmas tree?" Abby asked.

"We used to. Got so that everybody's schedule was too different. Now we buy one from a lot."

"Remember when we used to cut a tree near the cottage, how much fun it was?" Abby asked.

"I remember you complaining about the cold," Lizzie said.

"I only did that once when it was about zero out." Abby elbowed Lizzie.

"Hey, cut that out."

It turned into an expensive Christmas. They skied every day. Celie's sons went with them and Celie's friend, Ted. Celie's sons were terrific skiers, asking their cousins to go with them on the black diamond runs.

"No way," the young women said. "Maybe later," when pressed.

Celie was a good skier too, and she taught them a great deal.

"Want some help?" Ted asked. He'd been hanging around with them instead of the guys.

"No," Celie said, "I don't."

But he still hung around. He wasn't quite six feet tall, but he was lean and athletic with dark wavy hair and a rugged face. He had small brown eyes that Chelsea thought untrustworthy.

"Why don't you help me?" Chelsea said, sidestepping close to him on her skis. She needed to move to stay warm, despite the down jacket and long underwear under her ski pants. The snow blew low to the ground, like fog.

He looked at her and then at Celie. "Celie said she'd help you."

"She can help Abby and Lizzie. You said you wanted to help."

He leaned on his poles. "I did. I do."

"Okay, let's go. Show me how to be a better skier." Actually, Chelsea thought that would take a miracle worker. Heights terrified her. She lost her courage and screamed all the way down, forgetting to turn to slow her momentum.

Ted had no choice. Patiently, he worked with her until she managed to control her speed by sweeping turns—first by pointing her skis inward and putting weight on the downhill ski, then by just putting weight on her downhill ski. If she paid attention to what she was doing instead of the perilous downhill slope, she gained control. After several runs, she tired and went inside.

Abby and Liz were having a smashing time. They picked up a couple of guys, then ditched them for their cousins and whooped their way downhill until they got to the black diamonds. By then their mother and aunt were having a couple of drinks in the warming house. Ted was buying.

Around four Chelsea tapped Ted on the shoulder and asked him to come with her for a moment. They stopped outside the bathrooms, where Chelsea was really heading.

"You're fooling yourself, Ted. In fifteen years, Celie will look like your mother to you. You should be chasing my girls, not my sister. She has Mac, and she intends to stay with him."

Ted glared at her while she spoke, loud enough to be heard over the voices and music and a football game on TV. "I don't want to marry her. She's a better fuck than the younger ones." He turned and left.

Shocked, she went into the bathroom and then back to the table, where she told Celie what Ted had said. She was mad because Celie had lied to her, but hadn't she lied to Celie?

Celie smiled painfully. "He's not such a good fuck, and now he's dead meat. Watch out for the beautiful ones, Chelse. They aren't the best lovers. They don't always try to please, because they think you should please them." There were tears in her eyes.

Chelsea never saw Ted again during their five-day visit. When they hugged in the airport after the boarding call, Chelsea and Celie had tears in their eyes. Summer was a long way off, when they would see each other again.

At home, Chelsea lived her days hour by hour. She'd get up early, layer on clothes for the shuttle. When she got home, she read whatever manuscript was on hand, if any. Then she would sit in front of her computer. Hours sped by, unnoticed, as she lived in the world she was creating.

The doorbell startled her on New Year's Eve. Martha and Barb stood shivering on the doorstep.

"Did you forget about Cat's party?" Martha asked as she and Barb pushed their way into the warm house.

She had. "I'll shower quick and get dressed. Help yourselves to cookies."

"Don't mind if I do," Barb said. "I made them."

"Make yourselves a drink or have a beer," Chelsea called, appearing briefly wrapped in a towel.

Chelsea had been dreading the party. Jane would be there with her lover, and she really didn't want to see Jane. She still thrilled to her memories of their few times in bed together. It would be painful to see her with someone she loved. But go they must, else Cat would be mad.

Unlike last year's party, there was no snowstorm. They had yet to have a good snow. Lindsey opened the door, dressed in a red dress that showed off her budding figure.

"How lovely you look, Lindsey," Chelsea said.

Lindsey walked off without a word.

"That girl is going to have trouble socializing," Martha commented.

"She doesn't know what the word means," Barb said.

They were late, and Cat met them with a frown. "Where the hell have you been?" she whispered fiercely.

Martha and Barb looked pointedly at Chelsea. Barb's lofted eyebrows told the story.

"You like that damn book better than you like us," Cat said, but she was no longer angry. She went off to tend to her guests, and the three friends made their way to the bar.

The only one who had an inkling of an idea about how Chelsea had felt about Jane was Martha. When Cat brought Jane over to reintroduce her and to introduce her lover, Chelsea froze. She forced a stiff smile.

The girlfriend, Stacy Lee Cunningham, was stunning. Her dark hair, peppered with gray, curled around her shoulders. Her vivid green eyes sparkled with interest, but it was her sensuous mouth that Chelsea focused on. What she wouldn't give for that mouth, she thought, as Stacy bent forward slightly and took Chelsea's hand in hers.

Stacy's attention focused on Chelsea. "I hear you're writing a book. I've always wanted to write one myself. Actually, I've tried, and I get to about twenty-five pages and stall. Where do you get ideas to fill two or three hundred pages?"

Where the hell had she heard about the book? Jane? Chelsea asked, "How did you know?" She must have looked flummoxed because Stacy laughed, a lovely, bell-like sound. No wonder Jane went back to her.

"Jane told me." She glanced at Jane as if for help.

Jane stepped forward. "Jim Morgan. Cat told him. He wanted to know where you had gone. Were you trying to keep it quiet? I didn't tell anyone except Stacy."

"No. I'm just kind of astounded about how news travels. It's not really news," Chelsea said. "You know what I mean."

"I do," Jane said, "and it is news. When will it be available to read?"

"She's on her second book," Martha said. "The first one is coming out in September."

"She's some kind of genius," Barb put in.

Jane smiled at that. "She is, indeed."

"Congratulations!" Stacy said with a gorgeous smile. "We'll have to order it. What's the title?"

Slightly overwhelmed, Chelsea answered in a soft voice even as she thought, *What a stupid title.*

"We're going to have a book signing when *Misadventures* comes out. Chelsea will have copies to sell," Martha said.

Stacy looked thrilled. "Let's drink to it."

Jane smiled and met Chelsea's gaze. "I'm happy for you."

"Thanks," she said, looking away. She could get lost in the what-ifs, if she looked at Jane too long. "I'm always reading other people's books. I thought why shouldn't I write one?"

Actually, what she had often thought was that she could write a better book than the manuscript she was reading.

"I'll get the drinks," Barb offered. "Orders please."

At ten forty-five Lindsey passed out champagne, which Chelsea thought inappropriate. What was Cat thinking?

"Oh, but she's so cute. Don't you think?" Stacy asked. She had been hanging around their threesome, which meant Jane was also with them. Chelsea had not been able to shake her intense feelings for Jane. When she was around, Chelsea was unable to relax.

"Cute but it's dangerous to her health," Chelsea said. "I've seen her finish off partially empty glasses after a party." She knocked back the champagne as the ball fell in Times Square. Grabbing Martha, she kissed her.

Martha stiffened. She looked shocked when Chelsea kissed her again. 'I don't want to kiss Jane," she whispered.

"Well, find somebody else," Martha growled.

While she was kissing Barb, who also froze, Stacy tapped Chelsea on the shoulder. "My turn," she said.

Up close she was even more lovely—great skin and breasts. She tore her gaze away from the cleavage and caught Jane looking at them with a wry smile. Just then Stacy embraced her and pressed her soft lips against Chelsea's. Chelsea pulled back when the kiss went on too long.

"I know you want to kiss Jane," Stacy murmured.

People were staring at this cluster of women kissing each other. They were probably transfixed by Stacy's beauty, Chelsea thought, realizing with a touch of panic that Stacy was leading her to Jane.

Jane's arms were crossed. She leaned forward and gave Chelsea a peck on the cheek. "If you want her, you can have her," Jane whispered. "She likes to sample other women."

Chelsea backed away, embarrassed. She had heard the voices loud in celebration, but the din had been background noise. They were singing "Auld Lange Syne" and she joined in, hearing Barb's lovely voice harmonizing.

PART II

CHAPTER TWENTY-EIGHT

The books arrived the last Friday in August just as she was getting ready to go to the lake. She heard the knock on the door, went to answer it, and found three boxes, which she carried inside and left in the front hall. She continued packing and loading her car. When everything but the cooler was loaded, she opened one of the boxes.

The book cover was of a bright green station wagon, packed with suitcases and boxes, passing a sign that read Welcome to Wisconsin. Her name was on the bottom. She studied it for a long moment, before turning the pages—reading the publishing data, seeing the title again and her name under it. When she came to Chapter 1, her heart fluttered with angst as she began to read.

Seeing her own words on the pages made her feel exposed, as if she'd taken her clothes off in public. What if readers hated it? But it was better than she'd thought. It wasn't great writing, but the dialogue was well done and the people came across as real. She sat down. Before she realized how much time had passed, that her friends might get to the lake before she did, she had read one and a half chapters. She put the book back in the box, found a good pen and carried the box to the car and quickly followed with the cooler.

As she turned into the sandy driveway to the cottage, she saw Martha's car in the rearview mirror. She almost wished she was going to be alone this weekend so she would be the first to read her words in print. Cat wasn't coming, but Martha was already there, and Barb would probably not be far behind. She carried her weekend bag to the door and unlocked it. The interior was cool and smelled empty. She went back out for the cooler and met Martha carrying a box of dry goods.

"Are we still going out for fish?" Martha asked as she passed Chelsea on her way inside.

"I thought so. I don't have anything planned for tonight. Do you?" She'd have to wait till they got back from wherever they went for dinner before she could read any more.

As she slammed her trunk, Barb parked near the shed. "Hey, how the hell are you?"

"Same as I was when I talked to you yesterday." Barb had called to check if she was invited. "You don't have to double-check, Barb. I'd call you if something came up." That was Barb, though—not always sure of her welcome.

"I brought some appetizers—hummus, pita bread. Want to try it before we go out?"

"Sounds good. Thanks." She picked up the box of books and started inside. Over her shoulder she had a bag with wine and her library book. Her backpack was snug against her.

"Hey, let me carry some of that stuff," Martha said.

"No. I got it. Get your other stuff." Chelsea went inside and opened windows she'd have to shut when they left for dinner. Breathing in the smell of pines, she closed her eyes. What would she do without this place? *What most people do*, she told herself. Although an awful lot of people had cottages on lakes, more did not. They shared the public beaches, of which there were plenty.

She had dropped the box of books on her bed. She had thought to keep them to herself till she had finished reading one. If there were typos or other mistakes, she wanted to find them. When she looked up after dropping her backpack on the bed, she found two sets of eyes on her.

"What's in the box?" Martha asked. "Get a present?"

"Sort of. I'll tell you later. Let's have some hummus and pita chips and a drink. What do you say?"

"Where is Cat?" Barb asked, putting the snacks on the table.

"Lindsey was invited to a friend's birthday party, and her dad is out of town," Martha said, putting two bottles in the fridge.

"Chardonnay?" Chelsea asked.

Martha grinned. "No. Champagne. Just in case your books arrived."

"Oh," Chelsea said. How could she hide the books now? "They came today."

"Well, why didn't you say so? I'm so excited," Martha's face was alive with anticipation.

"Is that what's in the box?" Barb asked.

"Can we see one?" Martha asked.

"Sure." Chelsea got the one she'd been reading out of the box and handed it over.

Barb and Martha oohed over the cover. "I want to buy a copy," Barb said.

Martha handed the book back. "Have you read it?"

"They just came today."

"Well, you read one first and then tell us if it's worth the trouble," Barb said, hands on hips.

"I should knock you over the head with it," Chelsea said with a laugh.

Martha got the champagne out of the fridge and rummaged around for something to open it with.

"You two get free, autographed copies," Chelsea said, finding three juice glasses in the cupboard. "We might not be able to drive anywhere to eat tonight."

"Then we'll have hummus and pita chips and corn on the cob," Barb said.

"And brats," Martha added. "Let's just stay here and celebrate."

They took the champagne down to the lake and after she poured them each a glass, Martha put the bubbly in the water, the bases firmly stuck in the sand.

"I am so excited," Martha repeated after three glasses.

"Wait till you read it," Chelsea warned. "You might be excited for some other reason."

"Like what?" Barb asked, looking amused and confused.

Chelsea was high already. "Because it's got sex in it. It might get you all horny. You have to tell me if you are aroused, because that would be good."

"Aw, come on. How much sex can it have?" Martha questioned.

"Sheing and sheing?" Barb asked.

"You'll see."

"Damn. Here comes Dawn," Martha said.

"Don't tell her about the book," Chelsea said quickly.

"I think we better go up and fix something to eat," Barb said, grabbing the champagne out of the lake.

Dawn latched onto a pier post as they started up the stairs. "You leaving? I just got here."

"It's past dinnertime," Chelsea said. "Maybe we'll see you tomorrow."

"I'll just hang around and fish here. You're coming back down, aren't you?"

"Maybe, maybe not," Chelsea said. "We drank a lot of champagne."

"What are you celebrating?" Dawn yelled as they kept climbing.

"Another weekend in paradise," Barb hollered.

They managed to get a fire started and cooked the brats and steamed the corn. By then it was pitch black. The pounding on the door startled them all. Chelsea got up and went to see who was there.

"I got tired of waiting," Dawn said.

"Sorry. We're not coming back down. In fact, we're going to bed after we clean up."

"Clean up?"

"Dinner dishes. We're just now eating. Maybe we'll see you tomorrow." Chelsea had spoken through the locked screen door.

Dawn stood just outside, dimly lit.

"Careful going down the steps," Barb called.

"There's almost a full moon," Dawn said.

"I'll have to see it through the screens," Chelsea said. "I'm too tired."

"I've been looking forward all week to seeing you," Dawn persisted.

Chelsea felt bad for a moment, but it passed. *Sometimes,* she reflected, *it's best not to let someone in your life.* "Tomorrow," she said firmly and hiccupped.

"You're drunk on that champagne," Dawn said accusingly.

"Be glad you aren't," Martha said, joining Chelsea at the door.

"I want to see Barb," Dawn said.

"Tomorrow," Barb called again.

"Let's go to bed and read," Martha said when Dawn was gone.

However, even Chelsea couldn't stay awake to read her own book. It fell on her face, briefly waking her. Outside a huge moon hung over the lake and crickets filled the night with screeching chirps.

CHAPTER TWENTY-NINE

On the dining table snacks surrounded a full punch bowl borrowed from Cat. Chelsea sat behind a card table in the living room in front of the bay window with flowers in the yard as a backdrop—asters, purple coneflowers, blazing star, daisies.

She was nervous, chattering about nothing to Barb and Martha. The book reading and signing was to begin at four. She would read three pages from the beginning of the story and then autograph those books that sold. Martha would collect the money.

It never occurred to her to worry about anyone showing up. The day was fine, a little cool though, almost like fall. She wasn't ready for autumn, but she never had been. Fall had signaled the beginning of school and the termination of her freedom.

She glanced at her watch. Three fifty-five and no one had arrived. Books were stacked beside her and she had a new pen in hand. If she had to send back too many books, she would be embarrassed. Barb and Martha had claimed to love the book, but they were friends. Besides, anyone who came wouldn't know whether they would like the book.

She had sent out invitations—to Cat, of course, and Jane and Stacy and Dana and Mickie and the women at The Pivot—Sarah, Sue and Pat, Jeanine and Nan. She'd also sent invitations to Daph and Sally. She'd even sent one to Mimi Kincaid, but she didn't really expect her to show up. That wasn't a lot of people, but even Cat wasn't there. She thought at least she could count on her coming.

The doorbell rang, and Barb went to answer. Chelsea heard their voices and knew Cat had arrived. *God, what if there are only three people?* she thought—Barb and Martha and Cat. Well, they'd have a party. But then the doorbell rang again. This time it was Jane and Stacy. Chelsea looked at Jane and felt her body temperature rise. No matter how she tried she always thought of their time in bed when she saw Jane.

In another fifteen minutes the room was filled with lesbians. And then Mimi rang the bell.

"I had to come and congratulate you," she said to Chelsea, when Chelsea said she hadn't really meant for her to come all this way. She had only wanted to tell her of the book.

"Haven't you heard?" Mimi asked, and Chelsea shook her head. "It's number one on the lesbian book list in the *Lambda Literary Magazine.*"

"You're not serious," Chelsea said, but why would she make it up?

"I'm deadly serious." Mimi smiled. "Congratulations!" She gave Chelsea a hug.

Martha talked over the women, who were grouped around the dining table, drinking punch and eating appetizers. "Take a seat. Chelsea is going to read and then autograph books for those of you who want one."

Just before she started reading, Chelsea thought she heard Daph grumbling and nearly laughed. Daph would begrudge the time reading would take. She would want to buy a book and get out of there.

Whenever Chelsea bought a book, she always read the first few pages. If they drew her in, she purchased it. So that's what she was going to read.

They all listened quietly and then lined up at the card table. Stacy was first and looked stunning. She gushed about the pages Chelsea had read. Chelsea wrote on the title page—"Stacy Lee. Welcome to my home and my book. Thank you." And signed her name. Jane was next in line. She thanked her for coming and wrote the same thing she had in Stacy's book. It sounded dumb to her, but she really didn't know what to write. "Yours Truly?" "Hope you like the book?" "Best Wishes?" They all sounded stupid.

Then Cat was standing next to her. "Lindsey wanted to come. I told her it was only for adult women."

"She'll probably sneak the book from you and read it."

"Yes, she probably will."

"What do you want me to write?"

"What you wrote to Martha and Barb. 'To my friend, Cat Morgan.'"

So she did.

When everyone who was going to buy a book had done so, Chelsea stood up and made the rounds. Daph had left, saying she had things to do, but Sally stayed. Chelsea was talking to her when the doorbell rang. She answered it.

June and Karen stood outside. June was looking down the street, anywhere but at Chelsea, so Karen spoke. "I hope we're not too late to buy a couple of books."

She met Karen's gaze. They were still together, which surprised her. She pushed the screen open. "Sure. Come on in."

June walked in as if she still belonged there. She went to the dining table and filled a paper plate with appetizers—artichoke dip and chunks of bread, spinach balls, hummus and pita chips.

Karen bought the books, asking Chelsea to sign hers but not June's. "We won't stay. June is kind of torn."

Chelsea forced a smile and took her money.

"Look," Karen said, "if it makes you feel any better, I think I did you a favor."

"Cheating is never a favor. But thanks."

Karen took June by the elbow and steered her toward the door. June had been telling people that this had been her house, that Chelsea had forced her out.

When the others left, going out the door in twos, Chelsea thanked them for coming. "Let me know what you think of the book. I'd really like to hear," she urged.

She only relaxed when Jane and Stacy left. Jane put a hand on Chelsea's arm, and the hair on it stood straight up. "Congratulations, Chelsea," she said. Stacy told her not to be a stranger. Chelsea knew that was what she would be. It was too painful to be around Jane.

When there were only four of them left—Cat, Barb, Martha, and Chelsea—the partying began. "No champagne, but I have wine and vodka and tonic and cranberry juice," Chelsea announced.

The others toasted Chelsea and she smiled and smiled and smiled, recalling Mimi's news. Behind the smile, though, there was sadness. She loved her friends, but she missed the intimacy of being with someone. When they left, she would go to bed alone.

She had packed autographed books for her daughters, her sister, and Gina. Now she asked her friends if she should send one to Brad. They all begged off, saying they didn't know him.

"I'll ask Celie. She'll give it to me straight. Maybe he'll be hurt if I don't send him one. Maybe I should ask Gina too."

The chairs were stacked against the wall near the door, ready to go back to the rental place. She and her friends were sitting on the couch and the other two chairs in the room.

"When are we going to meet Gina?" Cat asked.

"Maybe next spring," she said, though she didn't want to share Gina when she visited. She imagined her here now, sitting with them and wondered what she would say.

She mailed the books the following Monday and then resumed her normal schedule. Only occasionally did she suffer a brief spell of panic. When a week and a half went by and she hadn't heard from Celie, she called her.

"Well?" she asked when her sister answered the phone.

"The book? Have you heard from the girls?" and without waiting for an answer, "I think you should send one to Brad." Chelsea had enclosed a note asking for her opinion.

"Why haven't you called?" Chelsea asked.

"It's a busy time of year and our summer help has gone back to school. I read it again, though. Finished it last night. Kudos, sister."

"Should I call the girls?" She could ask them if they'd gotten the book, but she hadn't the courage.

"Did you send one to Gina? I wonder what she thought. Were you really in love with her?"

She broke out in a worried sweat. "I never told her."

"You have now."

Why couldn't she have kept Gina and her daughters off her pages? She told Celie about the book being number one on the best-seller list in the Lambda magazine. "I don't know how much that means. It was only the lesbian list. There aren't too many lesbians to begin with and how many of them read?"

"Hey, that's wonderful. Wow! I didn't realize I was reading such an important book," Celie said enthusiastically.

Chelsea laughed. "Don't go overboard, Cele," but she felt a little thrill. She wanted to feel like an author of merit, that's what she'd like. *Get a little and want more*, she thought.

"You don't even know when you're famous. Who cares what the kids think, or Gina or how many lesbians there are. Your book is number one. You're a success."

Was she? Next week her book could be off the list, but today it was number one. She should be immensely pleased instead of worrying about what her kids and Gina would think. "Thanks, Celie."

"For what?"

"For giving me back my confidence. Give my love to Mac and the boys."

"Tom is gone, and Will has his own place. We are so busy. Come see me when you can, just not right now. And for crissake, be proud. I'll let you know what Mac says about the book."

"Don't let him read it." What the hell would he think? She'd never be able to look at him again.

"I already read some of the sex scenes to him. We had a pretty good time afterward."

"You didn't," she protested, trying not to picture it.

"We did. Let me know what Abby and Liz say. And Gina. Love ya."

"Love ya back," Chelsea said and hung up.

CHAPTER THIRTY

Gina called in the afternoon of that very same day.

Chelsea was working on her second book, immersed in the story, and it took her a moment to reorient. "Gina!" she said.

"You dropped a bomb, Chelse, and then you sound surprised to hear my voice."

"It's just that I was deep in another book, and I had to come out into the real world." Gina would understand. She was a reader.

"What book is that?"

"My second one."

"Is it like the first one?" Gina asked.

"Yes and no."

"Does that mean what I think it does? Same characters?"

Chelsea's heart had jumped into high gear. She longed to ask how Gina had liked the book, but she feared the answer. "Not really, but sometimes a bit of someone I know slips in. Yeah."

"Well, I can't wait to find out who's in this new book." She made the remark with some asperity.

"Gina, I didn't mean for her to be something like you. It just happened."

"Hmm," Gina said. "Why didn't you tell me how you felt?"

"Oh, come on. I couldn't take that chance. Your friendship was more important than anything else."

"And so was yours to me. It's a good book, Chelse. Don't let anyone tell you otherwise."

"You mean Abby and Lizzie?"

"I haven't talked to them. They will probably call, and I'll tell them their mother is a good writer."

"Should I send a copy to Brad?"

"I'd ask him first. His girlfriend is living there. You know that?"

"I do. I'm grateful for her. I want him to have a life again." She just didn't want him to love this new girlfriend more than he had loved her. "When will I see you?"

"Suze is getting married in May. You have to come and stay with me. Maybe I can make it to the lake next summer."

Chelsea told her about the best-seller list. "It's not like being on the *New York Times* best-seller list," she added.

"Congratulations! Send me the reviews. My best friend is a best-selling writer."

Chelsea only heard "my best friend." Her voice turned wobbly. "Your good opinion is so important to me."

"Well, you've got it. God, I miss you. You're the only one who doesn't talk nonstop about her kids. Now it's the grandkids they brag about."

She thought about Cat, who seldom talked about her kids. Lindsey was something of an embarrassment, she supposed. Was the boy, too? She couldn't remember his name.

"Love ya, girlfriend," Gina said before they hung up.

"I love you too," Chelsea said. She meant it in a whole different way. It was great to be able to say it, though.

Another week passed. Chelsea forgot to worry about what her daughters might think or say. She was talking with Martha on a Friday night after they'd gone out for fish.

Chelsea was obsessing about possibly having hurt Dawn. "I can't believe I was so cruel. All she wanted was to hang around with us. Was that so awful?"

"Yes," Martha said flatly. "We didn't want to hang out with her. You should be able to choose your friends." She took a sip of wine, frowning at Chelsea. "I know she towed us back to your beach that day, but that doesn't mean we owe her. It was a decent thing to do."

"I think she was lonely."

"Does that mean we befriend lonely people whenever we come across them."

Chelsea took a sip and set her wineglass on the end table, just as the phone rang, startling them both. She picked up the receiver. Abby was on the other end. It felt as if her heart stopped and started again.

"Hi, sweetie. How are you?"

"How do you know what I feel and think?"

"You're upset. That's how you are." She said it to lighten things up, but she should have known better.

"You bet I am. Liz is too. How could you, Mom?"

"That wasn't you. She didn't look like you, and as you pointed out, I don't know what you think and feel. When I'm writing, I use bits and pieces of people." She was keeping calm, trying to be informative, not apologetic.

Martha took her glass into the kitchen. Chelsea saw her rinsing it off. She didn't want her to leave. "Hang on a minute, Abby." She covered the phone with a hand. "Don't go home yet, Martha."

"It's late," Martha said. "I'll talk to you tomorrow."

"I'm back," she said brightly into the receiver.

"You were in love with Gina? How could you tell everyone? Did you send her a book?"

"Yes. She and I talked a week ago. We're still good friends. Abby, you can't help who you love." *Should it be "whom you love?"* she wondered, but that sounded so stuffy. "You know that."

"I can help it. I don't have to love you." Stunned silence followed. At least, it was stunned silence on Chelsea's part. "Is Lizzie there?"

"No. This is my apartment. Jeff's and mine. You left so Dad got a new girlfriend, and I don't belong at home anymore."

"But you already had an apartment."

"Yeah, but I often went home overnight."

"So, I'm at fault because your dad met someone, and she moved in."

"Well, he wouldn't have a new girlfriend otherwise," Abby said, but her voice wavered.

"Didn't this woman move in after Christmas? And does she have a name?"

"Carol," she said grudgingly.

"Is Lizzie not going home either?" she asked.

"Sometimes. Liz lives with Keith."

"How's the job?" her mother asked. "You are at Stratton and Stratton, right?"

"Yep. It's okay. Mom, I didn't mean what I said about not loving you."

Chelsea smiled. "I know, Abby. It's because you love me that you're having such a hard time."

"No, Mom. It's because you're a lesbian and you left Dad and you wrote this book about all of us."

"That too."

She poured herself another glass of wine after she hung up and sat in the living room to read. She would have to call Liz but not today. Liz might sound more reasonable, but Liz dealt with difficulty by ignoring it. Abby had been a mama's girl. Maybe she didn't want to share her mom with another woman?

Liz called her the next day. "Hi, Mom. I read your book. I knew you'd put Abby and me in it. I think you should go back home before Dad marries this woman." It all came out in a rush.

"This is my home, Lizzie. I'm glad your dad has found someone else. He deserves to be happy."

"Do I deserve to be happy?"

"Yesss, but everyone is responsible for their own happiness."

"Would I be responsible if I was in jail?"

"You're not in jail, Lizzie. You're free to make your own decisions."

Chelsea had a terrible feeling that Lizzie might sabotage her own happiness to punish her mother. "Don't hurt yourself trying to hurt me."

"I wouldn't be so stupid. I have to go." And she hung up.

They both were angry. She no longer felt so good about the book. Well, at least for a few minutes. Then the phone rang again. She answered with trepidation.

"Chelsea? Joan Gordon here. Your book is a big success. Congratulations!"

"Thanks, Joan. It wouldn't be without you and FemBooks."

"Have you started another book?"

"Yes. It's almost finished." Chelsea was smiling.

"Good. Send it in with a summary when it is. We'd like to publish you again."

This is what success feels like, she thought, so pleased. She thanked Joan and got back to the book, but her momentum was gone. The cursor blinked as she stared at the page. She didn't like this book as much as the other one.

The theme of this book was how difficult it was to be a lesbian in a straight world—always knowing you're different, sometimes hating yourself for it, often thinking you don't have to be that way. For her, sex reaffirmed who she was, but she hadn't had sex for a long time. What should have been a reassuring call from Joan had turned into a worry. She knew the next book wouldn't catch on like the first, but it wouldn't be her last book, she vowed. She had several more in her head.

The following morning, she was surprised to see Stacy Lee waiting for the shuttle at the dealership. It was the last run of the morning. "Anyone need a ride?"

"I do," Stacy said, and two other women stood up. They all filed outside to the Taurus. Stacy grabbed the front seat.

Chelsea asked for addresses and backed the car out of the slot. Stacy would be the last drop-off, only because she lived in Neenah on the Island.

The two women in the backseat struck up a conversation. "So, this is what you do when you're not writing," Stacy said.

"It is. I read manuscripts too," she said, although she hadn't read anything for a while.

"A woman of many talents."

Chelsea wished Stacy wouldn't go overboard on compliments. It made her uneasy. "This doesn't take much talent."

"But the others do. Jane and I were discussing your book last night. I've never had a signed copy of anyone's book."

She wanted to ask what they thought of the book, especially what Jane thought of it, but she only smiled and kept her eyes on the road. When she turned into the driveway of a two-story red brick house with a white two-and-a-half-car garage, she took a deep breath. This was where Jane lived. She wondered who owned the house or whether they both did.

"Why don't you come in?" Stacy asked. "Just for a few minutes."

"I can't," Chelsea said. "I'm working." At that moment the radio came on spewing static.

"What?" Stacy asked.

A voice gave out an address and names. "Gotcha," Chelsea said. "Got to pick someone up. Nice to see you, Stacy."

"We loved your book," Stacy called as Chelsea began to back out of the driveway.

She braked and opened the window. "Thanks. Say hello to Jane for me."

CHAPTER THIRTY-ONE

Fall was short. The trees turned crimson and yellow and dropped their leaves, except for the oaks at the lake. They clung to theirs as the leaves darkened and shriveled. Chelsea went with Barb and Martha to retrieve everything that would freeze, propped the fridge open, turned off the electricity and gas and water. The plumber would drain the water heater and blow out the lines for the winter.

How she hated the end of the season. It helped that Martha and Barb were with her. She wanted to get done and go home. When they were on their way back, they dodged deer leaping in panic across the back roads. Bow and arrow season had started. She would not be around when gun season began.

When Barb and Martha went home, her spirits took a dive. She sat in the dark with a glass of wine, wondering how she was going to live through another winter. The owners of the house were staying away at least until spring and were relieved that Chelsea could continue to house sit. She awoke in the middle of the night, chilled, her neck stiff and dragged herself to the bathroom and from there to bed, where she lay awake for what seemed hours.

Fortunately, the next day was Monday. She would have work, which would keep her busy. She checked the chart at the dealership. One person was waiting—someone called Taylor Davidson. She went to the waiting room door. A small woman, a bright blonde, nicely dressed, was poring over a large scheduling book.

"Hi. Need a lift?"

The woman looked up with a frown as if annoyed at the interruption. And then she smiled. "Yes, actually."

"Come with me."

Davidson got into the backseat, although there was no one else in the car. Whenever Chelsea looked in the rearview mirror, she was looking down at her schedule.

She dropped her off at the Becker Building, where they worked with out-of-control kids. "Thanks," Taylor said. "Can you pick me up at five? My car should be finished."

"I won't be working at five, but someone will. Call the dealership and they'll send a shuttle."

The woman nodded and turned toward the building.

Chelsea spent the afternoon in front of the computer. In the evening she picked up a manuscript she'd received in the morning mail and began reading. She found the comparisons between her manuscript and one she was reading interesting and sometimes helpful. Was that kosher? It would be hard not to be influenced, though.

The next morning when she picked up the sheet of those needing rides, Taylor's name was on for pickup after she dropped off those in the waiting room.

A few brightly colored leaves shaded Taylor's street. It was near the river and a cool wind shook the leaves, making them rattle. She parked in the driveway of a ranch house and got out to ring the doorbell.

Taylor was pulling on a jacket as she came out of the door. Her short blond hair blew around her head. Chelsea did something she'd never done. She held open the front door. "It's just you and me. May as well ride in the front."

The woman's hair shone like the sun. Her eyes were neither blue nor brown nor green, but a combination of those colors. She was younger than Chelsea, Chelsea guessed, but not by much.

"I didn't expect to see you again," Chelsea said.

"Yeah, well, they had to wait for a part."

Chelsea wracked her brains for something to say that wouldn't sound nosy or out of line and could think of nothing. Taylor seemed comfortable with silence.

"Do you like this job?" Taylor asked toward the end of the ride, as if she too had been trying to think of something to say.

"It's perfect. I'm writing my second book and reading another author's manuscript. I just need something to help pay for the groceries." She cringed because she sounded like she was bragging, but what did it take to snag the woman's interest?

"Really. What do you write?"

"Fiction." *Lesbian fiction*, she silently added. She didn't want to kill the conversation.

"What is your name?" She asked the question with that frown she'd first shown Chelsea.

Chelsea told her.

"And the title of your first book?"

"*Misadventures*," Chelsea said, her eyes on the road.

"Really?" Taylor said. "Congratulations."

Chelsea pulled into a parking space near the service door. "Have a good one."

"Thanks. You too." And the woman was out the door, walking into the dealership.

Chelsea followed her in, picked up the sheet with the names of those needing rides, and headed toward the waiting room. She figured she'd never see Taylor again. So why the hell had she been a show-off and told her about her writing.

Friday night she and Martha met at the Adler Brau shortly after five. Their plan was always to beat the Friday night crowds. They hadn't talked since the previous weekend.

The waitress brought their drinks—a beer for Martha and one for her, for a change. Chelsea leaned forward. "How was your week?"

"Okay. Yours?" Martha asked.

"I almost met someone." What was she saying? She didn't know if Taylor was a lesbian. It was just that vibe, that sense that someone else was like you. "Forget it. I made a fool out of myself."

"No! Tell me."

So she did. When she got to the part about telling Taylor that she was a writer, she faltered. "I wanted her to think I was more than a shuttle driver."

"And that's so terrible?"

"How many braggarts do you like?"

"You wanted to nudge her curiosity, right?"

She shrank a little. "But why? You know I'm never going to see her again."

"You know where she lives."

"I go up to her door and say what?"

"'Do you want to go out for dinner?'" Martha said brightly and laughed.

Chelsea was appalled. "I'd never do that and you know it. Besides, I might not even like her. She's kind of aloof."

Martha lifted her glass for another beer. "You're driving me to drink."

"Sorry."

"When you wanted to know Daph, you went to her door."

"I know, but this is connected to work. I could get fired."

"Hadn't thought of that." Martha took a deep swallow. "This tastes so good."

Chelsea glanced at the large doorway. Several people stood by the hostess's workspace. Chelsea leaned over and poked Martha on the arm. "Look toward the door," she whispered. "She's with that group of people. The blonde."

Martha turned her head. "You mean Taylor Davidson? Why didn't you just tell me her name?"

"Do you know everybody?" Chelsea asked. She watched as Martha waved a hand toward Taylor. She felt an odd thrill when Taylor said something to someone in the group and headed their way, weaving around tables.

Martha stood up and hugged the woman. "Let me introduce you to my friend, Chelsea Browning."

Taylor smiled and put her hand out for Chelsea to shake. "I thought you were Chelsea Danforth."

"Danforth is my given name. It's on my books." Had Taylor read her book? They knew her at work as Chelsea Browning.

"It's been too long," Taylor said, turning back to Martha. "You look good. How is everything?"

"Pretty busy at work. People are always looking for a job. How is it going for you? You look terrific."

Taylor laughed. "Yeah, yeah, but thanks. Work is madness. Fortunately, most of the kids are too small to harm me."

"Do you like it?"

"It's never dull."

Chelsea fought a jealous urge to thrust herself into the middle of their conversation, but she sipped her beer and politely kept her mouth shut. Taylor said goodbye to her before rejoining her group.

"Taylor works with difficult kids. I met her at a business function when she first came to town. The Chamber of Commerce put it on."

"Is she gay?" Chelsea asked.

"She lived with a woman before she bought that house near the river, but that doesn't make her a lesbian. I helped her move, and no one else moved in with her. I never saw the other woman again."

The waitress showed up and they ordered food.

"It sounds like you were good friends," Chelsea said, downing her drink.

"Not really. I was being uncharacteristically nice. She said she was moving and I offered to help."

"Why aren't you good friends?"

"She goes around with people she works with, I suppose. People with whom she has something in common."

"What do *we* have in common?" Chelsea asked.

Martha's mouth twitched. "We like fish fries."

The weekend was golden—the end of October, a harvest moon, cool nights, and warm days. Chelsea could not stay at the computer. She walked the streets and trails until she had to sit down on a bench facing the river.

"Hope you don't mind," someone said, sitting down next to her. "My legs are numb."

"I know what you mean." She turned to acknowledge the person sharing her bench and saw that it was Taylor. She stared.

"It's too nice a day to stay inside. And then as I was about to collapse, I saw you sitting here."

Chelsea smiled. "I couldn't stay inside either."

They sat in silence until Taylor got up.

"I'll walk with you," Chelsea said.

"I'm going home, which fortunately isn't too far from here as you know. Would you like to come with me? We could have a drink on the patio."

"Sure."

The patio was hidden from the neighbors by greenery—tall grasses, a lilac bush, a couple of spruce trees, and fall flowers like the ones in Chelsea's backyard. "It's lovely here."

"I read your book. I liked it," Taylor said.

"Thanks," Chelsea said, startled. "Before or after we met?"

"Before." A little smile played around her mouth, stretching it.

What a difference a smile makes, Chelsea thought. So, she was gay. Chelsea smiled.

"Was it autobiographical?"

"No! Well, yes, sort of. It didn't start out that way," she stammered, immediately on the defense.

Taylor nodded. "What is your drink?"

"Anything but gin," she said. "Can I help?"

"Sure. Come make your own." Taylor put out vodka and wine and a couple of mixers. She cut a lime into wedges.

Hesitant at first, Chelsea poured vodka over ice, added tonic, and twisted a bit of lime over it before stirring. She glanced around the kitchen. All the necessary modern appliances, plus a shiny wood floor.

Taylor poured herself a beer. "Shall we go back outside?"

"Sounds good." They settled on comfortable, padded, wrought-iron chairs that swiveled and rocked a little.

"What makes a person want to write a book?" Taylor asked.

Chelsea thought she was just making conversation. "I'm a reader for a lesbian publisher. Reading other authors' manuscripts made me think I could probably write too." She rushed on. "I know that sounds egotistical, but I don't mean it that way. I recognize how inferior I am to those who write literature."

"What makes something literature?" Taylor asked. She sipped her drink and looked at Chelsea with those indescribable eyes. What color did she put on her driver's license?

"I don't actually know. Maybe a book that concentrates on the quality of writing or has a lot of depth or talks about big issues or all three. Books where sometimes the reader doesn't even know what's going on."

She forced a smile. She didn't want to talk about her book or writing. The words came to her as she wrote. She wanted to know more about this woman. "Tell me about your work."

"On the weekends I try not to think too much about my job, but some kid always manages to sneak into my thoughts. It's difficult. Three-year-olds who attack you to get out the door. Beaten-down children who cringe if you get near them. Sad youngsters who won't even talk."

"It sounds heartbreaking." Just thinking about it hurt and made her heart pound with anger at the person or people who made these children afraid.

"It can be."

"Are you able to improve their lives?"

"Sometimes."

"Parents do these things to their children?"

"Not always. But you probably know the various forms abuse takes—emotional, sexual, physical—and the perpetrators have often been abused themselves. I am seriously considering counseling adults."

"I think I would if I were you." But she was worrying about the children who would lose a champion.

CHAPTER THIRTY-TWO

When Taylor called her late the next day, Chelsea's fingers were flying over the keys of her computer. Deep into Chapter 20, she almost didn't pick up, not wanting to interrupt her train of thought.

"Hi. It's Taylor. Would you like to go to a concert with me Thursday evening? By luck, I have an extra ticket to the St. Paul Chamber Orchestra performance at the chapel. The orchestra is exquisite." Then she added, "It's okay if you can't go. I know it's short notice."

"But I do want to go. Who wouldn't?"

"I have good seats."

"What time? I'll meet you there." Already she was wondering what to wear.

On Thursday afternoon, writing eluded her. She had thrown four pairs of slacks on the bed along with blouses. She ate a sandwich for supper and dressed finally in navy slacks and vest with a light-colored blouse and nice flats. It was still warm enough to wear a lightweight jacket.

She was pleasantly surprised to find a parking spot near the chapel, unlike the night of the *Messiah* last year when she had to walk for blocks. She was early, expecting a large crowd.

When Taylor walked through the door, the place was still relatively empty. Taylor was dressed in black slacks and a red blouse. She looked fantastic. Her hair was still bright from the summer sun and when she smiled at Chelsea and said how glad she was to see her, Chelsea glowed.

Their seats were in the tenth row. The audience was scattered. She leaned toward Taylor. "Where is everyone?"

"They're fools to miss this. They'll all show up for the *Messiah* in December, though."

"They did last year," Chelsea said.

The music was exquisite, as Taylor had promised, mostly J.S. Bach. It was played with such skill that Chelsea periodically closed her eyes in order to hear every note. She opened them once to see Taylor smiling at her. At the end she clapped and clapped to make up for the sparse audience, fearing the performers might be as insulted as she was for them. When they walked up the center aisle afterward, Chelsea thanked Taylor for inviting her. "Bach is my favorite composer," she confided.

"I could see that," Taylor said.

"Let me pay for my ticket," she said.

"Nope. My treat. It would have just gone to waste otherwise."

"The concert should have been sold out. Thank you so much," Chelsea said when they stepped outside. "Let me take you out to dinner then," she said.

"I'll go only if you let me pay my way." They were standing on the wide cement at the bottom of the steps, causing people to flow around them. "Where and when?"

Chelsea hadn't expected her to say yes. Her mind raced. "What is your favorite food?"

"Indian. Love that curry." Taylor's face was in shadow, but her smile was easy to see.

"Okay. Saturday evening. If you don't have other plans, I'll pick you up at six."

"All right."

It was as easy as that. Chelsea went home feeling pleased and called Martha.

"You missed the best concert ever. Did you suggest me in your place?"

"She called you then. I had to pick someone up for a meeting I had to go to. The meeting was boring as hell, but the head honcho at work was in town."

"I'm taking her out to dinner Saturday night for thanks. Well, at least we're going out. I don't know if she'll let me pay."

"Are we still on for Friday night?"

"Of course."

On Friday, she was once again tossing clothes on her bed, looking for an outfit. When the phone rang, she tucked it between her shoulder and chin.

"Hi, Mom, Abby and I are about an hour away. We thought we'd surprise you." Lizzie's cheerful voice filled her ear.

Panic struck. What was she going to say to Taylor? She remembered one of the girls calling with plans to visit when she and Jane were in bed. Jane had gone back to Stacy Lee, but who wouldn't go back to Stacy? It never occurred to her to tell her daughters she had plans. Their relationships with her were just too fragile. She didn't relish starting all over attempting to close the gap again. She was still standing holding a hanger and pair of slacks. She hung them back on the rod.

For half an hour she wracked her brain about what to do. Call Saturday night off? Take the girls with her? Then she called Martha with an idea.

"What's wrong?" Martha asked.

"Are you psychic?"

"You seldom call me at work. I've got about ten minutes, so what is it?"

She talked fast, explaining the problem. "What if I put on an Indian dinner here Saturday for me and the girls and Taylor and you and Cat and Barb."

"Can you cook Indian food?"

"No, but maybe I could get takeout from the Indian restaurant and heat it up."

"Your daughters surprised you, so they're going to have to share you? Is that the idea here?"

"No. I thought it might be a better scenario than the girls and Taylor going to a restaurant with me. That would be a pretty tense meal."

"So, Cat and Barb and I are buffers."

"Would you mind terribly?"

"For a free Indian dinner, I'll be glad to come. I'll even help. I gotta go now. I'll call you after work. Are we still going out tonight?"

"You bet."

She made phone calls before her daughters arrived. She'd have to order the food in advance and carry it out. She gave the date and ordered off a menu she had at home. It was going to be an expensive meal, probably cost her several days' pay, which she had been putting away for Christmas. As she hung up, her daughters drove into the driveway.

They would help, she decided. Maybe next time they'd give her longer notice of when they were coming. When they walked in the door, laughing, her bit of anger seemed overwrought and vanished. She opened her arms.

"Hi, you two. What's happening?"

"Just thought we'd surprise you," Lizzie said, her blue eyes shining.

Abby carried her bag into the spare bedroom. When she came back, she said, "You've got something going, don't you, Mom?"

"Yes. We're going out for fish tonight with a friend. And tomorrow we're serving an Indian dinner here."

"For friends," Abby finished.

"Yes. How did you know?"

Abby smiled. "All those clothes on your bed."

She loved Abby's smile, and it seemed like forever since she'd seen it. "Right," she said.

The girls were quiet at the restaurant. They were all quiet at first, until Martha began asking Chelsea's daughters questions about their lives to draw them out.

Lizzie said something about not exactly liking sharing an apartment with her boyfriend.

"I thought you wanted to marry Keith," Chelsea said.

"Yeah. That was before I started living with him. He never picks his stuff up, not even his underwear." She looked disgusted.

Chelsea looked at Martha, who lifted her eyebrows. Chelsea laughed.

"Why is that funny, Mom?"

"Because you didn't pick up your clothes," Chelsea answered mildly.

"Well, I'm not picking up after some guy," Lizzie said indignantly.

"And Jeff never makes the bed or helps with the cooking and cleaning up. I don't clean up after him either. His mom surprised us one day with a visit. She had something to say about her own son."

"What?"

"She said he was a pig and told me not to marry him till he started to clean up after himself. I think she'd make a good mother-in-law."

"Did he start picking up his stuff?" Lizzie asked. She was drinking beer out of a bottle.

"Not yet."

"I've got the perfect solution for that," Martha said. "You two should move in together."

"We just might," Abby said. "Was Dad that way, Mom?"

"Well, we had a dirty clothes basket in the room, so no. But he left nuts and bolts and little pieces of paper wherever he was standing when he emptied his pockets at night. He didn't help wash the dishes, but he carried them out to the kitchen. Best of all, though, he helped me learn to cook."

"Grandma didn't teach you how to cook?" Liz asked.

"I didn't want to learn when she wanted to teach me." She missed her mom. There were questions she wanted to ask her and things she wanted to talk about. She wasn't sure she'd ever let her know how much she'd loved her or told her what a good mother she'd been.

CHAPTER THIRTY-THREE

Chelsea got up at dawn to clean. She'd let things slide, like dusting and vacuuming and cleaning counters and washing floors. She scurried around the house with a rag, cleaning the furniture. She managed to wash floors and countertops. She even picked up the clutter before Abby came up behind her and asked about coffee.

Chelsea let out a small cry of surprise and told Abby she would have to make some and then wake Lizzie up, so they could help her. Before noon she and her girls had restored the house to its original state. She called the restaurant and checked on the order. Only then did she have another cup of coffee with her kids.

Chelsea picked up Taylor at six thirty. Once in the vehicle, Chelsea stayed in the driveway long enough for Taylor to ask if something was wrong.

"There has been a slight change in plans," Chelsea said.

"Oh. We don't have to go out to dinner, you know. You could come in and we can scrounge up leftovers."

"No, it's nothing like that. My daughters surprised me by showing up yesterday, and we're finally…beginning to close the gap I made by leaving home and writing a book…" She gave up.

"How old are your daughters?"

"In their twenties."

"Why don't you tell me what you have planned for this evening?" Taylor asked.

"We're having an Indian dinner at my house with my daughters and a few friends." She turned toward Taylor. "You have to come. I've worked my ass off all day."

"Cooking?" Taylor asked, her fair eyebrows arching. "It smells wonderful in the car. Is that you?"

"No, that's the food you smell. It's in the trunk."

Taylor laughed. "Well, then, what are we waiting for?"

Chelsea backed out of the driveway and headed toward her house. "I know most people think children as old as mine have no right to be upset with me for leaving their dad, who now has a girlfriend, and for moving far away. And then there is the book I wrote, which also disturbs them."

"I understand. They probably need time to digest all the changes."

"Exactly." Relief made her limp. She felt sweat drying on her body.

"Tell me why you felt the need to have dinner at home? Couldn't we go out?"

She couldn't explain that one. How could she tell Taylor what she'd said to Martha, that the silence at such a dinner would be too awful?

"Never mind. This sounds like a party. Martha will be there, I assume."

"Yes."

Martha opened the door. "Hi, Taylor," she said, walking past her toward the back of the car.

"I can help," Taylor said.

"No. You're the guest. Martha, would you mind introducing Taylor to the others? I'd be grateful. And send the girls out to help me."

"Why don't you play the hostess and send someone out to help me?" Martha asked.

Chelsea went in the front door, introduced Taylor to her daughters, and asked them to go help with the food.

"What would you like to drink?" Barb asked. "I'm the barmaid." She gave a little curtsy, and Chelsea laughed. "Actually, I once worked as a barmaid. Right after I graduated college."

"Do you have a beer?" Taylor asked.

"Oh, you're a hard one to please," Barb said, snatching a beer and glass from the fridge and handing them to Taylor.

"Where is Cat?" Chelsea asked.

"She has to take care of Lindsey." Barb's eyebrows bobbed.

Chelsea thought of calling Cat and telling her to bring her daughter, but she decided she couldn't handle Lindsey.

Lit candles and fall flowers adorned the tablecloth. The last of the daylight was gone and Chelsea turned on the stove light.

"This is like a romantic dinner without the guys," Lizzie said.

"You don't have to have guys," Martha said.

"You just need candles and flowers," Barb added with a jiggle of eyebrows.

Abby and Lizzie giggled. "We do."

"Well, I want to talk about your mom's book. Is that allowed?" Taylor asked when they were seated. She looked around the table and no one said anything. Martha and Barb gave quick nods. "You know it was the number one best seller in the Lambda magazine. How many people do you know whose book is number one in any category? Anyway, it was well received and well read and well thought of. When I found myself talking to the author in the Ford shuttle car, I was struck by how unreal this was. I want to toast Chelsea and her first book—*Misadventures*. It's a big success. May there be many more."

Abby and Lizzie looked at each other and their mother and raised their glasses. "Hey, Mama, congratulations," Abby said.

"Kudos to my famous mom," Lizzie added.

Six glasses waved in Chelsea's direction. If it had been a hundred, she would not have been more pleased.

Later, after Abby and Lizzie had gone to bed, Martha and Barb took their leave and Taylor and Chelsea stood in the front hall.

"I better take you home," Chelsea said.

"I suppose," Taylor said. "It was a nice evening."

"Thanks for saying all those nice things about my book."

"I meant all I said."

Chelsea squirmed a little. She wasn't good with praise. "I was pleased."

"When are your daughters leaving?" Taylor asked, stepping close enough for Chelsea to feel the warmth of her breath. She smelled of curry.

"Sunday, I suppose."

Taylor took another step closer and Chelsea resisted the urge to back up. She looked into Taylor's eyes.

"What color are your eyes?"

"On my driver's license they're blue." She leaned forward and kissed Chelsea. Her lips were warm and soft. It would have been so easy for Chelsea to pull her close, but her daughters were behind the wall next to them. Instead she drove Taylor home and kissed her goodbye in the car.

When her daughters left late Sunday, she sat down in front of her computer and got lost in the story. It was dark out and the phone was ringing when she looked up in a daze.

She picked up the receiver reluctantly, not wanting to lose her momentum.

"It's Taylor."

"What?" She felt disoriented.

"You do remember me. Right?"

"Oh. Hi. Sorry. I'm in a fog."

"I guess. Are you all right?"

"I was lost in my computer. What's up?"

"Nothing much. Thought maybe you might want to come to lunch next Saturday."

"I have to work." She was being pursued, she realized. A warm glow suffused her.

"When do you get off?"

"Right after the last pick up or delivery, but that could happen before or after noon."

"Come when you're free. Bring your kids with you if they're there."

"Okay. See you then." She was pleased.

She wore what she'd put on for work Saturday morning—jeans and a sweater. It was a cool, sunny day with a bit of a wind. She shivered as she rang Taylor's doorbell at twelve thirty. She'd been lucky to get off that early.

The door opened before the chimes stopped. Taylor stood squinting in a blot of sunlight, her hair shining, dressed in jeans and a pullover. "Come in out of the cold."

Chelsea did and stood on the doormat waiting for further invitation.

"Follow me," Taylor said cheerfully and led Chelsea to a table near the patio door, set with tableware and red grapes and sandwich meat and bread and condiments, along with a bowl of chips.

Chelsea was hungry. She pulled a chair up to the table and waited for Taylor to sit.

"Coffee?" Taylor asked. "It's decaf."

"Sure. It'll warm me up."

"How was the shuttle today?"

"It's not so busy on Saturday. People come in and wait for oil changes, but they don't usually leave their cars over the weekend."

"Why do they need a shuttle then?"

"There are always people picking up their vehicles from the day before."

They exchanged information over the food. Background stuff like where they were from. Taylor grew up in Milwaukee. Chelsea said she'd gone to college in Indiana. That was how she met and married Brad. She told her about Gina saving her from boredom.

"Is she still in Indiana?"

"It's home to her. She is still married and involved with horses."

"You must miss her." Taylor held her gaze.

"I do. A lot. My daughters are there. I love them, but I don't want to live there anymore."

"It must have been hard to leave, though."

Chelsea's throat began to close with emotion. "It was the hardest thing I've ever done."

"Was it worth it?" Taylor asked.

"Was it wrong to up and leave? Probably. I came out after my mom died. What was that all about? She was the most tolerant person I ever met. I waited for my kids to grow up, but did I really? I didn't even realize who I was until recently. How is that possible?" Was she trying to justify her behavior to Taylor?

"Denial is alive and well." Taylor got up to pour coffee. She brought a few chocolate chip cookies over. And smiled. "I can't imagine what that was like for you, but you seem to be doing all right."

"I thought maybe I'd lose my girls, but it appears otherwise." She smiled wryly. "You know the old warning, 'Be careful what you wish for'? I've thought of that more than once." She wondered if she was talking too much, all these words spilling out of her, but Taylor looked like she was interested.

"How so?"

"Well, I thought I loved this woman. I thought we'd make a life together. I left Brad. Actually, I did him a disservice." She was choking up, but she had to finish. "I left my girls, my best friend, the dog. Sold the horses." She shut up. Her eyes had filled with tears. "Six months after we moved into the house, she was cheating on me. It was lust I felt for her, not love."

Taylor gave her a minute or two to recover before saying, "Hey. It had to be very hard for you to leave, but you stayed for how long?"

"Over twenty-five years."

"I'd say you gave a lot of your life to Brad and the girls. Maybe you made a mistake with this woman, but without her you might never have left. You've written a book and are working on another. Do you get what I'm saying? It's your turn now."

Chelsea sniffed. She hunted in her pockets for a tissue and turned her head to blow her nose. Finally composed, she thanked Taylor.

"How long can you stay in the house where you live?"

It was such a jump that it took Chelsea a moment to catch up. "The owners are due back in March."

"You'll be looking for another place to live then. Are you buying or renting?"

"Renting." She wouldn't have the money to buy. She knew Brad was filing for divorce. He'd told their daughters. He and she would have to come up with a settlement they both could live with.

"Well, if you need a place to stay, I have room."

The surprise must have shown on her face.

Taylor shrugged. "I've rented a room before."

A business arrangement, she thought. "Thank you, but I think I'll get an apartment."

"Would you like to see the rest of the house?" Taylor asked. She stood, so Chelsea got to her feet.

There was a room with a kitchenette and bathroom at one end of the house. It even had a separate entrance. "Pretty nice," she said. "How much?"

"A couple hundred a month," Taylor said.

"That's a good deal, but I can't leave till the owners return."

"You might be interested?"

"Who wouldn't?" she replied.

EPILOGUE

Chelsea moved into Taylor's rental room a week before the owners returned. She rented a trailer to move her few possessions, and Martha and Barb and Taylor helped.

She had become accustomed to spending part of Saturday or Sunday with Taylor. As March warmed up, they took occasional walks or sometimes ate with each other at the house. She still went out for fish with Martha and sometimes Barb and Cat on Friday. She invited them over for dinners that Taylor usually joined.

Nothing physical had happened between the two women, so Chelsea was surprised when she turned around on April 1, a little more than a month after she'd moved in, and Taylor was right there. She took a step back and was stopped by a piece of furniture.

"I like you very much. Too much," Taylor said.

How can you like someone too much? Chelsea wondered. "I like you too."

"Do you think you could do better than like me?"

"I'm very grateful to you."

"I don't want gratitude," Taylor mumbled and turned away.

"Hey. I'm just a little bit cautious here. I mean, we're virtually living together. I don't want to get kicked out." Actually, she'd been cautious since her experiences with June and Jane. To be honest, she was more worried about getting hurt again than about being tossed on the street.

"I would never do that. It would be like breaking a contract," Taylor said, looking indignant. "It's okay. Forget I said anything."

Of course, she couldn't forget. She couldn't concentrate on her writing. She couldn't read. Finally, she walked the length of the River Trail and back again, weaving through the dog walkers, the bikers, and those who were out for a stroll or a run.

The house was dark, and Taylor's car was gone. She called Martha and told her what had happened. "What do you think she wants?"

"You."

"Because I'm handy?" she asked sarcastically.

"No, because she finds you attractive."

"Oh. How do you know?"

"Jesus, Chelse, she told me. If you're not interested in her, you should let her know."

"I do like her—a great deal." In fact, she felt chills when she thought of being in bed with Taylor.

"Tell her. See what happens. Hey, I wish some guy was interested in me like that."

She went to bed with a book, keeping her ears peeled for the sound of the garage door opening and closing. The window was open, and she heard an owl hooting when she awoke in the night. She had no idea what time it was.

When she was about to dress the next morning, there was a knock on the door. "It's open," she called, balancing on one foot, about to shove the other into her jeans.

Taylor walked in, dressed in a silky bathrobe and carrying two steaming mugs. "Coffee?" she asked, setting the tray with the cups on the bed.

Chelsea pulled on her jeans and sat on the edge of the mattress. "Sure."

Taylor sat down next to her, handed a cup to Chelsea, and took the other.

A shaft of sunlight turned Taylor's hair golden, and Chelsea reached out a hand to touch it. She took away Taylor's coffee cup, set it with hers on the tray, and put the tray on the bedside table.

It was easy then. They moved toward each other until they were near enough to kiss. Chelsea wriggled out of her jeans and untied the belt on Taylor's robe. Her breasts fell out and Chelsea buried her face in their softness while she gently explored Taylor's body. Desire swept through her when she found what she wanted. Taylor was so ready. She slid her fingers inside and out in a slow caress.

Taylor gasped and arched toward Chelsea's touch. She began stroking Chelsea in return. It was all over so quickly that Chelsea wondered at her desire. She hadn't known she was so ready.

"Wow. All because of a cup of coffee," Chelsea said, breaking the silence as they lay apart.

"I better heat it up," Taylor said.

"First, I want a hug." She gathered Taylor in her arms and felt her softness against her own. She loved the feel of skin on skin.

It was too nice a day to spend in bed, though. After an hour, they got up and Chelsea fixed breakfast. They looked at each other over the small table. This morning Taylor's eyes had a bit of gold in the greenish blue.

"What do you want to do today?" Chelsea asked.

"You choose. I'd just go back to bed."

"Later," Chelsea said. "It will be better. I promise. Let's take a shower and go for a walk somewhere different, like High Cliff. I need to stretch my legs."

"All right. I'll go get ready."

"Can't we shower together?"

"I'll get my clothes then," Taylor said. She was smiling.

But the shower caused another delay. While the water pounded down on them, they moved into each other's arms.

After washing each other's hair and bodies, they hurriedly dried and went to the bed.

"What about the walk?" Taylor asked as she looked up at Chelsea. Her pupils were huge.

"It can wait." Chelsea's hand moved over Taylor's smooth skin, raising goose bumps. "You feel so good."

"Mmm, that feels good." She pulled Chelsea down for a kiss that ended in a gasp as Chelsea entered her.

Chelsea worked her way down Taylor's body, kissing, tasting, until she reached the joining of her legs, which she gently pushed apart and began lightly teasing her with her tongue. The sounds Taylor made and the rise of her body only fueled Chelsea's desire. Then Taylor pulled Chelsea down to do the same. They were done almost before they began.

Chelsea worked her way up to hold Taylor, who said, "Wow! I never expected it to be like this."

"It will get better and last longer with time," Chelsea said. She was guessing, although it made sense.

"How about that walk now?" Taylor said.

After parking near the tower, they hiked to the top of the bluff overlooking the lake. Chelsea remembered the last time she had been here and how bleak the future had looked. She wanted to put an arm around Taylor, but of course, she couldn't, although the guy next to them had his arm around a girl.

Life was good, though. She had a lover now, her daughters still loved her, as did her sister and Gina. And then there were her friends, Martha and Barb and Cat. And her writing. All this good fortune almost scared her, but she'd do her damnedest to keep it.

She met Taylor's smile with her own. "Ready to go home?" she asked.

Bella Books, Inc.

Women. Books. Even Better Together.

P.O. Box 10543
Tallahassee, FL 32302

Phone: 800-729-4992
www.bellabooks.com